T0153114

RUM SPRING

Visit us at www.boldstrokesbooks.com

By the Author

In Medias Res

Rum Spring

RUM SPRING

by

Yolanda Wallace

2010

RUM SPRING

© 2010 By Yolanda Wallace. All Rights Reserved.

ISBN 10: 1-60282-193-3
ISBN 13: 978-1-60282-193-4

This Trade Paperback Original Is Published By
Bold Strokes Books, Inc.
P.O. Box 249
Valley Falls, NY 12185

First Edition: December 2010

THIS IS A WORK OF FICTION. NAMES, CHARACTERS, PLACES, AND INCIDENTS ARE THE PRODUCT OF THE AUTHOR'S IMAGINATION OR ARE USED FICTITIOUSLY. ANY RESEMBLANCE TO ACTUAL PERSONS, LIVING OR DEAD, BUSINESS ESTABLISHMENTS, EVENTS, OR LOCALES IS ENTIRELY COINCIDENTAL.

THIS BOOK, OR PARTS THEREOF, MAY NOT BE REPRODUCED IN ANY FORM WITHOUT PERMISSION.

CREDITS
EDITORS: CINDY CRESAP AND STACIA SEAMAN
PRODUCTION DESIGN: STACIA SEAMAN
COVER DESIGN BY SHERI (GRAPHICARTIST2020@HOTMAIL.COM)

Acknowledgments

Writing is often a labor of love. I couldn't do what I do without the woman who gives me all the love and support anyone could ask for. Thank you, Dita, for always being in my corner. Thank you also to Radclyffe and the Bold Strokes family, who have made this only child feel like she has found dozens of long-lost sisters. Last, but not least, thank you to the readers who make the long hours in front of the computer worthwhile. Your feedback is invaluable and much appreciated.

Dedication

To Dita. Thank you for choosing me.

CHAPTER ONE

Rebecca Lapp dropped sautéed onions and celery into a bowl filled with day-old bread that had been cut into cubes. She added milk, salt, and pepper, and blended the ingredients with her fingers. Then she set the warm mixture aside to cool.

"You do that so well," Rebecca's sister Sarah said. "Maybe you should be the one getting married instead of me."

Rebecca smiled at the note of approval in Sarah's voice. Sarah was great help around the farm, but she wasn't much of a cook. With that in mind, Rebecca and their mother Mary were teaching Sarah how to prepare her fiancé's favorite dish—roast chicken with bread stuffing. When their mother placed the raw chicken on the table, Sarah looked as if she wanted to sink through the kitchen's wooden floor.

"You'll be fine." Rebecca handed Sarah a large spoon. "Joshua loves you so much you could probably burn every meal and he wouldn't care."

Sarah wrinkled her nose in disgust as she spread the chicken's legs and gingerly filled the cavity with the bread stuffing Rebecca had prepared.

"Don't be afraid," their mother said. "Nothing in the bowl is going to bite you. And if the chicken manages the feat without a head, it will be a miracle."

Rebecca and their mother shared a laugh, but Sarah remained stone-faced. Rebecca couldn't remember the last time she had seen her sister laugh or even smile. Sarah had not seemed herself for quite some time. Rebecca had hoped the wedding preparations would bring as much joy to Sarah's life as they had to hers. Instead of being energized by the plans for the nuptials, Sarah seemed to grow even more anxious with each passing day.

"I have to get this right," Sarah said. "This is the dish I want to prepare for Joshua on the day we're published."

On the Sunday of fall communion, the names of all the couples who planned to marry would be announced. At the end of the service, their cousin Peterli, acting in his official capacity as the *Armendiener* of their Amish community, would call out the names of each girl along with the name of the man she would soon marry. Each of the girls' fathers would then stand one by one to give the date and time of the respective wedding and invite the congregation to attend. This year, Sarah's name would be on the list.

Sarah's announcement wouldn't come as a surprise. Even though their courtship was supposed to be a secret, everyone knew Sarah and Joshua King had been sweet on each other all their lives.

Joshua and Sarah would not attend church on the Sunday they were published. As tradition dictated, they would spend the day with each other. Sarah would cook and she and Joshua would share a private dinner for two at her parents' house.

"I don't want Joshua to be doubled over in pain when you come home from church and I introduce him to you as my fiancé."

Rebecca looked forward to the day she could join her life with someone else's as Sarah was about to do. She didn't feel drawn to any of the boys she knew—she felt more comfortable with Thomas Mahoney's daughter Dylan than she did with them—but she had time to find the boy who was right for her. The decision wasn't one she could afford to take lightly. Once she married, she could not be divorced. Such a thing was against the *Ordnung*, the mostly unwritten set of rules that governed all facets of Amish life.

She watched Sarah season the chicken, wincing a little when she noticed her sister was being too liberal with the salt. Sarah was going to need much more practice before she would be able to craft a decent meal on her own.

The thought of eating the salty chicken made Rebecca's mouth dry. She poured herself a glass of water from the pitcher on the baker's rack next to the gas stove. As she turned to resume watching the cooking lesson, she detected movement out of the corner of her eye. She pushed the curtains aside and looked out the window.

She knew something was wrong by the way Mr. Mahoney's truck kicked up dust as it barreled down the dirt road. Mr. Mahoney was a careful driver. It wasn't like him to be in a hurry without reason.

The glass of water slipped from Rebecca's hands and shattered on the floor.

"Butterfingers," Sarah said.

"Don't tease your sister," their mother said. "Accidents happen."

"Mama?" Rebecca tried to keep her sense of dread at bay so she wouldn't alarm her mother and sister, but she could feel her voice quaver. She was fourteen, two years shy of the official beginning of her search for a mate. She didn't feel like the woman she would soon become. She felt like a little girl who needed her mother to tend to a scraped knee or comfort her after a bad dream.

Her mother's cheerful expression quickly changed to one of concern when she saw Rebecca's face. "What is it?" She wiped her hands on a towel and joined Rebecca at the window. She drew back immediately. Her hands were shaking, but her voice was even. "Go fetch your father from the pasture."

Rebecca left the shards of broken glass on the floor and rushed out the front door. Holding up the hem of her calf-length dress, she took the steps two at a time and dashed across the yard just as Mr. Mahoney turned into her driveway.

Dylan stuck her head out of the passenger's side window and called Rebecca's name, but Rebecca kept running.

In school, Rebecca had been the fastest runner on the softball team. When she tried to steal a base, no one could throw her out. She missed running. Feeling the wind in her face and the ground flying beneath her feet. But those days were over. Her formal schooling had ended when she completed eighth grade. Now her father was in charge of her education, a task he scheduled in between the chores they each had to perform on the farm.

When she finished school the year before, everyone in her close-knit community expected her to act like an adult even though she wouldn't be considered one until she had gone through *rumspringa* and been baptized in the church. That was still years away. Her *rumspringa* years wouldn't start until she turned sixteen and wouldn't end until she was twenty or twenty-one, when she decided she was ready to join the church or leave her family and friends behind to live among the English.

She rounded the barn and skidded to a stop. Her father Samuel and her uncle Amos were tending to the crop of sweet corn that covered nearly five acres of their jointly owned land.

With the clomping of the horses' hooves, the squealing of the metal wheels, and the whir of the steel blades, Rebecca knew her father couldn't hear her over the sound of the thresher. She waved her arms over her head to get his attention. Her uncle Amos saw her first.

Uncle Amos jumped on the thresher's running board with a sprightliness that belied his sixty years. He tapped on her father's shoulder until he drew his gaze away from the horses.

When Uncle Amos pointed at Rebecca, her father signaled the horses to stop. He handed the reins to Uncle Amos and climbed down. Then he gripped Rebecca's shoulders in his calloused hands. "What's wrong, child?"

Rebecca gasped for breath. She didn't think she had ever run so far so fast. "Mr. Mahoney," she said, fighting to draw air into her lungs.

"What about him?" A rare note of impatience found its way into his voice.

"Mr. Mahoney is up at the house. Something's wrong and he needs to talk to you right away."

Rebecca's father and uncle looked at each other but didn't speak. Her father was the head of the local congregation. Uncle Amos was one of his assistants, a *Diener zum Buch*. In addition to providing spiritual leadership, her father preached and performed baptisms, marriages, and ordinations. He also excommunicated congregants who broke the *Ordnung*. Uncle Amos and his fellow minister Micah King did not dole out discipline. They concentrated on preaching and teaching instead. The role suited Uncle Amos's personality. He seemed to enjoy being a mentor, a counselor. He had never aspired to be anything else. Nor had he expressed a desire to be a leader of men. He was a better follower than a leader.

Her father rested a soothing hand against Rebecca's cheek. "Stay here," he said as Rebecca reached up to secure the prayer covering that held her long brown hair—uncut since childhood—in place. "Amos, come with me."

Rebecca watched them walk away. She was torn between following them and delaying the inevitable. *Ignorance*, she had learned in school, *is bliss*. Standing among the ripe cornstalks that towered over her head, she enjoyed her last few moments of bliss. *On such a beautiful day*, she thought, staring up at the bright blue sky, *what could possibly go wrong?*

She waited. Dylan would come soon.

She had known Dylan for six years. They had watched each other grow up and, when Rebecca was twelve, Dylan had saved her life. Not literally, but to Rebecca, it had certainly felt like it at the time.

It was a day much like the present one. Bright and beautiful with not a cloud in the sky. A Saturday. Rebecca and Sarah had ridden with their father to town. He had dropped them off at the shoe repair shop before continuing on to the hardware store. Rebecca and Sarah had pooled their money to buy their father a new pair of work boots for his birthday, but he had deemed the footwear too fancy and had refused to wear them. So the girls had taken a pair of his old shoes to the cobbler to be resoled. They had picked up the refurbished shoes and were waiting for their father to return when a group of boys had surrounded them.

Clutching her brown paper–wrapped package under one arm,

Sarah had protectively draped the other arm across Rebecca's shoulders. "It's okay," she had told Rebecca in Pennsylvania Dutch. "Just ignore them and they'll go away."

Cowering in fear at her sister's side, Rebecca had tried to do as Sarah asked.

The boys had bullied them for several minutes—blocking their path, calling them names, pulling at the strings on their bonnets. Eyes downcast, the girls hadn't attempted to defend themselves. They had simply waited for the torment to end. Rebecca had prayed for someone to come to their rescue. Dylan, who had been hanging out with her brother Matthew in front of a sandwich shop, had been that person.

Dylan had waded into the middle of the circle of teenage boys and given the ringleader a two-handed shove in the chest. "Why don't you pick on someone your own size?"

Rebecca had been more afraid for Dylan than for herself. She had tried to move forward, but Sarah had held her back.

"Who's going to stop me?" the boy had scoffed. "You?"

"Not me. I might hurt you." Standing her ground, Dylan had folded her arms in front of her chest and stood with her feet apart like she was prepared to take on all comers. "But why don't you try my brother on for size?"

"Ooh, I'm shaking," the boy had said. "Who's your brother?"

With a smile, Dylan had pointed to the spot where Matthew Mahoney was continuing to hold court. "My brother's the one in the red shirt."

The boy's smile had vanished in the blink of an eye. "Maniac Mahoney's your brother?"

Dylan had nodded.

The boy had stared at Dylan for a long moment before apparently deciding it was better to lose face than to have it rearranged. "Come on, guys. They're not worth it, anyway."

Rebecca had stared at Dylan in disbelief. No one had ever done anything that brave—or that crazy—on her behalf. No one except for Dylan Mahoney.

❖

Dylan crashed through the cornfield. She swiped at the drooping stalks as if she were a machete-wielding explorer trying to clear a path through dense jungle. She felt trapped in the figurative maze of her emotions and the literal one formed by the overgrown plants that surrounded her. Rebecca was at the center of both.

A few days a week, Rebecca assisted the teacher at West Nickel Mines School with her classes. The same school that had been the site of a shooting earlier that morning. When Dylan's father had come to her school to tell her about the incident in Nickel Mines before she could hear it from someone else, she had been hysterical, certain Rebecca had been seriously hurt or worse. She had insisted on accompanying him to the Lapps' house. To be there when he delivered the tragic news. If she could be there for the hurt, she could be there for the healing.

"Rebecca!" Dylan shouted her name with unexpected force as her tenuous hold on her self-control began to give way. Again.

"Over here."

Feeling like a character in a Stephen King novel, Dylan turned left and headed deeper into the rows. Finally coming face-to-face with Rebecca, she let out a deep breath. "You're all right." The overwhelming sense of relief that washed over her nearly caused her knees to buckle. "You're all right," she said once more as she launched herself into Rebecca's arms.

Rebecca staggered from the force of Dylan's hug. "Of course I am. Why wouldn't I be?"

Dylan pulled away. Not completely. Just far enough so she could see Rebecca's face. So she could look into her eyes. She ran her fingers over Rebecca's face—the most beautiful sight she had ever seen. "I thought you were helping at the school today."

"With Sarah about to be married, there is too much to do at home for me to be able to work at the school."

Dylan finally let go. "You don't know, do you?" Shaking her

head, she answered her own question. She kept forgetting how out of touch the Lapps were. Like most Old Order Amish families, the Lapps didn't have a phone. Some of their neighbors had installed phones in their barns or outlying structures in their yards in case of emergency, but the Lapps had not been willing to make even that small concession to the modern world. They preferred to do everything the old-fashioned way. The way it was done hundreds of years ago. "Of course you don't."

She took Rebecca's hands in her hers, then sat her down and tried to put in words what had happened.

"I don't have all the details. I only know what I heard on the radio and on the scanner in Dad's truck. The guy on the radio said the story was still developing, but it's bad."

"How bad?"

"A couple of hours ago, a man drove to the school in Nickel Mines and barricaded himself and ten girls inside." Rebecca tightened her grip on Dylan's hands. Dylan hesitated, uncertain if she should go on. She forced herself to move forward, knowing it was too late to turn back. "The man shot each of the girls, then turned the gun on himself."

Rebecca's face turned ghostly pale. "Is he— Are they—"

Dylan tried to make her voice as gentle as possible. "The man and several of the girls died at the scene. The rest of the girls were taken to the hospital, but I don't know what condition they're in. My dad and I passed dozens of ambulances and news crews on the road. It's a madhouse out there."

"How could anyone do such a thing?"

"I wish I knew." In Dylan's opinion, no explanation was reason enough to prompt an action so heinous. "I'm sorry," she said. She didn't know why she was apologizing, but it felt like the right thing to do. The right thing to say. She had to let Rebecca know not all English were bad. Not all of them wished her people harm or made fun of them and their ways. She didn't profess to understand their traditions, but she was sure the Amish probably felt the same way about some of hers.

She held her hand against Rebecca's cheek. She couldn't stop touching her—and she didn't want to. She had to keep proving to herself that Rebecca was real and what she was feeling wasn't a mirage. She wanted to hold Rebecca in her arms and never let go. But she couldn't. It wasn't the time or the place. Not after what had transpired only a few miles away.

"Are you okay?" Dylan asked.

Rebecca nodded but didn't speak. She was fine physically, but what about emotionally? The Amish were pacifists. Opposed to war, the military, and all forms of violence, they were a peace-loving people. How would she—and they—recover from the shock of something so violent happening to ten of their own? What would it mean for their friendship? Would Dylan and the rest of the English become someone to vilify, or would their two worlds continue to coexist?

Hot tears rolled down Dylan's cheeks, mirroring the ones that glistened on Rebecca's. Dylan's tears were born of relief that the precious friend she feared she had lost had been found to be unharmed. Dylan thought Rebecca was crying for the victims—innocent girls she had grown up with and seen almost every day. Some girls who were gone forever and others who, if they survived, would never be the same again. She moved to comfort Rebecca, to put her arms around her and take the sorrow away, but what Rebecca said surprised her.

"Can you imagine the kind of pain he must have been in to commit such an act? We should be grateful his soul is at peace now."

"Grateful? For what he did, he deserves punishment, not peace."

"That isn't for my people to decide," Rebecca said softly. "He is not one of us, so we are not allowed to judge him or his actions. Our judgment is limited to those who have pledged to follow the *Ordnung*. He did not make such a pledge. Therefore, we must forgive this man, not judge him."

Dylan rocked back on her haunches, unable to believe what she was hearing. "Then why are you crying?" She barely knew the girls and it was all she could do to keep it together. To keep from taking out some of the pain and frustration she felt on someone else.

"I'm crying because it hurts to forgive, but I know it is what we must do."

Dylan, who had never professed to understand Rebecca, now looked at her as if she had never seen her before. She felt, for lack of a better word, unworthy. She felt like the bond she and Rebecca shared went much deeper than friendship. It went beyond life. And beyond death. But could it outlast the church?

Dylan wiped away Rebecca's tears with her thumb.

"I almost lost you today." The thought terrified her. So did the idea that, in a few years, her friendship with Rebecca would have to come to an end. After Rebecca joined the church, her forays into Dylan's world would become even more limited than they already were. The rules that governed Rebecca's religion would curtail her interactions with people not of her faith.

"Do you think I could stay with you tonight?" Dylan asked.

Rebecca wanted nothing more, but she knew her father would not allow it. He had granted permission for Dylan to sleep over on rare occasions, but Rebecca didn't think that night would be one of those times. If she knew her father like she thought she did, he was making plans to visit the families and offer them words of comfort. She didn't know if he would want his family to accompany him, but she had to be available in case he did. More likely, she and her mother were about to spend endless hours in the kitchen preparing meals for the affected families so they would have one less thing to worry about.

Dylan held Rebecca's face in her hands. She lowered her head until their foreheads touched. "I don't want to leave you. Please don't make me." She drew herself up to her knees and pulled Rebecca into another hug.

Dylan's arms were around her neck, squeezing tight and getting tighter, but Rebecca didn't think that was the only reason she felt so light-headed. Her heart pounded in her chest as she brought her arms up and circled them around Dylan's waist. She had hugged

Dylan before, but she had never held her. Not like this. Not with their bodies touching up and down and their hearts racing at light speed. Racing in time. Holding Dylan this way felt different. It felt good. Rebecca didn't want to let go. She wanted to hold on to her forever. She turned to smell Dylan's auburn hair. It smelled like fresh green apples and sunshine. Better than any perfume.

Dylan rested her forehead against Rebecca's once more. "May I stay?"

Rebecca stared at Dylan's full lips, just inches away from her own. She wanted to know how they would feel pressed against hers. What it would be like to feel them part and—

"What are you doing?"

Sarah's shrill voice cut through Rebecca's reverie. "N-n-nothing," Rebecca stammered as she and Dylan hastily moved apart.

"I was just—" Dylan began, but Sarah cut her off.

"Mr. Mahoney asked me to come and get you. He says it's time for you to go."

"So soon?" Dylan scrambled to her feet and brushed dirt off her jeans.

"Not soon enough, if you ask me," Sarah said under her breath. She grabbed Rebecca by the arm and roughly pulled her to her feet. "Mama needs you up at the house. She wants you to help her make chicken and corn soup to send with Papa."

"Where is he going?" Rebecca asked, even though she had a good idea what the answer would be.

"He and Peterli are going to visit the Englishman's widow." Sarah's words dripped with scorn.

"What about Uncle Amos?" Rebecca had assumed Uncle Amos or his fellow minister would accompany their father on such a mission. Peterli was just a deacon and a newly ordained one at that. Uncle Amos had been a minister for over twenty years, Joshua's father Micah for almost fifteen.

"He's gone home to prepare a sermon on forgiveness. He and Mr. King are going to lead a special service tonight to honor the ones who were killed." Sarah turned to Dylan. She rubbed her belly as if she sought to calm the child growing inside her, but her words were far from soothing.

"I don't know what my sister sees in you. Because your mother sells Rebecca's quilts to outsiders who think my people are nothing more than a tourist attraction doesn't mean we have to put up with you hanging around all the time, does it? Don't you have better things to do? Other friends you could spend time with? Or are you smiling in our faces and laughing behind our backs like all the others? Go home, English. We don't need you here. Hasn't your kind done enough today?"

Rebecca had never heard Sarah say such harsh words to anyone, Amish or English. She rushed to defend Dylan. "Dylan had nothing to do with what happened at the school. She doesn't deserve such spite. No one does."

"Some deserve a lot more." Sarah's expression was one of defiance. "Well," she said when Rebecca and Dylan didn't move, "what are you waiting for?"

Rebecca and Dylan dutifully began walking toward the house, Sarah close behind. Their fathers were shaking hands when the girls approached.

"I insist on paying you, Thomas Mahoney," Rebecca's father said, wiping his sweaty brow with a cotton handkerchief.

Rebecca quickly surmised Mr. Mahoney had agreed to drive Papa and her cousin Peterli to Nickel Mines. Though the Amish could not own cars, they were allowed to ride in them. For journeys that covered long distances and could not be feasibly made via horse-drawn carriage, they often paid their English neighbors to drive them.

Mr. Mahoney held up his hands. "I wouldn't dream of charging you. Not for something like this. And please, call me Thomas. All the other families do."

"We are not like the other families. In this house, we pay respect where it's due."

"Daddy," Dylan asked, "may I stay until you get back?"

Mr. Mahoney held out his arm, an apparent sign he wanted Dylan to join him at his side.

"Your mother closed the shop early today," he said. "She's already on her way home. I'm sure she wants to spend as much quality time with you as she can. I'll see you in an hour, Samuel."

Her father raised his arm in a gesture of farewell. "An hour it is." He ushered Sarah and Rebecca toward the house.

❖

Dylan broke away from her father, ran up the steps, and drew Rebecca into her arms in a bear hug so strong it would have taken five grown men to pull them apart.

"I'm so glad you're safe," she whispered in Rebecca's ear. "I don't know what I would have done if anything had happened to you." She kissed Rebecca on the cheek and ran back to the truck.

Dylan's head swam as her father drove them home. She had been attracted to girls for as long as she could remember, but this was different. This was Rebecca. This was someone she could never have. Did Rebecca feel the same way? Even if she did, it made no difference. An English and an Amish couldn't be together. Everyone knew it was against the *Ordnung*. But was it possible? Could she and Rebecca be together? Dylan had never wanted anything more.

Chapter Two

Two years later

Dylan consulted The List. She thought of it in capital letters because it was that important. It had started out as one page of scribbled notes that quickly became two, then five, then ten. She eventually migrated it to a notebook—a leather-bound tome she kept with her at all times. The List consisted of all the things she wanted to share with Rebecca. All the things she wanted to experience with her but couldn't because of the strict rules that guided Rebecca's faith.

The List encompassed everything from the mundane to the magnificent. The simple to the sublime. From food to drinks to movies to travel destinations to everything in between. Some of the things on The List would be easy to accomplish, others virtually impossible. Money was a factor, but so was time.

As The List grew, Dylan realized it would take the rest of her life to cross off all the items. Limited to three days a week for the next few years, she and Rebecca wouldn't have that long. They would always be playing catch-up. Unless—

Dylan stopped herself before the fantasy went too far. Because that's what it was. A fantasy. She and Rebecca would have four years. Five at the most. They could spend every weekend together with no one to tell them what they could and could not do. For once, the rules would not apply. But what about after that? What would they do when Rebecca inevitably decided to "join church"? Dylan didn't want to think that far ahead. Not yet. She forced herself to put thoughts of the future in the back of her mind. She had been waiting two years for this day. She wasn't going to let anything spoil it.

Flipping through the pages of her journal, she tried to decide what to do first. It was a no-brainer, really. The first thing they had to do was watch *Witness*, the achingly romantic 1985 drama starring Harrison Ford as an undercover police officer who falls in love with Amish widow Kelly McGillis as he tries to protect her and her son Lukas Haas from vengeful dirty cops. Dylan had seen the movie dozens of times. Each time, she found herself wishing the ending were different. That instead of driving away, Harrison's character John Book would hit the brakes, put the car in reverse, and turn around. It's what she would have done. If she ever established bonds that strong, she would never let them break. Not for anything or anyone.

Dylan ran her finger down the list of movies. Maybe they could start with *Bound*, the 2000 thriller with an ending they wouldn't have to handicap. No, despite the unquestioned charms of Jennifer Tilly and Gina Gershon, the plot was too violent for Rebecca's first time out. The bloodshed would probably remind Rebecca of that awful day in Nickel Mines. A day Dylan and everyone she knew would always remember but longed to forget.

Desert Hearts would probably be better. Patricia Charbonneau and Helen Shaver falling in love in 1950s Nevada and looking hot while they did it. Or perhaps *Casablanca*, followed by *To Have and Have Not* and *The Philadelphia Story*. Who could provide a better introduction to the magic of cinema than acting legends like Katharine Hepburn, Cary Grant, Jimmy Stewart, and Bogie and Bacall?

Dylan was a film buff of the highest order. She could name the release date, director, and stars of every noteworthy film since the medium was invented. Instead of the latest teen idols, posters of classic movies covered her walls. To feed her habit, she had a part-time job as an usher in a theater in her Lancaster hometown. Tearing tickets in half wasn't the most exciting way to earn spending money, but during breaks, she got to sneak up to the projection room and watch movies while she kept her friend Willie company.

Minus the thick black glasses and pierced eyebrow, Wilhelmina "Willie" Sgoda was a dead ringer for Anne Hathaway, the comely star of 2001's *The Princess Diaries* and 2006's *The Devil Wears Prada*. In addition to working together at the Rialto Cinema, Dylan and Willie were also colleagues on their high school newspaper, where Willie was a photographer and Dylan a columnist.

Several of Dylan's friends—Willie included—had suggested she should become a filmmaker one day. She didn't want to make movies. She wanted to talk about them for hours on end. She wanted to write about them. When she went to college the following year— she had already applied to Villanova, Temple, and Penn State, and was trying to decide between them if she was accepted—she planned to major in journalism with an eye on becoming a film critic so she could get paid to see movies instead of the other way around. Carrie Rickey of the *Philadelphia Inquirer* and Roger Ebert of the *Chicago Sun Times* were her heroes. After she wrote a review, she always took a peek at her favorite critics' take on the same film in order to grade herself. They had the occasional difference of opinion but, much to her delight, they were usually on the same page.

The weekly column she wrote for *The Chronicle* only served to whet her appetite. She often found herself writing reviews for films she wasn't assigned to cover. Besides being good practice, it helped enrich her moviegoing experience. It reminded her to go beneath the surface and examine the movie from every angle. To parse every line for hidden meanings, even the throwaways. Now she would get to share the experience with Rebecca. What could be better than that?

Dylan forced herself to hit the brakes. Rebecca had been controlled her whole life. Told what to say, what to do, what to wear, and what to think. The time had come for her to be allowed to make her own decisions. Dylan would leave it to Rebecca to plan the evening. Whatever Rebecca decided to do was fine with her. All Dylan wanted to do was be close enough to see the look of wonder cross Rebecca's face as she finally discovered what she had been missing for so long.

Dylan slid her journal into her messenger bag and reached for her car keys. When she picked Rebecca up, she wanted to hold the door open for her and say something gallant like "Your chariot awaits, my lady," but she didn't think she could pull it off. Not with a straight face, anyway. For her sixteenth birthday the year before, her parents had bought her a VW, a bright yellow new Beetle that was like a happy face on wheels. That didn't exactly scream gallant.

Her father looked up when Dylan headed downstairs. He was standing in front of the mirror in the foyer trying to make sure his tie was straight. Dylan's mother Grace was running around making sure she had turned everything off. They had reservations at her mom's favorite Italian restaurant, which meant, Dylan knew, that her dad was probably going to return home with sauce stains all over the tie that currently occupied so much of his attention.

"How do I look?" he asked, buttoning his gray sport coat.

Dylan gave him the once over. At fifty-six, he no longer possessed the size 30 waist he had sported all through high school and college, but he was still in relatively good shape despite his admitted weakness for cheese steaks and garlic fries. The touch of gray at his temples gave him a distinguished air that was offset by the boyish glint in his bright blue eyes. "Not half bad. Even borderline handsome." She reached up and gave his tie a final adjustment. "If you play your cards right, you might get lucky tonight."

He waggled his strawberry-blond eyebrows mischievously. "You think?"

"Who knows? Maybe I will, too."

His expression turned serious. "You do know this isn't a date, don't you? If you have feelings for Rebecca, she can't possibly return them."

"I know."

"I hope you mean that and you're not just saying what you think I want to hear. I don't want to see you get hurt, Dylan."

"Neither do I. And I won't."

"Rebecca is a sweet girl and I wish things could be different. For her and for you."

"Dad, I know you mean well but you're kind of bumming me out. Can I enjoy tonight without worrying about tomorrow? Or next week? Or next year?"

"Sorry, honey. I just want to make sure you aren't expecting more from your friendship with Rebecca than she will be able to give. Has she ever said she wants to be more than friends?"

"I don't know if she has even allowed herself to believe such things are possible, but I think it's telling that she wants to spend the first night of her *rumspringa* with me, don't you?"

"She couldn't have chosen a better escort," her mom said. She was wearing a beaded black cocktail dress, a white silk shawl thrown over her shoulders. Her lustrous red hair was swept up and away from her face, which was framed by a pair of dangling emerald earrings. She looked stunning. Dylan was blown away. So was her dad. He let out a piercing wolf whistle.

With a broad grin, her mom twirled like a runway model on the end of a catwalk. "You like?" she asked, enjoying the attention.

"Wow, Mom. You look great."

"You think so?"

"I know so."

"No curfew tonight, right?"

Her mother's grin disappeared. "You wish. Just because Rebecca gets to break all the rules doesn't mean you do, too." She kissed Dylan on the forehead and gave her a hug. "Be home by eleven, and no drinking and driving."

"And don't forget to watch out for the other guy," her father said.

Dylan headed for the door. "Have fun tonight, Dad. Don't do anything I wouldn't do."

"I thought you said you wanted us to have fun."

While she made the short drive from Lancaster to Lutz, Dylan reflected on the conversation she and her father had just shared. Was he right? Was she expecting too much?

"I know you want what's best for me, Dad, but this time I think I'm in a better position to judge that than you are."

Her father was the reason Dylan and Rebecca had met. When she was a kid, Dylan used to ride along with him while he made his propane deliveries. She would remain in the truck while he hopped out to check the levels on the gas tanks and refill them as necessary. At the Lapps' house, she had waved shyly at Rebecca, who was playing Parcheesi on the front porch with her sister.

Like most Amish children, Rebecca's primary language was Pennsylvania Dutch. She didn't begin to learn English until her first day of school. Dylan knew enough Pennsylvania Dutch to say hello and good-bye, but not enough to have an entire conversation.

"Guder mariye," she had said in Pennsylvania Dutch.

"Good morning," Rebecca had replied in heavily accented English.

"Wie bischt du heit?"

"I am fine," Rebecca had said slowly, the frown on her face indicating how much effort it took for her to form the words. "How are you?"

The girls had continued their give-and-take on each subsequent visit, Dylan picking up more Pennsylvania Dutch and Rebecca learning more English. Their conversations had grown longer and longer as time passed. Because of the restrictions imposed on interactions with outsiders, however, they had remained little more than acquaintances until Dylan took part in Take Your Daughter to Work Day when she was ten.

Dylan remembered the day well.

Her heart had skipped a beat when the door to My Souvenirs opened. Her first customer. And it was Rebecca. As Rebecca approached the counter, Dylan tried to remember all the things her mother had told her during their brief training session that morning. What was the most important thing? Oh, yeah. Greet the customer with a smile in your voice to match the one on your face.

"Good morning, Rebecca. Good morning, Mrs. Lapp."

Rebecca's mother nodded in reply and quickly turned her

attention to several wood bread boxes on display. Rebecca returned Dylan's greeting. "Good morning, Dylan. May I speak to your mother?"

"She's in the back checking inventory. I'm running the register today. Is there something I can help you with?"

Rebecca looked back at Mrs. Lapp, who gave her a nod of encouragement. Clearly nervous, Rebecca placed a folded quilt on the counter. "I finished this yesterday. The other quilts your mother has for sale are so beautiful that mine might not belong. Do you think you could find a place for it in the shop?"

Dylan spread the quilt on the counter and examined the intricate patterns. She might not be able to tell one stitch from another, but she recognized talent when she saw it. Rebecca was only nine years old. How had she managed to create something so accomplished? Dylan couldn't imagine duplicating the feat. For her, coloring without going outside the lines was accomplishment enough.

"This is beautiful. You did this by yourself?"

Rebecca nodded, her cheeks turning bright red. "I would like to begin earning my keep. I have more quilts at home and I could make another in a few weeks' time. If I brought them in, do you think someone might want to buy them?"

"I think they'll walk out of the store as soon as you bring them in."

"Really?"

"Yes, really." Dylan carefully refolded the quilt. "What kind of machine did you use?"

Rebecca held up her hands and smiled as if Dylan had just told the world's funniest joke.

"Duh," Dylan said, feeling her cheeks burn. "No electricity, Dylan."

"My mother has a machine she runs by tapping her foot against a pedal, but I'm better with my hands."

Dylan thought Rebecca's comment was meant more to ease her embarrassment than to impart information. She appreciated Rebecca's thoughtfulness.

Rebecca darted her eyes at her mother, then leaned forward. "That didn't sound like pride, did it?" she asked in a whisper.

Dylan had smiled, simultaneously touched and amused by Rebecca's desire to downplay her obvious gift. "It sounded like a statement of fact to me. But I won't tell if you won't. It'll be our secret."

Dylan wondered how many other secrets she and Rebecca shared. When Rebecca's thoughts turned to the future, did she dream of having a husband and children, or did she want to see what the world had to offer?

They had not been able to have an intimate conversation since that day in the cornfield two years before. Most of Dylan's time was taken up by school and her job at the theater. In addition to her chores on the family farm, Rebecca had a job of her own.

She worked at the Sunrise Bakery, which was across the street from the restaurant where Marian Schlabach worked as a waitress. She and Marian met on the road each morning and made the three-mile walk together. In the afternoon, they walked home or hitched a ride with friends if one of their buggies happened to be passing by. The journey wasn't so bad in the spring and summer when the weather was nice, Dylan thought. Come winter, though, Rebecca and Marian would turn into human Popsicles before they reached their destinations.

Marian had been Sarah's best friend for years, but Dylan couldn't remember the last time she had seen them together. Was it before Sarah's marriage or after? Either way, Dylan never seemed to see Rebecca any longer unless Marian was around.

Time alone had become a precious commodity. That was about to change. Now they were going to have all the time in the world.

Dylan turned onto a dirt road. Half a dozen cars and trucks were parked haphazardly along the embankment. Dylan pulled in next to a gray buggy and checked the address to make sure she had come to the right place. Rebecca had asked Dylan to meet her at Marian Schlabach's house, but the house Dylan was parked in front of was dark except for a single gas lamp that flickered in an upstairs window. Downstairs, a side door was slightly ajar, signaling the crowd of boys milling in the yard that there were girls inside who might be persuaded to go out courting.

Most of the boys were Amish, but Dylan couldn't tell them from the English friends they had brought with them. Their bowl haircuts had been shaved off or allowed to grow long and they had tossed their dark suits, black socks, and black shoes aside in favor of T-shirts, jeans, and tennis shoes.

Dylan watched as one of the boys aimed a flashlight beam at the upstairs window. A few minutes later, Marian appeared in the open doorway and invited some of the boys inside. Dylan didn't know if she was supposed to join them so she stayed put and waited for Rebecca to show up. She didn't have to wait long. Less than five minutes passed before the boys came back downstairs, followed by about twenty girls dressed in a traditional manner.

Dylan looked through the sea of faces until she spotted Rebecca's. Resisting the urge to honk the horn, she flashed her headlights and climbed out of her car.

Rebecca waved and came running over. "Did you bring them?" she asked, giving Dylan a quick hug.

Dylan nodded. "Right here." She reached into her messenger bag and pulled out a pair of jeans and her favorite blouse. She and Rebecca were roughly the same size. The jeans might be a little big, but with the belt cinched a little tighter, they should be fine.

Rebecca looked at the clothes in her hands. "All my dresses are solid colors. This is the first time I'll wear something that bears a pattern."

"I'm sure the blouse will look great on you. Even better than it does on me."

"I doubt that, but thank you for letting me borrow it."

Rebecca gave Dylan another hug, then pulled off her bonnet and loosened her flowing hair. Dylan had to restrain herself from running her hands through it.

In the other cars, girls were smoking, drinking, and cranking up the radios. Country, rock, and rap artists fought for dominance of the airwaves. Under normal circumstances, music of any kind was forbidden for fear it would stir up the listeners' emotions. The members of the caravan that snaked up the road aimed to put the theory to the test.

"Where are they going?" Dylan kept her eyes averted as Rebecca changed clothes in the backseat. She couldn't see much anyway. The new moon didn't provide enough illumination for her rearview mirror to be used as a spyglass, but that didn't stop her from trying.

"To the Kwik Stop so the girls can change clothes and the boys can buy beer. There's a hoedown in Casey. Everyone's going to be there."

All the more reason to stay away, Dylan thought. She wanted Rebecca all to herself. She smiled as Rebecca climbed into the front seat. She had expected Rebecca to look different when she changed clothes, but she hadn't expected this. Someone who strived to be plain had turned into someone breathtaking. "Well, hello, gorgeous," she said, mimicking Barbra Streisand in *Funny Girl*.

Rebecca blushed. "I've never been called gorgeous before. What am I supposed to say?"

"How about thank you?"

"Thank you."

"You're welcome. What do you want to do tonight?"

"Don't you have anything special in mind? What about The List?"

"The List can wait. This is your night, not mine."

"Maybe we could go to Casey for a while. Perhaps it's best if I stick with my own."

My own. Dylan latched onto the words. Why did their lives have to be separate? Hers. Mine. Why couldn't it be theirs?

"I thought *rumspringa* was about pushing past your boundaries, not remaining inside them."

"It is, but we don't have to push them tonight, do we? I don't want to end up like Sarah, forced to marry before I'm ready."

"Do you think she made a mistake?"

"I don't, but if she does, that could explain the unease I sense in her soul."

Dylan looked at Rebecca out of the corner of her eye. "When do you think you'll be ready to get married?"

"Not for a while yet. Four years, at least."

"Four years can seem like a long time when you're looking forward to something, but time passes in the blink of an eye."

"That's why it's so important I make the right decisions now. I don't want to make a choice I'll spend the rest of my life regretting."

"Is that what Sarah's doing?"

"She doesn't seem as happy as I thought she would be, but Joshua is a good man. Sarah made the right choice when she decided to marry him."

"Perhaps she doesn't feel the same way. Only she knows what's best for her. The same way only you know what's best for you and only I know what's best for me."

"What do you think is best for you?"

"Freedom. Freedom of choice. Freedom to love who I want and how I want."

Rebecca frowned. "Don't you want to get married and have children?"

Dylan hesitated, unsure whether she should answer the question or deflect it. The rules of Rebecca's religion forbade many things and allowed limited use of others. Alcohol was okay in moderation, smoking was tolerated as long as there were no cigarettes involved, and so on and so on. The rules on homosexuality, however, were unequivocal. Expressing romantic love for someone of the same sex was expressly forbidden.

Dylan turned on her blinker and pulled her car to the side of the road. Ahead of her, a string of taillights continued to head out of town.

"Why are you stopping? We aren't there yet."

"I want to tell you something first. After I do, I'll gladly take you anywhere you want to go—even if it's away from me."

"You're one of my closest friends. Why would I want to leave you?"

"You might not have a choice."

Dylan looked down at her hands. Her fingers gripped each other so tightly her knuckles were white.

Rebecca placed her hands on top of Dylan's. "You're scaring me. What's wrong?"

"I would say nothing's wrong, but your father and the rest of your church might not agree."

"What do you mean?"

"When I get married—and I do want to get married—it will be to a woman instead of a man." Dylan waited for her words to sink in. "Do you understand what I mean by that?"

"You're saying you like girls instead of boys. You're saying you would prefer to commit yourself to a woman instead of a man."

Rebecca's voice was flat, betraying no emotion. Dylan examined Rebecca's face but couldn't unravel the mystery hidden in Rebecca's brown eyes. "How does that make you feel?"

Rebecca fidgeted in her seat but didn't let go of Dylan's hand. Dylan was grateful for the continued contact. If Rebecca didn't shy away, that meant there was still hope. There was still a chance what she was feeling wasn't one-sided.

"Papa says it's wrong for a man to lie with a man as he would a woman. He says it's wrong for a woman to love a woman as she would a man."

"I'm not asking you what your father thinks. What do you think?"

"I think I'll love you no matter who you choose to spend your life with."

Dylan's heart skittered when she heard Rebecca use the verb *love* in a sentence in which she was the object. "What if I said I wanted that someone to be you?"

Rebecca pulled her hand away. "Are you— Do you think I am like you?"

"I was hoping you were."

Rebecca leaned against the passenger door. As the physical distance between them widened, Dylan felt the emotional chasm grow as well.

"Have I ever shown any sign that I might feel as you do?" Rebecca asked.

"That day in the cornfield, I thought—I hoped—there might be something between us. A spark that could grow into something bigger than either of us ever imagined. When I go to bed each night, your face is the last thing I see. When I wake up each morning, your name is on my lips. My father tried to tell me not to think of this as a date, but—"

"Your father knows about you?"

"My parents and I talk about everything. We always have."

"When you told them, they didn't...punish you?"

"No, they loved me. So would yours."

Rebecca looked out the window. "My parents aren't like yours. They can't be. They love me, but there are rules they must follow."

"Do those rules say your parents have to stop loving you if you do something that displeases them? I doubt that. You're their daughter. They'll love you no matter what you do. Maybe our parents are more alike than you think. Maybe you and I are, too."

Dylan held out her hand. Time stopped while she waited for Rebecca to respond. If Rebecca took her hand, it would mean the beginning. If she didn't, it would be the end. After what seemed like an eternity, Rebecca bridged the distance between them. Her palm slid across Dylan's. When Dylan spread her fingers, Rebecca curled hers around them and squeezed. Rebecca's grip felt strong and sure. It felt like acceptance. Dylan's heart sprouted wings and threatened to fly out of her chest.

"So do you want me to take you home, or are you ready to party?"

Rebecca giggled. "Let's party."

Dylan eased back into traffic. She felt like she and Rebecca had just passed their first test. How would they do on the next one?

"Can we go shopping tomorrow?" Rebecca picked at a seam on the baggy jeans. "I can't possibly borrow your clothes every weekend. I'll need some of my own."

"Of course we can go. I'll invite Mom along. I'm sure she would love to have a girls' day out. We haven't had one in years.

If I ask nicely, I think I could convince her to take us to the spa for massages and mud baths."

"A mud bath?" Rebecca wrinkled her nose. "I can get one of those on the farm."

Dylan laughed, glad to see Rebecca was finally starting to get comfortable. "It's not the same. This one is a lot more expensive. It smells a lot better, too."

❖

Dylan pulled into the parking lot of the Kwik Stop, where Marian was holding court with four boys huddled around a battered Trans Am. Dressed in tight jeans and a short top that bared her navel, Marian flirted brazenly with each of the boys. They competed for her attention. "Relax, fellas," she said when the competition threatened to turn physical. "There's enough of me to go around."

"I wish I could be more like her," Rebecca said. "Wild and free and unafraid. She's always willing to speak her mind and do or say whatever is on it."

"And that's a good thing?"

Marian headed over to Dylan's car and knocked on the driver's side window. Dylan pressed the switch that lowered the glass. Marian leaned inside, her unfettered breasts nearly spilling out of her shirt. "Nice car." Her words were already slurred even though it was barely nine o'clock.

"Thanks."

Rebecca noticed Dylan leaning away from the smell of alcohol on Marian's breath. Marian was just nineteen, but she looked twice that as years of hard partying started to take a toll on her prematurely haggard face.

Dylan often referred to *rumspringa* as Rum Spring since so many participants used the opportunity to introduce themselves to drinking. For Marian, it was more like Rum Spring, Rum Summer, Rum Fall, and Rum Winter.

Marian looked over at Rebecca. "Having fun, little simmie?"

Simmies was the term used to describe the kids who were new

to *rumspringa*. The older kids made fun of them because the young ones were so anxious to prove they belonged they usually ended up embarrassing themselves by trying too hard to fit in. Meaning "foolish in the head," the label was one Rebecca wanted to be rid of as soon as possible. "So far."

"Just wait," Marian said. "It gets better. As long as you're able to hold your liquor, you'll be fine. If you're anything like Sarah, that shouldn't be a problem for you. I haven't seen much of her lately. How is she?"

Rebecca held back an exasperated sigh. Marian asked her the same question every time they saw each other. Perhaps Marian thought the answer would change one day and she wanted to be there when it did. Rebecca didn't know what had happened to cause Sarah and Marian's falling-out—she and Marian were now closer than Sarah and Marian were—but she wished they would make things up so she wouldn't feel caught in the middle.

"She's fine," Rebecca replied, parroting the same answer she always gave. "Her son keeps her pretty busy. He's a real handful."

"I'm sure," Marian said. "Isaiah looks just like his father, don't you think, Dylan?"

"To me, he looks more like Sarah."

"Sarah has fine, straight hair. Joshua, too. Isaiah has a head full of curls. Where do you think they came from?"

"I think they're a gift from God," Rebecca said.

"You're probably right," Marian said. "You usually are about such things. Are Sarah and Joshua still staying at your uncle's place?"

"For a few more months, then they're going to get a place of their own." Dylan looked confused, so Rebecca tried to fill in the gaps in her knowledge. "When Sarah and Joshua first got married, they planned to live with Mama and Papa for a few months before finding a place to call their own. When spring arrived, the price of land was so high they couldn't afford to buy the lot they had their eye on. They didn't want to keep imposing on Mama and Papa, so they moved in with Uncle Amos. He has never married and he doesn't have any children. He lives in a big house all by himself.

I was glad when Sarah and Joshua moved in with him because it meant he wouldn't have to be alone all the time. I don't get to spend as much time with Sarah, Joshua, and Isaiah as I would like. Most days, I only see Sarah and Joshua in passing—before work when they arrive to help with the chores on the farm and after work when they're headed home."

"You'll see plenty of them at the barn raising next year. Make sure you invite me, okay? I wouldn't miss it for the world." Marian returned her attention to Dylan. "Do you have a boyfriend, English?"

Rebecca sat straighter in her seat, anxious to hear the answer. Marian was a gossip. If Dylan told her she was gay, the word would spread like wildfire. Rebecca could be considered guilty by suspicion.

"Why do you want to know?" Dylan asked.

"Because my little brother wants to ask you out." Marian pointed out her brother Zeke, who was coming out of the convenience store carrying two bags filled with junk food. "He has a thing for English girls. English boys like Amish girls because we know how to party. English girls like Amish boys because they have lots of money."

"So why does your brother like me?"

"He thinks you're cute." Marian shrugged as if to say there was no accounting for taste.

"Tell him thanks but, yes, I am seeing someone."

"What's his name?"

"Willie."

"Little Willie or Big Willie?" Marian asked suggestively.

"I wouldn't know yet. We're taking it slow."

"If you say so. Did Rebecca tell you we're thinking of renting an apartment in town?"

"No, she didn't say anything about it." Dylan looked over at Rebecca for confirmation.

"It's Marian's idea. Moving into town would put us closer to work and it would make life more convenient for both of us."

"We just have to convince her father that it's a good idea."

The boys in the Trans Am honked the horn, signaling that everyone was ready to go.

"It's time to go, simmie," Marian said. "Let's see if you can keep up." She skipped over to the Trans Am, climbed in the front seat, and sat in a dark-haired boy's lap.

Dylan turned her key in the ignition but left the car in neutral. "We don't have to do this, you know."

"I know, but I want to." Rebecca felt like she had something to prove—to Dylan, to Marian, and to herself.

Dylan watched Rebecca drain her second cup of Blue Hawaii—pineapple juice spiked with liberal doses of vodka, coconut rum, and blue Curacao—and tried to determine whether Rebecca would get sick before, during, or after she drove her home. Dylan was leaning toward before. To her credit, Rebecca was holding out longer than the other simmies—who were puking their guts out all over the field—but Dylan didn't think Rebecca would be able to last much longer. The fragrant concoction in her cup looked like glass cleaner and smelled like fermented fruit. Dylan hadn't drunk any but she felt like she had a contact high from the fumes.

The hoedown was much bigger than she had expected it to be. Nearly five hundred people were spread around the huge bonfire that dominated the field and made the hot August night even hotter. Music blasted from portable stereos hooked to car batteries.

Near the edge of the cornfield, a couple of English boys had erected a makeshift stand and were doing a brisk business selling marijuana, cocaine, and homemade crystal meth. As an added bonus, the entrepreneurs threw in free glow-in-the-dark condoms if the purchase exceeded twenty dollars. Dylan watched as several couples, prophylactics in hand, disappeared into the pitch-black rows of corn or sneaked into the barn that sat atop the hill on the other side of the field.

Though unsteady on her feet, Marian managed to make her

way across the rutted cornfield without spilling a drop from the three cups of punch in her hands. "Ready for a drink, English?"

"It's *Dylan*," Dylan said, tired of feeling like an outsider. "And no, thank you."

"Sorry, your highness. I didn't mean to offend your delicate sensibilities."

"I'll take one." Rebecca reached for one of the cups, leaving Marian to two-fist the other drinks.

"That's the spirit. Drink up, simmie." Marian raised one cup in a toast before leaving to greet a group of newcomers.

Rebecca took a sip of her fresh drink. Dylan reached up to wipe away the drops of Windex-blue alcohol clinging to Rebecca's upper lip, but Rebecca slapped her hand away. "I can do it," she said defiantly. "I can take care of myself. I don't need you to look after me."

Dylan was stung by the vehemence behind Rebecca's words. "Maybe you ought to slow down a little."

Rebecca downed half her drink in one long swallow. Then she swayed as if the wind rustling the corn stalks were a nor'easter instead of a gentle breeze. "I'm confused. If you like girls, who's Willie?"

"My best friend."

"Your best friend is a boy?"

"Willie may dress like a boy from time to time, but, underneath the clothes, she's all girl."

"Is she your girlfriend?"

"No."

"Then why did you let Marian think Willie was more than a friend?"

"Because my personal life is none of Marian's business. And I don't want her to make assumptions about you based on what she knows about me."

"Oh."

Dylan watched Rebecca try to process the information she had just been provided. She understood Rebecca's obvious eagerness to get wasted. It couldn't be easy to have everything be so brand new. To have every experience be one you had never undergone before.

From the looks of things, Rebecca was about to experience something else—her first hangover.

Rebecca's lips went from blue to green to gray. She shivered despite the intense heat generated by the blazing bonfire.

"Are you okay?"

Rebecca pressed a hand to her stomach. "I think I'm going to be sick." She barely got the words out before she bent over double and spewed blue liquid on the ground.

"There goes another one!" Marian yelled, prompting a round of mock cheers.

Dylan rubbed Rebecca's back but made sure to stay out of the line of fire. "Better?" she asked after Rebecca purged the contents of her stomach a second time.

"I think so." Rebecca wiped her mouth with the back of her hand, nearly spilling the rest of her drink all over her borrowed blouse.

Dylan took the plastic cup out of Rebecca's trembling hands and dashed the contents on the ground. "Let's get you something a little less potent." They made their way over to the concession stand. "How much for a bottle of water?"

One of the boys reached into a nearby cooler and pulled out a bottle of spring water. "Five bucks," he said, setting the bottle on the counter.

Dylan did a double take. Earlier, she had seen a sign saying water was only a dollar. She had thought the prices would go down as the night wore on. They had multiplied instead. "You're shitting me."

"I shit you not. It's all about supply and demand. They're demanding and my supply is dwindling. E makes you thirsty, you know."

"No, I don't know."

"I'll make you a deal." The boy's eyes drifted from Dylan to Rebecca and back again. "Make out with her and I'll give you the water for free."

Dylan pulled a $5 bill out of her pocket and slapped it on the counter. "Sorry. I don't do floor shows." She handed Rebecca the bottle of water. "Let's go home."

❖

Dylan looked in the refrigerator. "Are you hungry? We have some leftover spaghetti. I'll split it with you if you like."

"Yes, please." Freshly showered and changed into a T-shirt and a pair of Dylan's pajama bottoms, Rebecca felt like a new person. No, she felt like herself instead of a simmie who didn't know when enough was enough. "What time will your parents be home?"

Dylan put the plastic container of spaghetti in the microwave. "They'll call the house phone before my curfew to make sure I'm here, then they'll probably show up a half hour later. That's their usual pattern anyway. Did you have fun tonight?"

Rebecca watched the food spin around on the carousel. "Before or after I threw up?"

"Before."

"I liked being with you, if that's what you're asking."

"It's not, but thank you. I liked being with you, too." Dylan took the spaghetti out of the microwave, gave it a quick stir, and sprinkled Parmesan cheese on top. She grabbed two forks out of the cutlery drawer and handed one to Rebecca. "What would you like to drink? We've got water, soda, juice, and lemonade. No Blue Hawaii, though."

Rebecca wadded up a napkin and tossed it at the back of Dylan's head.

Dylan tossed it back. "Nice arm, but we need to work on your aim." She grabbed two bottles of water and set them next to the plate of spaghetti. They ate standing next to the island in the center of the kitchen.

When Dylan licked spaghetti sauce off her lips, Rebecca flashed back to the day two years before when Dylan had almost kissed her. What would have happened if they had kissed? Would their lives be drastically different or would they be the same? Rebecca couldn't change the past. She could only hope to learn from it. Her faith said Dylan and people like her should change their ways or remain celibate. They should live a life without love. But how could love—in any form—be wrong?

"Kiss me."

Dylan's eyes widened. "What?"

"Kiss me."

"Are you sure?"

Rebecca met and held Dylan's gaze. "*Rumspringa* is about pushing your boundaries. Isn't that what you said? I want to push mine. Will you help me?"

"Gladly."

Dylan put her hands on Rebecca's waist and pulled her closer. When their lips met, Rebecca felt her body come to life. Dylan's lips were soft and warm. They were amazing. No, *miraculous* was a better word. She circled her arms around Dylan's neck as Dylan's hands slowly slid up and down her back. Chills ran down Rebecca's spine. Did kissing a boy feel this good? Or could she feel this way only when Dylan Mahoney's lips were pressed against hers?

When Dylan pulled away, Rebecca felt a part of herself go with her. She couldn't believe what she had just done. And she couldn't wait to do it again.

"Have you ever seen *Lady and the Tramp*?" Dylan asked. "It's an animated Disney film about a pampered cocker spaniel and the streetwise mutt she befriends. It's not the first movie that comes to mind when I think of romantic scenes, but there's one scene in particular that— Well, it's better if I show you. Follow my lead."

Dylan picked up a spaghetti noodle and put one end in her mouth. She directed Rebecca to take the other end. They slowly worked their way through the noodle until their lips met in a kiss.

"That kiss was even better than the first one." When Rebecca lowered her eyes, Dylan put a finger under Rebecca's chin and tilted her head up. "You're safe here. You don't have to hide how you feel. You don't have to be scared. Not with me. I will protect you."

Rebecca desperately wanted to believe Dylan's words were true, but how could they be? If word of her behavior were to get back to her family, the impact could be devastating. She hadn't yet been baptized so she couldn't be shunned, but she was still subject to her father's will. If he forbade her from seeing Dylan, she would have no choice but to comply.

"That would be my parents," Dylan said when the phone rang. She gave Rebecca a quick kiss, then crossed the room and picked up the phone. She quickly filled her mother in on her evening, assured her everything was fine, and returned to Rebecca.

"Do your parents really know about you?" Rebecca asked.

"Yes, they do."

"What did they say when you told them you were going out with me tonight?"

"They told me there was no way you could feel the same way about me as I do about you. If you tell me you could live the rest of your life without kissing me again, maybe I'll believe them."

Rebecca replayed their first kiss. And the second. And the third. "I don't think I could live five more minutes."

"Neither could I."

"When did you first realize you liked girls?"

"I was seven. I had a crush on the librarian at my elementary school. She didn't feel the same way, but I think she did have a bit of a soft spot for me. She used to try to teach me about the Dewey Decimal System. I never learned how to catalog books, but I did learn one very important thing: I loved the way her legs looked in fishnet stockings."

A librarian. Surrounded all day by thousands of books. To Rebecca, it sounded like the most wonderful job in the world. She wondered what she would have to do to get a job like that. She knew she would have to go back to school, but for how long? And how much would it cost? She enjoyed working at the bakery but she didn't want to do it forever. Before she met Dylan, she had never allowed herself to dream such things. Now dreams were her constant companion.

Dylan pulled a pint of butter pecan ice cream out of the freezer. "Sweets for the sweet." She fed Rebecca a spoonful of ice cream. "Am I the only girl you've ever wanted to kiss?"

Rebecca savored the luxurious sweetness of the ice cream before swallowing it down. She immediately opened her mouth for more. "I've kissed other girls before."

"The way you kissed me?"

"Of course not, silly."

"Did you like kissing me?"

"Yes." Rebecca's stomach felt funny. She couldn't determine if the cause was the alcohol she had drunk, the strange food she had just eaten, or Dylan Mahoney standing so close.

"Can you still be friends with me knowing what you do about me?"

"My feelings for you won't change, no matter who you choose to love."

"Wow. I'm supposed to be the writer, but you have an eloquence I could only hope to possess."

"Speaking the truth always sounds better than making up a lie." Unaccustomed to staying up so late—her day usually ended at nine and began at four—Rebecca stifled a yawn.

"You must be exhausted. Let's get you to bed."

"I can help you clean up."

"There's nothing to clean up." Dylan tossed the empty water bottles into the recycling bin, put the rest of the ice cream back in the freezer, and placed the dirty dishes in the washer. "See? All done." She showed Rebecca to the guest room upstairs and kissed her good night. "Sweet dreams."

Rebecca grabbed Dylan's hand. Alone in a strange environment, she clung to the familiar. "Stay with me."

Rebecca crawled under the covers and Dylan slid in behind her. "Close your eyes," Dylan said, gently stroking Rebecca's hair. Rebecca did as she was told. Dylan softly sang a lullaby several centuries old.

"What's that language?"

"Gaelic," Dylan said. "Grandma Siobhan, Mom's mother, is

from Ireland. She taught me that song when I was a little girl. She used to sing it to me all the time. Two verses and I was out like a light. I'd love for you to meet her. Even more, I'd love to show you where she grew up. Her village is filled with rolling green hills that go on forever. My family and I went there on vacation once. It was so beautiful I didn't want to come back home. Sharing that journey with you is item number five on The List."

Rebecca rolled over in bed. She was face-to-face with Dylan, their heads just inches apart. "If taking me to Ireland is item number five, what's the most important thing you want to show me?"

Dylan grinned. "We took care of item number one when you asked me to kiss you. I've been waiting two years to cross that one off."

"And what's next?"

Dylan grew tongue-tied when she thought of the entry on the second page of her journal. The experience she wanted to save until she was old enough to fully appreciate it. "I don't think we're ready for item number two yet, so we'd better skip to item number three. Would you like to learn to drive?"

"A car? You're going to teach me how to drive a car? *Your* car?"

"My car is a stick shift, which is harder to learn. My dad's truck is an automatic. It's a lot easier to practice on. Next weekend, I thought we could go out to the country and I could give you a driving lesson. Would you like that?"

"Very much." Rebecca wrapped her arms around Dylan's neck and kissed her cheek. "Thank you, Dylan."

"You're welcome." Dylan could feel Rebecca's body thrumming with excitement. Adrenaline coursed through her own veins. *If you're not careful, Mahoney, she's going to break your heart.*

"Is everything okay?" her mother asked when she and her father stuck their heads in the room thirty minutes later.

"Everything's fine."

"So it went well?"

"It went great."

"Then go to sleep. She'll still be here in the morning."

"Hey, Dad?" Dylan called out when he started to close the door.

"Yes?" He stuck his head back in the room.

"Did you get lucky?"

He grinned and turned to watch her mother walk down the hall. "Not yet. Give me a few minutes," he replied in a conspiratorial whisper. "What about you?"

Dylan looked down at Rebecca's sleeping form. "Give me a few years. Then ask me again."

Rebecca stood under the shower spray until the hot water turned tepid. She loved the way the water felt as it pelted her head and streamed down her body. At home, she had to fetch water from the well and heat it on the wood stove in the kitchen in order to have a hot bath. At Dylan's house, all she had to do was turn on the tap.

"Running water is my new favorite thing," she said as she pirouetted in the shower. "No, kissing Dylan is my new favorite thing. Nothing is better than that, not even a sewing bee. Perhaps I should start a list of my own. Kissing Dylan would come first. Running water would be a close second."

Laughing, she shut off the water and toweled herself dry. When she pinned her hair up, she felt her demeanor start to change. She felt herself grow quiet. She watched herself become plain. Her black dress and stockings were laid out on the bed. When Dylan saw her wearing them instead of the worldly clothes she had sported all weekend, would Dylan still think she was gorgeous?

Rebecca wrapped a towel around her body and gathered her things. When she opened the door that separated the bathroom from the guest room, she discovered she wasn't alone. Dylan was placing folded clothes in a dresser drawer. How long had she been there? Had she heard Rebecca musing to herself?

Dylan looked up after Rebecca gasped in surprise. Her eyes

slowly traveled up Rebecca's body. Rebecca watched Dylan's eyes darken, the emerald orbs filling with an emotion Rebecca didn't recognize. Rebecca's skin prickled from the heat.

"Hello, beautiful," Dylan said, her voice husky and low.

"Hello." Rebecca felt the loose knot holding the towel closed begin to loosen. She hurriedly grabbed the towel before the halves separated and fell to the floor.

Dylan cleared her throat and turned away. "I didn't mean to scare you. Mom washed and dried the clothes you bought yesterday. I was just putting them away for you. I want you to think of this as your room. Whenever you're here, this space is yours. Even when you're not, it will still feel like yours to me." She pushed the drawer shut and cleared her throat again. "I'll let you get dressed." She headed for the door.

"Dylan?" Rebecca waited for Dylan to face her before she continued. There was so much she wanted to say but she didn't know where to start. Or where to end. "Thank you."

"I don't know what I did, but you're welcome. When do you have to be back?"

"Services don't begin for a couple of hours yet, but I want to get home in time to feed the horses. I love taking care of the animals. Especially the babies."

"I can totally see you doing that. You're going to make a great mother someday."

"So will you."

"I don't know about that. But with you around, I can learn from the best. I'll wait for you downstairs. I'll take you home after we grab some breakfast. Next week, maybe you can stay longer."

"If you're not tired of me by then."

"Not a chance."

The time had come for Rebecca to leave Dylan's world and return to her own. She had thought the transition into Dylan's world would be harder than the one out of it. Who would have thought that it would be the other way around? Though she looked forward to going home, she couldn't wait until she could return to the Mahoneys'. They had opened their home and their arms to her. And

Dylan had opened her heart. No matter what happened in the future, Rebecca knew she would treasure the Mahoneys' hospitality for the rest of her days.

After breakfast, Dylan drove Rebecca to Lutz and pulled to a stop next to the winding road that led to the family farm. Dylan could go no farther. Rebecca's family tolerated intrusions from the outside world during the week, but not on Sundays. The Sabbath was reserved for worship or visits with family or their Amish neighbors.

"Thank you, Dylan. For everything." Rebecca looked around to make sure no one was nearby. Then she gave Dylan a quick kiss. "You made the first weekend of my *rumspringa* one I shall never forget."

"Neither will I." Dylan held her fingers against her mouth as if her lips burned. "Where do you want me to pick you up on Friday? Marian's again?"

Rebecca noted the look of displeasure that crossed Dylan's face. It was obvious Dylan hadn't enjoyed herself at the hoedown. To be honest, Rebecca hadn't, either. Just thinking about those few hours made her stomach queasy. "No, one weekend like that was enough. I did it once. I don't have to do it again. Drinking and partying aren't for me. I just want to spend time with you and your family. Is that okay?"

Dylan's eyes glowed as if they were lit by a fire from within. "What do you think? Of course it's okay. I'll pick you up at the bakery and you can tell me where you want to go from there."

"Can we do item number ten?"

"You want to go to Philadelphia?"

"I want to see the Liberty Bell. I learned about it in school but I've never seen it in person. Is it really and truly cracked?"

"Yes, it is, but the bell itself is much smaller than you might think. I thought it would be huge, but it's only three feet tall."

"Do you think we can go?"

"I don't think my parents would let me drive to Philly without an adult in the car, but I'm sure my dad would tag along if we agree to buy him a cheese steak."

"Can I have one, too?"

"You can have anything you want. If the Phillies are in town and we can get tickets, we can cross off item number twenty-seven, too. Your first professional baseball game."

"I love baseball. When I was little, Sarah bought a battery-powered radio we kept hidden in our room. Late at night, after our parents were asleep, we would listen to music and learn the words to all the latest pop songs. She left the radio behind when she moved out. I use it to listen to broadcasts of the Phillies games. The announcers make me feel like I'm sitting in the ballpark with them. I never imagined I would be able to see the team play in person. You make me feel so special, Dylan."

"You *are* special. I know you believe no one is better than anyone else, but you're special to me, Rebecca."

Her parents made Rebecca feel loved. Dylan made her feel wanted. Dylan seemed to be courting her. Rebecca didn't know whether to ask her to stop or encourage her to keep going.

"See you next weekend."

Rebecca got out of the car and waved good-bye to Dylan. She skipped up the road, pausing once to watch Dylan's little yellow car head toward town.

"Was that Dylan Mahoney?"

Rebecca squealed in fright. "Who's there?" she asked, resisting the urge to run.

Esther Hershberger, a basket of blackberries in her arms, stepped out of the wooded area next to the fence. "Only me."

"Esther, I didn't see you there." Rebecca let out a deep breath but didn't allow herself to relax. How much, if anything, had Esther seen?

Esther had chosen to spend her *rumspringa* participating in activities organized by the church. Hay rides, volleyball tournaments, and Sunday sings. While Rebecca ventured into the world, Esther would remain behind.

"I've been waiting for you. Mr. Lapp said you should be home soon and I wanted to be the first to greet you. Do you think we could make a blackberry pie after church?"

"I don't see why not."

"Was that Dylan Mahoney's car you were riding in?"

"Yes, it was."

"You didn't pay her to drive you, did you? You know we're not allowed to exchange money on the Sabbath."

"I didn't have to pay her. She drove me for free."

"She has always been a good friend to you."

"As have you."

Esther linked her arm around Rebecca's as they walked up the road. "Did you enjoy your time away?"

"Very much."

"What did you do?"

Rebecca hesitated. She wasn't obligated to tell her parents or anyone else what she did during *rumspringa*. They could ask, but she didn't have to answer. Her weekends were her own. She could do with them what she wished, spend them wherever she pleased.

Rebecca regarded her friend and saw no cause for concern. Esther was the daughter of her family's closest neighbors. They had known each other since they were very young children and were constant fixtures at one another's homes. She felt certain Esther would never wish her harm, no matter what the *Ordnung* dictated.

"There's something I have to tell you."

"What?"

"Can you keep a secret?"

Esther tilted her head, a tendril of blond hair spilling out of her bonnet. Her eyes glittered at the prospect of a shared confidence. "Of course I can."

"Promise me."

"I promise. What's the secret?"

"I was kissed."

Esther clapped her hands in delight, then abruptly began to pout.

"What's wrong?" Rebecca asked.

"Tobias will be jealous."

"Your brother? Why would he care that I was kissed?"

"Rebecca, are you really so blind? Tobias has always fancied you. He was planning to tell you so tonight at the sing." Esther blushed. "I guess I can't keep a secret after all."

As they walked up the road, Rebecca thought about what Esther had said. Tobias was a nice boy—hardworking and firm in his faith—but Rebecca had never thought about him as anything other than a friend. The love she felt for him was one a sister might feel for a brother. Could she grow to love him as a wife would a husband?

Rebecca didn't know how to reconcile her conflicting emotions. On one side, there was Dylan and the promise of an uncertain future. On the other, there was Tobias and the certainty that life as she knew it would not change. Which side should she choose?

Kissing Dylan—spending time with her—was fun. But it felt unfair. When she kissed Dylan, she felt it in her body. Dylan seemed to feel it in her heart. Rebecca felt as if she were toying with Dylan's emotions. Such behavior was unacceptable. It was settled. There would be no more kisses unless they meant as much to Rebecca as they obviously meant to Dylan.

"You've returned."

Rebecca smiled at the evident relief in her father's voice. "Were you worried?"

He held her at arm's length, a twinkle of delight in his soft brown eyes. "I knew you would be safe with the Mahoneys. Your mother, on the other hand—"

"Nonsense," her mother said, shooing him away so she could give Rebecca a hug. "I knew I could count on you not to get into mischief. You did behave yourself, didn't you?"

"Yes, Mama."

Undoubtedly remembering Rebecca's confession about being kissed, Esther giggled and pressed the basket of blackberries into Rebecca's arms. "I'll see you at services, Rebecca. I'll come back later to help you with the pie. If you would like a ride to the sing tonight, Tobias and I would be happy to take you."

"That would be fine."

"Good-bye, Mr. and Mrs. Lapp. See you soon, Rebecca."

Rebecca noted the pleased look her parents shared at the mention of Tobias's name. The beginning of courtship was a subject not openly discussed with family or friends. Parents respected their children's privacy and, if need be, pretended not to know their offspring had begun the selection process.

Rebecca valued her parents' opinions. Their expressions indicated they approved of Tobias and his yet-unstated intentions to woo her. If they considered him a worthy lifemate for her, why didn't she?

Tobias was the spitting image of his sister. He was as handsome as Esther was beautiful. They had the same corn silk-colored hair and bright blue eyes. When Rebecca looked into those eyes, though, she didn't feel the same way she did when she looked into Dylan's. She felt fondness when she looked into Tobias's eyes. When she looked into Dylan's, she felt something close to—

"I'm going to see to the horses."

Rebecca walked out of the house and headed to the barn. She heard voices when she approached the half-open door. On second thought, she heard only one person speaking, not two. Uncle Amos was talking to himself. He seemed to be practicing a speech. Listening a little longer, Rebecca gathered that Uncle Amos was rehearsing his sermon. He would give the short lecture that opened services; her father would deliver the longer one later in the day. During the time between the two talks, worshipers would comment on what was said and sing selections from the *Ausbund*, an ancient book of hymns.

"*Guder mariye*, Uncle Amos," Rebecca said, making her presence known.

"*Guder mariye*, Rebecca. Have you come to help your old uncle or humor him?"

"Both." Rebecca held a burlap bag open while her uncle filled it with a combination of oats and sweet feed. One of Uncle Amos's horses nudged her shoulder with his muzzle. "Coming, Goliath," she said, reaching up to stroke the white patch on the big horse's face. "Be patient."

She watched as Uncle Amos picked up the feed bag and strapped it around Goliath's neck. The horse crunched on the bag's contents as if he had not eaten in a week. Rebecca knew better.

"Slow down, greedy. I know Uncle Amos fed you yesterday. Have you brushed and combed the horses yet, Uncle Amos?"

"Not yet," he said, filling another feed bag. "I was saving that chore for you."

Rebecca selected a brush and comb from the collection of tools that hung on one wall of the barn. She slipped the comb into the pocket of her apron and began to brush the horses, a task that gave her nearly as much pleasure as it did the animals. Rebecca could almost feel Goliath sighing as she ran the brush over his coarse hair.

"Uncle Amos?"

"Yes, child?"

"We have always been close, have we not?"

"Ayuh."

The one-word answer perfectly summed up their relationship. Rebecca fondly remembered the many nearly wordless afternoons they had spent fishing, reading, or tending to the animals. Uncle Amos didn't talk much, but his meaning was always clear. When he did speak, his words were powerful. They carried much weight. Both in his family and in his community.

"May I ask you a question?"

"Of course, child. What is it?"

"You're older than Papa, but he is the one who is married with children. Why are you still clean-shaven after all these years while Papa is the one who has a beard down to his chest? Could you find no one to marry?"

Uncle Amos was quiet for so long Rebecca began to think she had offended him. She was trying to concoct a suitable apology when he finally answered her question.

"There was someone dear to me when I was a young man, but we were not meant to live as one."

Rebecca combed Goliath's thick black mane. "Was it not God's will for you to be together?"

"You've heard the story of the country mouse and the city mouse? That is what we were. I could never leave the country for the tumult of the city. I tried to leave once, but the noise and excitement proved too much for me. I prefer the quiet of the farm and our people. In the city, I felt lost. It was rush, rush, rush all the time and I couldn't hear myself think. I returned to the life I knew best. The only life I will ever know."

"If you had the chance to make the choice again, would you make the same one?"

"The decision you will have to make is yours and yours alone. Don't live your life based on what I would or would not do. Live *your* life, Rebecca, not mine."

Rebecca had long admired her uncle. She wanted to be like him in every way—kind, gentle, understanding. Would she also be as he was now—alone with no one to love?

❖

Dylan poked her head into the projection room. "What film are you showing?"

"Typical summer blockbuster," Willie Sgoda replied with a shrug. "Lots of car chases, explosions, and bad dialogue."

Dylan tilted the book in Willie's hands so she could read the title. "That explains why you're so riveted on *A Tale of Two Cities*. 'It was the best of times, it was the worst of times.'"

Willie used her finger to mark the page she was reading and closed her book. "Speaking of the best of times, how was your weekend with Rebecca?"

"It started out inauspiciously. We went to a hoedown, she got blitzed, and she nearly threw up on me."

"Sounds romantic."

"It wasn't so bad. We went back to my house and talked things out. Then I stayed up half the night watching her sleep." Dylan checked her watch to see how much of her fifteen-minute break remained. Ten minutes. Plenty of time. She pulled up a chair and sat next to Willie.

"At any point in the evening, did you take the time to tell Rebecca you're a card-carrying lesbian?"

"I haven't done anything to earn my card yet. I'm still a big old virgin just like you."

"Speak for yourself."

"Are you trying to tell me you finally made it with the Anderson twins?"

"No, but it's just a matter of time."

"Right. To answer your question, yes, I told Rebecca that I'm a lesbian. I did that before the evening started, thank you very much. I wanted her to know what she was getting into."

"And that you wanted to get into her?"

"I'll be so happy when you finally grow out of your adolescent phase."

"Coming soon to a theater near you. What happened when you told Rebecca? Did she run screaming for the hills? Or is it the farm?"

"Neither one."

"She was okay with it?"

"She was more than okay. She kissed me."

"Shut up. She kissed you? On the lips?"

"More than once."

"Are we talking a 'Hello, how are you?' kind of kiss or a 'Hey, sailor' kind of kiss?"

"It was more like an 'I think I like you but I don't know what the hell I'm doing' kind of kiss."

Willie nodded in commiseration. "Yeah, that's usually the kind I get. So is she going to see you again or is her science experiment over?"

"We've made a date for next weekend to see the Phillies play the Dodgers. Dad bought the tickets this morning. He got great seats, too. Close to Harry the K's restaurant with a clear view of the field."

"You bitch. I hate you."

"I was going to say I popped for an extra ticket and you could come with if you want, but—"

"I love you, Mahoney."

"You say that to all the girls."

"Isn't that what horny teenage bois are supposed to do? But, seriously, D. I hope you know what you're doing. Please tell me you're just having a good time and there are no thoughts of fairy-tale endings running around that head of yours."

Dylan patted the whirring projector. "We're in the movie business, Willie. Don't you believe in happily ever after?"

❖

"Tobias is here," Rebecca's mother said, looking out the front window. "Look, Papa. See how clean his horse and buggy are. He reminds me of you when you were his age."

Her father moved his pipe from one side of his mouth to the other. He held a lit match over the pipe's bowl and inhaled until the tobacco began to emit a steady stream of smoke. "I certainly hope not." He blew out the match. "If he does, Rebecca will have to stay home tonight."

"You're riding to the sing with Tobias Hershberger?" Sarah asked. She, Joshua, and Isaiah had come to visit after church and had not yet returned home. "Are you going to pair up with him tonight?"

At a sing, boys and girls from congregations in neighboring districts sat on opposite sides of a long table. Each person took turns selecting a hymn, the more solemn songs ignored in favor of those with a faster pace. The boys and girls conversed between songs. A boy who did not have a girlfriend paired up with a girl who was also unattached. After the sing ended, the boy—who had ridden to the sing accompanied by his sister or one of his sister's friends—drove his prospective girlfriend home in his courting buggy.

"Sarah, leave your sister in peace. You know such questions are not encouraged."

"I'm sorry, Papa."

Rebecca tied her cape around her shoulders when she heard Esther bounding up the front steps. "I'll be going now." She could feel everyone's eyes upon her as she walked to the door. Was it too late to change her mind? Perhaps Uncle Amos had the right idea after all.

Tobias Hershberger touched his fingers to the brim of his straw hat. "Good evening, Rebecca."

"Good evening, Tobias."

"Would you like to sit in the middle next to Tobias or would you prefer to sit next to the road?" Esther asked.

Rebecca looked up at Tobias's earnest face and lowered her eyes. "Sit next to your brother, Esther. I'll take the outside seat."

Esther climbed into the buggy. Rebecca followed her. Tobias waited for them to settle into their seats.

"Giddap!" he said with a click of his tongue. He lightly flicked the reins against his horse's haunches, stirring the animal into motion.

The horse trotted down the driveway and headed for the road as if it knew where it was going. Perhaps it did. Sunday sings were traditionally held in the same home that hosted the day's services. The horse was being asked to repeat the journey it had made that morning.

Rebecca sat with her hands folded in her lap. She looked down at her laced fingers and was immediately reminded of her time with Dylan. Sitting in Dylan's car on the side of the road. Holding hands. Listening while Dylan revealed her innermost secrets. She was thankful Dylan had shared something so personal with her. And grateful for her friendship.

Esther leaned to whisper in Rebecca's ear. "Is there a reason for the smile I see on your face?"

"Yes, someone is the cause."

"Someone I know?"

"Yes," Rebecca said, allowing Esther to believe the someone was Tobias.

Now she had a secret of her own.

CHAPTER THREE

R ebecca clutched Dylan's hand and glued herself to Dylan's side. The stadium had a capacity of over forty-five thousand. Most of the seats were filled. Rebecca had never seen so many people gathered in one place at one time. The noise they made was deafening and the game had barely begun.

Dylan gave Rebecca's hand a gentle squeeze. "It's okay. I'm right here."

Rebecca looked up at the huge scoreboard suspended over her head. The Dodgers were up 1–0 in the bottom of the first inning. Mr. Mahoney had spent the top of the first trying to find a place to park in a lot that looked bigger than her father and Uncle Amos's entire farm.

Dylan, Rebecca, and Willie took their seats while Mr. and Mrs. Mahoney made a trip to Harry the K's for food and drinks.

"Dylan said you used to do some teaching. Is that true?"

Rebecca told herself not to stare at the silver hoop that pierced Willie's left eyebrow, but her eyes kept returning to it like a moth to a flame. Even when she had stood in front of the Liberty Bell, the nearly three hundred-year-old symbol of freedom, she had been more fascinated by Willie's unusual accessory than the storied crack she had heard so much about.

"I helped out," Rebecca said. "I was never a teacher myself."

"But if I asked you to teach me Pennsylvania Dutch, do you think you could?"

"Why would you want to learn that?"

"So I can finally understand what Dylan mutters under her breath when she's pissed at me about something," Willie said, taking a good-natured swipe at Dylan. "I love languages. The more, the better. I want to spend my junior year of college abroad. I keep trying to convince Dylan to come with me so we can take France by storm, but she seems to have found a reason to stay."

Rebecca felt guilty. Was Dylan holding herself back because of her? She didn't want to keep Dylan from fulfilling her dreams.

"How many languages do you speak, Dylan?"

"I know parts of six, but I'm fluent in three—English, Gaelic, and Spanish. My Pennsylvania Dutch is still spotty, but it's a lot better than it used to be, thanks to you. My French and German are pretty good, but not as good as Willie's."

"How many languages do you speak, Willie?"

"Four, not including English. I know Spanish, French, German, and a little bit of Italian. Right now, I'm teaching myself American Sign Language. It's just for fun but you never know when it might come in handy."

"German and Pennsylvania Dutch are very similar, so I wouldn't have very much to teach you."

"Why don't we give it a try and let me be the judge of that?"

Rebecca wanted Dylan's friends to like her. She was overjoyed she and Willie were getting along so well. If Willie was serious about the lessons, Rebecca now had something else to look forward to. She rose with the rest of the crowd after the Phillies' lead-off hitter smacked a home run to tie the game.

"How much are you planning on charging?" Dylan asked after they sat down again.

"Nothing." Rebecca wouldn't consider charging any of Dylan's friends for any services rendered. And definitely not for something like this. If someone wanted to learn about her way of life, she would gladly show them for free.

"It's pro bono," Willie said.

"Kind of like charity work?" Dylan said.

"So *that's* why she's with you."

"Ha ha."

"Did someone order cheese steaks?" Mr. Mahoney handed a steaming sandwich and a bag of chips to each of the girls. Mrs. Mahoney passed out the drinks.

Rebecca picked up her sandwich. Her fingers sank into the soft roll as she bit into the layers of chopped steak, sautéed onions, and melted cheese.

"Careful," Dylan said. "It's hot."

Before Dylan could complete her warning, intense heat hit the roof of Rebecca's mouth. The melted cheese seared her soft palate as if it were molten lava turning hard pavement into bubbling tar.

"Here. Drink this."

Rebecca sucked at the proffered straw and filled her mouth with ice-cold soda. She burped loudly after the carbonated liquid forced her stomach to expand.

"That was a good one, dude." Willie raised her right hand, the palm facing Rebecca. "You're not going to leave me hanging, are you?" She lifted Rebecca's right hand and slapped their palms together. "That is what we English call a high five."

"A high five?"

"It's primarily used in team sports," Dylan said. "To celebrate a good play or to pick up a teammate when she's down."

Rebecca looked at her hand as if it no longer belonged to her. She had been one of the smartest people in her school. In the real world, though, there was still much for her to learn.

❖

"I'll never get the hang of this."

Rebecca pounded the steering wheel in frustration. She had just hit the gas instead of the brakes, causing the truck to veer off the road and lurch to a stop in a ditch.

"Sure you will. Like everything, it just takes a little practice. Remember, your right foot is the gas pedal and your left foot is the brake pedal. Right means..."

"Go," Rebecca said, filling in the blank.

"And left means…"

"Stop."

Dylan grinned. "See, it's not as hard as you think. Ready to give it another try?"

Rebecca took a deep breath to slow her racing heart. "I think so."

"Let me turn the truck around and we can have at it."

Dylan climbed out of the passenger's seat and walked around the truck while Rebecca slid over so she could take the wheel. Dylan put the truck in reverse and hit the gas but the truck didn't move.

"Uh-oh."

"What is it?" Rebecca asked.

Dylan stuck her head out the driver's side window and hit the gas again. Rebecca heard the truck's tires spin as they searched for purchase in the sandy soil.

"I think we're stuck."

Rebecca's heart sank. "I'm sorry. I didn't mean to do anything wrong."

"Relax, it's not anyone's fault."

"What do we do?"

"I'll call my dad. He can use our neighbor's Hummer to pull us out." Dylan patted her pockets, then her face turned bright red. "Crap."

"What now?"

"I forgot my cell phone."

Farmland stretched for miles but Rebecca didn't know any of the owners. The nearest town was miles away. "So what do we do?"

"Wait until the cavalry shows up."

Dylan got out of the truck, stepped on the front bumper, and sat on the hood. Rebecca followed suit.

"You're not mad at me?"

"You just bought us even more time alone. Why would I be mad at you?"

"It can't be easy for you having a friend who doesn't know

anything about the world. I can't even drive ten feet without doing something wrong."

"Don't be so hard on yourself. No one's perfect, Rebecca. When I was learning to parallel park, I spent three weeks flattening all the orange cones my parents set up. It got so bad I couldn't even look at an ice cream cone without wanting to cry."

"You're just saying that to make me feel better."

"No, I'm not. You can ask my parents when we get back."

"*If* we get back, you mean."

Dylan slipped her arm around Rebecca's waist. "You don't have to be scared. Nothing's going to happen. And you're not in trouble."

Rebecca *was* scared. Petrified, even. What frightened her was not the thought of what might happen to her and Dylan if no one came along but the realization of how good it felt to have Dylan's arm wrapped around her. To sit with her on a lazy summer day with nowhere to go and nothing to do.

Dylan wanted to be more than her friend. Did Rebecca want the same thing?

"How was the sing last week?"

"It was okay."

"Only okay?"

Rebecca had not told Dylan about the sing because talking about it would mean telling Dylan about Tobias. But Dylan deserved to know she wasn't the only person who was pursuing her affections.

"Tobias Hershberger drove me home from the sing. Do you know what that means?"

"That he's a nice guy?"

"It means he's courting me." Dylan stiffened and pulled her arm away, but Rebecca did not regret telling the truth. "Tobias is sweet on me. He has been for a while. He hasn't told me so, but his sister says it's true."

"Perhaps he's still trying to find a way to say what's in his heart."

Was Dylan talking about Tobias or herself?

"Are you sweet on him?" Dylan asked.

Rebecca and Tobias had made small talk during the sing and she had allowed him to drive her home afterward, but she didn't know if or when she would spend time with him again. He had told her more than she ever wanted to know about the inner workings of his family farm and the land he was saving up to buy, but he had not managed to capture her attention the way Dylan had. The way Dylan continued to do. But Tobias was a nice boy and he meant well. Perhaps he deserved another chance. Dylan had given her a second chance. The least she could do was offer Tobias the same courtesy.

"I don't think I could make a better choice for a husband."

"Then I guess you can stop looking." Dylan jumped down off the truck and kicked one of the tires. Dust quickly covered her tennis shoes, turning the sneakers from black to gray. "I've never attended an Amish wedding. What's it like?"

"The preparations take weeks. The wedding feels just as long. First, you send invitations to three hundred relatives, friends, and church members. Then you have to sew the wedding dress as well as dresses for each of the *newehockers*—what you would call bridesmaids. The wedding itself starts at eight thirty a.m. and lasts for three hours. The women in the wedding party wear blue, the men black suits, white shirts, and bow ties. No one carries flowers and there's no maid of honor. All the attendants are considered equally important. After the ceremony, everyone gathers for a feast that lasts most of the afternoon. By the time the day is over, everyone is filled with food and with love."

Rebecca allowed herself to imagine her own wedding. When she did, she pictured Dylan at her side instead of Tobias. She giggled at the thought of Dylan—now busy throwing dirt clods at a nearby fence post—in a dress. Blue, white, or otherwise.

Dylan cocked her head. "Do you hear that?"

"Hear what?"

"It sounds like a tractor." Dylan walked to the middle of the road. A few minutes later, a dust-covered tractor topped the hill. Dylan waved her arms over her head to get the driver to stop.

The farmer wrapped a chain around the truck's trailer hitch and pulled it back onto the road. Dylan and Rebecca thanked him profusely before he continued on his way.

Dylan held up the truck's keys. "Ready to get back on the horse?"

Rebecca had never heard the expression before, but she assumed Dylan was asking her if she wanted to continue her driving lesson.

"Why don't we try something else for a while?"

"Like what?"

"Anything would be easier than this."

Dylan opened the driver's side door of the truck and guided Rebecca into the seat. "You're doing great. Don't let one setback shake your confidence. You can do whatever you set your mind to."

Dylan said the words with such conviction she almost managed to convince Rebecca they were true.

"Right means go and left means stop," Rebecca said to herself.

She pressed the brake and put the truck in gear. She bit her lip as she released the brake and the truck eased forward.

"Driving is about constant correction," Dylan said. "If you feel the truck start to drift to the left, turn your steering wheel to the right. If you feel it moving to the right, turn to the left. Pretty soon, it will become so automatic you won't even be aware of what you're doing."

Rebecca flexed her aching fingers. She was gripping the steering wheel so tightly she was surprised she didn't leave her fingerprints behind.

"See. I knew you could do it."

"I'm driving. I'm really driving." Rebecca turned to give Dylan a high five and nearly drove into another ditch.

Dylan grabbed the wheel and steered the truck back onto the rutted road. "What's the most important part of driving?"

"Never take your eyes off the road."

"And the second?"

"No drinking and driving."

"And the third?"

"Always look out for the other guy."

"My dad made up a couple of those rules, but in my family, they're appropriate."

"Because of your brother, you mean? How did he die?"

"TJ was killed in a car accident when I was seven. He was driving back to college from spring break when he was hit head-on by a drunk driver. The loss devastated my parents and forced me to grow up much faster than I might have wanted. My brother Matt went in the opposite direction. He went from being the sweetest guy you could ever hope to meet to being angry at the world. Instead of dealing with his pain, he tried to inflict it on others or dull it with drugs and alcohol. His behavior got even worse when he was in high school. He was constantly picking fights and getting into trouble. That's why his friends called him Maniac Mahoney."

"Where is he now?"

"He and a friend of his share an apartment in Reading. They do just enough to get by. I keep hoping he'll get his act together, but so far that hasn't happened."

Rebecca looked at Dylan out of the corner of her eye. Dylan always got so sad when she talked about her brothers. Rebecca wished she could take that sadness away, but she didn't know how. She was glad to know, though, that family was as important to Dylan as it was to her.

"Is TJ's death the reason you don't drink?"

"It's one of the reasons. I've tried alcohol, but I don't like the taste. Even more than that, I hate being out of control."

"Now I'm even more embarrassed."

"For?"

"Getting drunk at the hoedown. I was definitely out of control. I said some things—"

"That are already forgiven and forgotten. Let's leave the past where it belongs. In the past. It's the future I care about. From where I sit, the future looks pretty bright."

Rebecca was inclined to agree.

CHAPTER FOUR

Drive-in theaters, much to Dylan's dismay, became obsolete years before she was born. Her parents often regaled her with tales of the two of them sitting wide-eyed in the dark watching movies from the backseat of their respective family cars. Dylan wished she could make a similar memory of her own. The closest she could come to replicating the experience was participating in her high school's annual Hollywood Under the Stars program. On Saturday nights, attendees spread blankets on the football field while the event's organizers showed family-friendly films on the scoreboard.

The movie of the week was *Footloose*, the music-filled Kevin Bacon vehicle from 1984. Dylan had seen the movie dozens of times, but this was the first time the storyline hit home. She was struck by the similarities between the forbidden Ren-Ariel romance and her own. But how much of a romance could hers be if all of the emotions were one-sided? Rebecca still had not expressed her feelings for her—if she had any—and it had been weeks since they kissed. Or was it months? Days. Weeks. Months. It didn't matter. Dylan felt like it had been years since the last time her lips touched Rebecca's.

Now there was Tobias Hershberger to deal with. How was she supposed to compete with a walking, talking Ken doll, a straight girl's vision of the American dream?

She kept telling herself to be patient, but her patience was wearing thin. If there wasn't a chance for her and Rebecca to be together, even temporarily, she needed to know. And she needed to know now. Before she invested any more of her heart in a relationship that was never going to develop.

❖

Rebecca clapped as the movie's closing credits rolled across the screen. Dylan introduced her to at least one film each weekend. She enjoyed them all, but this one struck a chord with her. The characters in the movie were banned from dancing or listening to rock music. So was she. Most of the characters in the movie were the children of farmers. So was she. But the kids in the movie learned how to dance and even held a school prom. She would never do either of those things.

Her applause petered to a stop. She could feel Dylan's eyes on her. The intensity of Dylan's gaze unnerved her. Dylan had been staring at her for a while now, but not in the usual way. Dylan normally looked at her as if she were a precious jewel to be admired. Tonight, Dylan was scrutinizing her as if she were someone who could not be trusted. What had happened to cause Dylan to lose faith in her and their friendship?

"Is something wrong?" Rebecca asked as Mr. and Mrs. Mahoney folded the oversized blanket the four of them had used as a buffer between themselves and the damp grass.

"Why would something be wrong?"

"You seem…not yourself tonight."

"I'm fine."

Rebecca didn't believe her. Dylan had been tense and edgy all night. She had kept up her end of the conversation, but she wasn't her usual good-natured self. Darkness hovered over her like a storm cloud. Rebecca prayed the storm wasn't about to unleash its fury. She didn't like seeing Dylan unhappy, especially when she suspected she was the cause of that unhappiness.

Rebecca pulled Dylan aside while Mr. and Mrs. Mahoney talked to some people they knew. "What can I do to fix it?"

"Fix what?"

"Whatever's wrong."

"Nothing's wrong."

"Talk to me, Dylan."

"What do you want me to say?"

"Whatever's on your mind."

"You don't want to hear what's on my mind," Dylan said after a moment's pause.

"Yes, I do. Please tell me what's bothering you."

"I'm just worried, that's all."

"About what?"

"I'm going to be graduating next year, which means I'll have to leave you. I don't want to go somewhere you're not going to be."

"But you have to. I know how important your education is to you."

"You're important to me, too. Aren't you going to miss me, even a little?"

"Of course I will. I'll think of you every day."

"I don't want to be thought of. I want to be loved. If you can't do that, please let me know and I'll find someone who can."

❖

Dylan watched Rebecca's face fall. She wanted to kick herself for taking her frustrations out on Rebecca, but the targets that were easiest to hit were usually the most convenient—and the most inopportune.

"Don't mind me. You're right. I'm not myself today, but there's no excuse for what I said to you. I'm sorry."

"Don't apologize for being right. You deserve someone who can love you as much as you love…her."

When Rebecca stumbled over the word, Dylan realized she had been deluding herself for the past two years. She and Rebecca weren't having some kind of storybook romance. She had a crush on a straight girl who could never reciprocate her feelings.

Dylan flinched when her father clapped her on the back.

"Call me crazy, but I feel like dancing. Who's with me?"

"I never learned how," Rebecca said.

"We can show you a couple of moves," her mother said. "I'm sure Dylan would love to be your instructor. Wouldn't you, honey?"

Dylan forced her mouth to curve into a smile. "I can't wait."

❖

Mr. and Mrs. Mahoney moved the furniture in the living room aside to form a makeshift dance floor.

"What should we start with?" Mrs. Mahoney asked.

"How about something classic like the Twist?" Mr. Mahoney stood on the balls of his feet and twisted them into the carpet as if he were trying to squash an insect.

"How about something she could actually use one day?" Dylan said.

"So I guess that means the Charleston's out, too?" Mrs. Mahoney wagged her index finger in the air while she gyrated through what Rebecca assumed was once a popular dance.

Mr. Mahoney snapped his fingers. "I've got it."

"Should I be afraid?" Dylan asked.

Rebecca couldn't tell if Dylan was really getting into the spirit of the evening or if she was only pretending to in order to please everyone else.

"You should be very afraid."

Mr. Mahoney searched through the collection of CDs until he found the one he wanted. He took the disc out of its case and put it in the player. Dylan groaned when music began blasting out of the speakers.

"You can't go wrong with the Chicken Dance. It's a staple at wedding receptions everywhere."

Rebecca tried to follow along as Mr. Mahoney demonstrated the dance. She felt ridiculous mimicking his actions, but the way everyone was laughing, maybe that was how she was supposed to feel.

The waltz was next.

Mr. and Mrs. Mahoney held each other close as they glided around the room.

"I'll never be able to do that."

"You never know until you try." Dylan held out her hand. "Do you want to try?"

"Yes, I do."

Rebecca tried to mirror Mrs. Mahoney's position. She gripped Dylan's left hand with her right and put her left hand on Dylan's shoulder. Dylan's right hand rested on Rebecca's waist. Rebecca responded to Dylan's cues as Dylan subtly directed her to move left, right, forward, or backward.

"See," Dylan said when the song ended. "I knew you could do it."

Rebecca couldn't breathe. All she could see was Dylan. All she could hear was Dylan. All she wanted was Dylan.

"Teach me more."

"You two have at it," Mr. Mahoney said. "I'm beat."

"Me, too," Mrs. Mahoney said.

"Party poopers. Let's go to my room, Rebecca. I'll teach you everything you need to know."

Rebecca followed Dylan upstairs.

Dylan closed her bedroom door behind them and switched on the lamp next to her bed. Then she turned on the stereo. Music, loud enough to be heard but not loud enough to disturb Mr. or Mrs. Mahoney, drifted out of the speakers.

"This one's called the Electric Slide. It's a group dance, so it's more fun when you have a lot of people participating."

Dylan demonstrated the steps. Rebecca tried to keep up. Halfway through the song, she had the moves down pat.

"There you go. You got it."

The song ended and another one began.

"Give me your hands."

Rebecca allowed her hands to be guided to Dylan's shoulders. Dylan circled her arms around Rebecca's waist and taught her how to slow dance.

"Feel the music. Relax and let your body move to the rhythm. That's it. Just like that."

Rebecca felt her self-consciousness begin to abate as Dylan continued to offer encouragement. She moved forward. Rebecca heard Dylan's breath catch when Rebecca molded her body against hers.

Dylan tried to pull away but Rebecca held fast.

"Don't. Stay with me."

Rebecca could hear someone panting. She realized with a start that the sound was coming from her. She shivered involuntarily when she saw the hungry look in Dylan's eyes. Why was she shivering when she was so hot? Her body felt as if it were on fire. When Dylan's lips brushed against her ear, the feather-soft touch made the fire grew hotter.

"It's been weeks since you let me kiss you."

Rebecca melted in the crucible that was Dylan's gaze.

"I told myself I wouldn't kiss you again until it meant as much to me as it does to you. May I kiss you now?"

Dylan licked her lips as if her mouth was dry. "Please."

Rebecca tentatively lifted her mouth to Dylan's. Dylan returned the kiss, then took the lead. She backed Rebecca against the wall and slowly parted her lips with her tongue. She slipped one leg between Rebecca's and pulled her closer.

Rebecca moved against Dylan's leg. How had she known to do that? And why did it feel so good? Needing more, she clutched at Dylan's hips with one hand. She slipped the other under Dylan's T-shirt and slid her palm over the smooth skin of Dylan's back. She had never felt anything so soft.

Dylan stroked Rebecca's hair, then buried her fingers in it. "I want to feel your hair on my skin," she said as she nuzzled Rebecca's neck. "I want to see you."

Rebecca remembered the day she had walked out of the bathroom wearing nothing but a towel. She remembered the way Dylan's eyes had crawled over her body. She longed for them to make the journey once more. She moved her hand from Dylan's hips to the back of her neck and pulled Dylan's mouth down to hers. When their lips met, Rebecca felt their souls become one.

❖

Dylan shuddered and groaned deep in her throat. "We have to stop."

"Why?"

"Because I don't want to stop." She crossed the room and turned off the music, then stood with her back to Rebecca. "Do you have any idea how hard this is for me?" she asked without turning around. "To want you as much as I do and not be able to have you?"

Rebecca put her arms around Dylan and rested her head on the back of Dylan's shoulder. "Is it always like this?"

Dylan leaned into Rebecca's embrace. "I don't know. I've never felt anything like this."

"Neither have I."

Dylan turned to face Rebecca. Did Rebecca just say what she thought she said? "What about Tobias? What about your family?"

"I don't know the answers to your questions."

Dylan kissed Rebecca on the tip of her nose. "So let's figure them out together."

CHAPTER FIVE

The night Dylan turned eighteen, she watched *The Age of Innocence*, Martin Scorsese's 1993 period piece starring Michelle Pfeiffer and Daniel Day-Lewis as ill-fated lovers in 1870s New York.

"Who is that?" Rebecca asked when the actress appeared on screen.

"That," Dylan replied, pleased Rebecca was impressed by one of her favorite actresses, "is Michelle Pfeiffer."

"She's beautiful."

"If you think she looks good in this, you should see her in *Batman Returns*. The scene where she licked Michael Keaton's face in the alley made me want to run out and buy some heavy-duty white thread, some latex, and a sewing needle. Before that movie came out, I thought the perfect Catwoman had Julie Newmar's playfulness and Eartha Kitt's purr. After the film was released, I realized no Catwoman could be complete without Michelle Pfeiffer's lips."

Rebecca reached for another handful of popcorn. "So when do I get to see that one?"

"I'll rent it next weekend."

"You don't have it already?" Dylan's movie collection, housed in a built-in bookcase that doubled as an entertainment center, took up nearly an entire wall of her room. "It looks like you have a copy of every movie ever made. How could there possibly be one missing?"

"*Batman Returns* was okay and Catwoman's part of it was

terrific, but the Penguin's backstory kind of turned me off. The writers spent half the film developing it and it didn't really go anywhere. Or, at least, not far enough. If there's a villain, I want to love him or hate him, not feel sorry for him."

"I love how excited you get when you talk about movies. Your whole face lights up."

"That's because you're here."

Dylan hoped the comment would lead Rebecca to step out of her comfort zone and share her feelings for once. She didn't have to tell Dylan she was madly in love with her or anything, though it would have been nice to hear. Instead, Rebecca changed the subject.

"What do you want to do for your birthday?"

"I'm doing it."

"Watching a movie you've seen a hundred times?"

"No," Dylan replied, bumping Rebecca's shoulder with her own. "Spending time with you."

"But don't you want to do something special?"

Dylan bumped Rebecca with her shoulder again. "I am." When she noticed the funny look on Rebecca's face, she paused the movie. "What did you do?"

Rebecca looked sheepish but didn't say anything.

"Rebecca."

"Your parents told me they want to take you to dinner and I kind of said we didn't have anything planned."

Dylan grimaced. "Please tell me you didn't do that."

"Sorry, I did. Is that a bad thing?"

Normally, Dylan didn't mind family time, but this group outing would take away from her time with Rebecca. She didn't want to make Rebecca feel worse than she already seemed to, though, so she tried to put a positive spin on things. "I've finally convinced Mom and Dad that Chuck E. Cheese is no longer my first choice for dining out, so it should be okay. And I'm sure being cooped up with me can't be your idea of fun."

"I don't care what we do when we're together as long as we're doing it together, but I don't want to keep you from doing the things you normally do."

"You aren't keeping me from anything. Don't ever think that way. I want to be with you every moment of every day. When something or someone gets in the way of that, I get a little upset. I don't mean to be so selfish or to sound like a stalker, but I live for these moments with you. I want them to be perfect."

"They are. I want to share my life with you. All of it. The good and the bad."

"So you know what that means, don't you?"

"What does it mean?"

Dylan dragged Rebecca toward the door. "It means you're coming with us."

❖

"Where do you want to go?" Mrs. Mahoney asked after everyone piled into her car.

"How about Shogun?" Dylan said. "I love that place. We used to go all the time but we haven't been there in forever."

"What's Shogun?" Rebecca asked.

"It's a Japanese restaurant in the Keystone Shopping Center. Since it's teppanyaki-style, it's the kind of place where you sit around a really big table and the chefs cook the food right in front of you. It's really cool. You'll love it."

"So no hot dogs and French fries?" Mr. Mahoney asked.

"More like spring rolls and cream cheese wontons," Mrs. Mahoney said.

Mr. Mahoney stuck out his tongue the way Rebecca had the night Mrs. Mahoney introduced her to Brussels sprouts. "Make it Yakiniku steak and we have a deal."

Mrs. Mahoney drove into town and found a spot in the crowded parking lot.

"Follow me, please." The greeter led them past several open tables and toward the area traditionally reserved for private functions.

"What's going on?" Dylan asked.

Mr. and Mrs. Mahoney shrugged as if they didn't know what

she was talking about. Rebecca played innocent, too. She couldn't wait to see how Dylan reacted to what was in store for her. Rebecca's anticipation had been building for weeks. Ever since she dropped off a quilt at My Souvenirs and Mrs. Mahoney told her she wanted to plan a surprise party for Dylan's birthday—and she needed Rebecca's help to pull it off. Mrs. Mahoney always made Rebecca feel welcome, but her request had made her feel like part of the family.

Rebecca's role in Dylan's life was getting bigger. So was Dylan's role in hers. Would they continue to play a part in each other's lives in a few years, or would they become more like strangers than friends?

The greeter opened the panel door that led to one of the two banquet rooms. The space was filled with dozens of people—Dylan's friends, classmates, and coworkers, along with a few of Mr. and Mrs. Mahoney's friends. "Surprise!" they yelled.

Dylan covered her face with her hands.

Mr. Mahoney squeezed Dylan's shoulders and pushed her forward. "Gotcha."

"Happy birthday, buddy," Willie said.

Dylan gave her a hug.

"This room looks just like a scene from *Rashomon*. I feel like I'm standing in the woods where most of the action took place. I know you did the artwork, so don't even deny it. So this is what you've been up to the past month. Every time I tried to make plans with her, she blew me off and said she was busy," Dylan explained to Rebecca before turning back to Willie. "I thought you were hooking up with someone new and you were here busting your ass for me?"

"Guilty as charged."

"How did you know we'd end up here?"

"Because I know you. Nice job on the misdirection, Rebecca."

"You were in on this, too?" Dylan asked.

"Guilty as charged," Rebecca said, borrowing Willie's phrase. Her lessons with Willie were proving to be mutually beneficial. Rebecca taught Willie Pennsylvania Dutch. In return, Willie taught Rebecca English slang. Dylan had helped Rebecca learn English, but she hadn't taught her how to curse. Willie took care of that during their very first class. Now Rebecca could, in Willie's words, "curse like a sailor." Whatever that meant.

"Way to go, teach." Willie held up her hand for a high five. Rebecca slapped her palm against Willie's. "Go mingle, D. I'm sure everyone wants a piece of you. I'll take care of your girl while you're gone. Come on, teach. Let's grab something to eat before all the food disappears."

Rebecca trailed Willie to the buffet table. Following her lead, Rebecca piled her plate high with one exotic dish after another. She avoided the baby octopus salad, though. Rebecca could barely believe such a creature existed and had no idea why Willie or anyone else would want to eat one.

"How's it going, Mrs. Ziegenfus?" Willie tapped an impatient finger against her plate while the woman ahead of her in line piled hers with fried rice.

"Fine, Willie. Just fine." The woman added two more scoops of rice before she replaced the spoon.

Willie provided introductions. "Rebecca, I'd like to introduce you to Mrs. Ziegenfus. She just moved here from Florida. Dylan and I are in her French class. Mrs. Ziegenfus, Rebecca Lapp."

"Pleased to meet you, Rebecca. Are you Dylan's little Amish friend?" Rebecca winced when Mrs. Ziegenfus pronounced it *Ay-mish* instead of *Ah-mish*. "Where's your bonnet and your cute little apron?"

"She left them outside in her buggy," Willie said.

Mrs. Ziegenfus laughed, then abruptly stopped when she realized no one was laughing with her.

"Rebecca is Dylan's *friend*," Willie said. "Mine, too."

"Thanks for coming to my defense," Rebecca said after she and Willie sat down.

"Not a problem. Mrs. Ziegenfus is a great teacher, but she has a bit of a superiority complex. No one is allowed to make my friends feel 'less than.'"

"How long have you and Dylan been friends?"

"Since we were in diapers."

"And you've always been…friends?"

"That's a cute way of asking if we've ever been more than that."

Rebecca sampled the spicy chicken. The peppers immediately set her tongue on fire and she reached for a glass of water. "Have you?" she asked after choking it down.

"No. I like blondes and she likes brunettes."

Remembering her experience with the spicy chicken, Rebecca tentatively picked up a Philadelphia roll. The combination of salmon, cream cheese, and cucumber was surprisingly good. Refreshing, even.

Rebecca took in Willie's long brown hair and feminine features. "I still don't think you look like a boy."

Willie flashed a wicked grin. "I have my moments."

"Does Dylan like bois?"

"She likes *you*. I like you, too. Not in the same way, of course. But I think you're cool."

"Did you not expect to become fond of me?"

"Before I met you, I spent hours trying to think of polite responses to Dylan's inevitable 'So what did you think?' Thankfully, I didn't have to use any of my prepared lies. I found you curiously captivating. A year later, I still do."

"Because I'm so different from you?"

"Because you're so much like me. Dylan's my best friend and I love her to death. I think you do, too. Not in the same way, of course. If you ever need anything, give me a call, okay?"

"But I don't have a phone."

Willie smiled. "It's an expression, teach. It means if you ever need a friend, you've got one in me. No matter what happens with you and Dylan."

Rebecca covered Willie's hand with her own. "Thank you. I appreciate that."

Dylan joined them at the table. "What are you two plotting now?"

"Nothing that involves you," Willie replied with a wink. "Not this time, at least."

❖

"How did I get so lucky?" Dylan asked.

"You have a lot of things here."

Rebecca looked at Dylan's impressive haul. It had taken two trips to bring all her gifts in from the car. Almost all of them. After hearing about a historic theater scheduled to be demolished, Mrs. Mahoney had gone online, purchased two of the seats, and had them reupholstered. Those prize possessions were sitting under a tarp in the garage, where they would remain until Mr. Mahoney could find the time to install them in Dylan's home theater/bedroom.

Dylan put her arms around Rebecca and pulled her close. "I don't mean the things. I mean you. You and everyone else who showed up tonight. You worked for weeks to sew me a quilt. Willie put hours and hours into painting that backdrop. Then my parents came up with all this subterfuge in the first place. Why did you do all this for me?"

"Because we love you."

Dylan cupped her hand around her ear as if she hadn't heard. "Say that again."

"Because we love you," Rebecca repeated.

Dylan leaned forward. "One more time?"

Rebecca put her lips next to Dylan's ear. "Because I love you," she whispered. She kissed her the way she had seen Humphrey Bogart kiss Ingrid Bergman in *Casablanca*, a movie she didn't need Dylan to tell her was the most romantic of all time. "Happy birthday."

"It is now."

CHAPTER SIX

Rebecca bent to examine the stitching on a patchwork quilt sewn in 1890. The colors were still vibrant despite the fact that the materials were over a hundred years old. She consulted her program to read the artist's biography.

"Perhaps your name will be in there one day," Dylan said.

"I don't think so. These quilts are spectacular. Mine pale in comparison."

Dylan had driven Rebecca to the Philadelphia Museum of Art to see the thirteen antique and contemporary African American quilts on display. Rebecca was awed by the endless variety of the quilts and the unquestioned creativity of the women who had sewn them.

"Which one's your favorite?"

"That one." Rebecca pointed to a quilt covered with cutouts shaped like stylized human hands.

"Mine, too. It was commissioned for the movie *The Color Purple*."

"Is that why it's your favorite?"

"No, it reminds me of you learning to high five."

Rebecca felt her cheeks redden. "Everything reminds you of me."

"Just about." Dylan pulled out a map of the museum. "The Matisse exhibit isn't too far from here. Would you like to see it?"

"Yes, but I'd like to talk to you first."

"That sounds ominous."

"No, I think you're going to like what I have to say."

They went outside and sat on the stone steps that led to the entrance of the museum. Rebecca watched as one person after another ran up the steps, thrust their arms in the air, and did a triumphant dance.

"They all think they're in *Rocky*," Dylan said. "These are the steps from the movie."

"The one about the boxer?"

Dylan chuckled. "If you want to describe a movie that won three Oscars as 'the one about the boxer,' yes."

Rebecca enjoyed the gentle ribbing. When Dylan teased her, she could feel how much Dylan cared about her. When others did it—like those boys who tormented her and Sarah and mischief makers who threw bricks and beer bottles at passing buggies—she could feel their mean spirits coming to the fore. Why did people feel the need to make fun of what they didn't understand? And why was Dylan so different?

"Thank you for being my friend."

Rebecca squeezed Dylan's hand. Dylan squeezed back.

"Thank you for being mine. What did you want to tell me?"

"I'm moving in with Marian."

Dylan's eyebrows knitted. "I know it's convenient, but why would you want to live with someone who is as unpredictable as she is? Her friends are just as bad. All they do is party and get wasted."

"I know Marian has a problem with drink, but I hope I can be a steadying influence on her. And if I'm living in the city, it will give you and me more time to be together. Time without anyone to tell us what we can and can't do."

Dylan slowly unspooled a smile. "When is moving day?"

Rebecca returned Dylan's smile. "Marian moved in last night. I will join her Wednesday after work."

"I'm supposed to work that night. I'll see if I can switch with someone so I can help you move."

"If you do that, you'll probably end up having to work over the weekend and we won't be able to go fishing. I'm looking forward to showing you something that *I* like to do for a change. I'll ask someone else to help me."

"Who, Tobias?"

"No, I shall ask Papa. He agreed to let me move into town because he doesn't want me on the road all the time. He has not asked to see the apartment, but I know he would like to so he can assure himself I will be as safe there as I would at home."

"I could use the same assurance."

"You'll have it. You can visit as often as you like." Rebecca grinned.

"What's so funny?"

"I never thought I'd have a place of my own. Not without having a husband and children first." A veil descended over Dylan's eyes the way it did every time Rebecca mentioned becoming a wife and a mother. To lift the shroud, Rebecca moved to less weightier matters. "I like Philadelphia."

"You should," Dylan said with a laugh. "We're here practically every weekend." Her expression turned serious. "Could you see yourself living here one day? Could you see yourself living with me?"

"I'm like Uncle Amos. I can visit the city, but I couldn't live there."

"What if I were there to help you?"

"You would quickly tire of having to lead me by the hand."

"If you think I would ever get tired of having you in my life, you need to think again. But it sounds like you've made up your mind. When your *rumspringa* ends, so will we."

Rebecca heard the air of finality in Dylan's voice. End? They had barely begun. "I have made no such decision."

"Then why can't you talk about the future with me? Why can't you talk about *a* future with me? Tell me honestly. Where do you see yourself in five years?"

"Married to Tobias and learning to love him."

Rebecca didn't know she was going to say the words until they tumbled out of her mouth. Once they were said, she couldn't take them back. She had known from the first weekend of her *rumspringa* that she would choose Tobias. The day Esther had told her Tobias was interested in her, Rebecca had felt fated to become his wife.

Tobias was calm and steady. Life with him would be untroubled, devoid of the emotional peaks and valleys that characterized her relationship with Dylan. Tobias was the easy choice, but was he the right choice?

Dylan's eyes filled with tears. "You would marry a man you don't love and have his children in order to fit in instead of remaining true to yourself?"

Rebecca thought of Uncle Amos living by himself because he couldn't be with the one his heart desired most. "I don't want to be alone."

"You don't have to be alone. You can be with me. Why should you have to learn to love Tobias when you already know how to love me? You can have the life you want."

"The life *I* want or the one you want for me? How do you know what I want?"

"Because I feel it every time you kiss me."

Rebecca sighed. "You're not making this easy for me."

"I don't intend to. Tell Tobias not to make those wedding plans yet. I'm not letting you go without a fight."

❖

Rebecca's father stood in front of the open refrigerator. "There is more food in here than you girls will eat in two lifetimes."

"That's Uncle Amos's fault," Rebecca said. "He gave me three boxes of vegetables because he didn't want me eating out of cans."

Marian tossed a plastic container of macaroni and cheese into the microwave. "Canned food is better. You don't have to cook it as long and you don't have to worry about it going bad after a week. Hello again, Mr. Lapp."

"Marian."

Rebecca was embarrassed by Marian's immodest attire. Why was she wearing skimpy shorts and a tank top when she knew her father was coming to help her move in?

"I'd best be going," he said.

"So soon?" Rebecca asked.

"I want to get home before dark. Neither I nor my horse see as well as we used to."

Marian sat on the counter, causing her short shorts to ride up even higher on her long legs. "Come back when you can stay longer, Mr. Lapp."

Rebecca shot Marian what she hoped was a baleful look. She would discuss Marian's disrespectful behavior later. "Let me walk you out, Papa."

"No need. I'm sure I can find my way."

Rebecca didn't want him to rush off. She tried to prolong his visit. "What do you think of the apartment?"

He rapped his knuckles against the living room wall. "It is well-made. It should do nicely." His eyes flicked toward the kitchen, where Marian was singing an off-key version of a rap song. He turned back to Rebecca. "If you decide not to stay, your room will be waiting for you at home."

"Thank you, Papa, and thank you for your help today."

"It seems like just yesterday you were a newborn babe and I was holding you in my arms. Now you're nearly grown. How quickly time passes."

He kissed her cheek. A lump formed in Rebecca's throat as she watched him walk away.

"I thought he'd never leave," Marian said. "Break out the beer, simmie. It's time to celebrate." She picked up the phone and began calling all her friends. "Party at my place. Be there or be square."

When Marian's friends showed up, Rebecca quickly tired of their drunken antics. She retreated to her room. Rowdy laughter seeped through the locked door. Rebecca plugged her ears with wadded tissues and opened a book.

"So much for being a steadying influence."

❖

Dylan baited her hook and, with a quick flick of her wrist, cast her line into the water. The red and white bobber floated on the water's surface, then quickly sank beneath it. "I've got a bite." She braced her legs underneath her and strained to reel in the fish. "Get the net. I've got Moby Dick on the line."

Rebecca set her own rod aside and picked up the fishing net. When Dylan pulled her quarry closer to the creek bank, Rebecca dipped the net into the water and captured the fish. She held up a brook trout only slightly longer than her hand. "Did you say you had Moby Dick on the line or Nemo?"

"I will never show you another movie as long as I live."

"I'll believe that when I see it." Rebecca gently pulled the hook out of the small trout's mouth and released the fish into the water.

Dylan grabbed a chicken salad sandwich out of the cooler and sat on the soft grass. "Dad and I haven't gone fishing in ages. I had forgotten how much fun it could be."

"So this was a good idea?"

"This was a great idea."

"I'm glad you're enjoying yourself. Some of the best times I've shared with Uncle Amos were spent with fishing poles in our hands. We could go all day without uttering a word, but I never felt like we ran out of things to say. Do you ever feel that way? No, you're the kind of person who has to be doing something at all times or you go stir-crazy. You're always in a hurry."

Dylan tapped her watch. "The clock is ticking. We have only so much time."

"Don't remind me." Rebecca reeled in a five-pound trout and placed it in the fishing basket at her feet.

Dylan took a peek in the basket. Six large trout lay inside. She had caught two. Rebecca was responsible for the other four. Fresh fish for dinner. Yum. Rebecca had volunteered their services to cook, but Dylan feared Rebecca might not be the only one who would need help figuring out how to use the temperature controls on her mother's electric stove.

Dylan took a bite of her sandwich and debated whether to bring up the subject that had been preoccupying her thoughts for weeks. "I want to ask you something. Your answer's probably going to be no, but I'm going to ask you anyway."

"What is it?"

"You don't have to look so serious. It's not life and death."

"Then what is it?"

"Will you go to the prom with me?"

"As your date?"

"Ideally, but if you'd like to go as friends, we could do that, too."

"What would you do if I said no? Would you ask someone else?"

"There is no one else I'd rather be with. If you say no, we'll find something else to do that night. But I'm not going to ask someone else to go to the prom with me just to be able to say I went. One thing I'm never going to do is settle for second best. It wouldn't be fair to me or whoever I ended up with."

Rebecca thought for a moment. She had an opportunity to go to a dance on Dylan's arm. She could think of nothing better. But what if someone saw her? What if word got back to her mother or father or someone else in her community? What was she supposed to say if they asked her to explain her relationship with Dylan? Her relationship with Dylan was a mystery even to her. Wondrous and magical but oh-so-confusing.

If someone accused her and Dylan of being more than friends, she wouldn't be able to deny the accusations, but how could she possibly confirm them? But she couldn't keep saying no every time Dylan suggested they engage in a public activity without Mr. and Mrs. Mahoney around. If she kept doing that, Dylan would eventually get fed up and find someone who wasn't afraid of her own shadow. No matter what she said about not "settling" for someone else.

"I would love to go with you."

"But?"

"I don't have anything to wear."

"I know where you could find the perfect dress." Dylan's face lit up. Hope blossomed in her eyes. Rebecca loved seeing that look on Dylan's face. Moreover, she loved knowing she had put it there. She didn't want to be responsible for taking it away.

"When is the prom?"

"Next Saturday night. Should I buy tickets?"

"Would we be the only ones..." Rebecca's voice trailed off. She couldn't say the word most people would use to describe what she was. Did she need to? She loved Dylan and Dylan loved her. Why did there have to be labels attached?

"Would we be the only people like us? No. Willie's taking a girl from our French class and my friend Brendan is going with his boyfriend James. We can all sit at the pink table." Dylan tossed the sandwich wrapper in the cooler and rested her arms on her knees. "You don't have to go if you don't want to. I won't get mad. I won't be upset. Don't say yes just because you think it will make me happy. What do *you* want to do?"

Rebecca weighed the pros and cons. The negatives outnumbered the positives, but the weight of Dylan's smile tipped the scales in her favor. "I would love to go to the prom with you." Dylan whooped and Rebecca began to gather her things. "But right now, I want to go driving."

Dylan's smile widened. "Driving or parking?"

"Both."

Dylan grabbed the cooler and the fishing rods. "Let's go."

Lately, they spent more time parked by the side of the road than they did driving on it. Their lessons had devolved into makeout sessions—fifteen minutes of driving followed by thirty minutes of kissing and feeling each other up. Rebecca could sit in Dylan's lap and kiss her forever, but when Dylan's eyes darkened and her voice grew husky, that was Rebecca's cue to stop. If she didn't take the cue, Dylan would gently put an end to their feverish kisses. Rebecca preferred to be the one who pulled away. If Dylan had to do it, Rebecca knew she had pushed her too far.

Rebecca longed to take the next step. At least, her body did. When Dylan touched her, she felt like she was on fire. A fire that Dylan had started—and only Dylan could extinguish. Reluctantly, she took her cue. She climbed off Dylan's lap and slid into the passenger's seat.

"Let's find you something to wear."

Dylan took the wheel. While she drove, she pulled at her clothes as if they were too tight. Rebecca knew the feeling.

❖

Rebecca looked at her reflection in the full-length mirror. Was that really her?

That afternoon, Mrs. Mahoney had taken her to get her hair and nails done. Then Mrs. Mahoney had shown her how to apply makeup. Rebecca ran her hands over her strapless white gown. When she tried on the dress, the lady in the formal wear store had told her she looked like a princess. Now Rebecca felt like one. The tiara-shaped spray of flowers in her upswept hair added to the impression.

Rebecca pulled on the black shrug that matched the black bow sewn into the waistline of her dress. She still had misgivings about the evening but, screwing up her courage, she pushed her fears aside and opened the guest room door.

Dylan was waiting for her at the foot of the stairs. Rebecca's breath caught when she saw her. Dressed in a tuxedo with a red rose pinned to the lapel of her jacket, Dylan looked like she could have been a star in the classic movies she loved so much.

Dylan's mouth fell into a round *O* of appreciation as Rebecca slowly descended the stairs. Her eyes spoke the words her mouth could not form.

"How do I look?" Rebecca asked in a shy whisper.

"Beautiful."

The word came out in a croak. Rebecca smiled, glad to see she wasn't the only one who was nervous. "Is that for me?"

With a start, Dylan seemed to remember the box she was holding. She opened the container, removed a corsage, and slipped it around Rebecca's wrist. "The limo's waiting outside. Are you ready to go?" She offered her arm.

"Yes." Rebecca put her hand in the crook of Dylan's elbow.

"You two look amazing," Mrs. Mahoney said.

Rebecca noticed Mr. and Mrs. Mahoney for the first time. They were beaming. Practically glowing with pride. For Dylan and for her. Rebecca's heart swelled with love.

Mrs. Mahoney held a digital camera in the palm of one hand. "May I take a picture?"

Rebecca felt all eyes turn to her. The decision was hers to make. Possessing or posing for photographs was forbidden. But why should she deprive Dylan of a lifelong memory because of a rule neither of them had pledged to follow?

"One picture couldn't hurt."

Mrs. Mahoney quickly took a picture and checked the display on the back of the camera. "Gorgeous. One more for safety and off you go."

"No curfew tonight, right?" Dylan asked.

"I don't know how you talked us into it, but no curfew," Mr. Mahoney said.

"Have fun." Mrs. Mahoney gave them each a kiss on the cheek. "But by all means, be careful."

"We will. Thanks, Mom." Mr. Mahoney pulled some money out of his wallet and pressed it into Dylan's hands. Dylan's eyes widened when she saw the folded hundred-dollar bills. "And thank you, Mr. Franklin."

The chauffeur tipped her cap while she stood next to the open back door of the long black car idling next to the curb. "Ladies, my name is Ashley and I'll be your driver for the evening. Where may I take you?"

"Lolita. I have the directions." Dylan reached into the inside pocket of her tuxedo jacket.

"No need. I'm quite familiar with the restaurant. My girlfriend and I have eaten there several times. I highly recommend the glazed pork carnitas." She waited for them to climb into the car. "There's bottled water and soft drinks in the refrigerator. Sit back and make yourselves comfortable. I'll have you in Philadelphia before you know it." Ashley closed the door and pulled away from the curb.

Rebecca stuck her arm out of the window to wave good-bye to Mr. and Mrs. Mahoney. "Is Willie going to meet us at the restaurant?"

"No, we're going to hook up at the prom and hang out afterward, but we decided to do dinner on our own. She's taking Danielle to the Italian restaurant Mom adores."

"And what kind of restaurant are we going to?"

"Lolita is a lesbian-owned nouveau Mexican restaurant famous for its home-brewed margarita mixes as well as its food. Diners are even encouraged to bring their own tequila to pair with their favorite mix. We can't do that, but we can have a couple of virgin blood orange margaritas and pretend they're the real thing."

"How long have you been planning this?"

"From the second you said yes." Dylan reached for Rebecca's hand. "And I'm so glad you did. Are you?"

So far, Rebecca thought.

The small restaurant was filled with couples, both gay and straight. When the greeter showed her and Dylan to their table, Rebecca felt like they were the center of attention. Rebecca suddenly longed to be somewhere—anywhere—less public. Dylan apparently sensed her apprehension.

"Look at me."

Rebecca looked into Dylan's eyes and found immediate reassurance.

"This is going to be one of the best nights of our lives. You'll see."

When the bill came, Rebecca finally began to believe Dylan might be right. *Paid in full* was written at the bottom where the amount should be.

Dylan called the waitress back to the table. "There must be some mistake."

"No mistake. Your meal is compliments of the women at table

three." The waitress pointed to a pair of silver-haired ladies, who raised their colorful drinks in acknowledgment. "They said to tell you they're glad to see the future is in good hands."

Dylan gave the waitress a twenty. "I'd like to return the favor. Tell them thank you and their next round's on us. Better yet, we'll tell them ourselves."

"We can't just walk up to their table," Rebecca said. "We don't even know them."

"No time like the present."

The women introduced themselves as Paula and Evelyn, "just a couple of married ladies from South Philly."

"Thank you for dinner," Dylan said.

"You look so cute together we couldn't resist," Paula said.

Dylan's hand in hers helped loosen Rebecca's tied tongue. "How long have you been together?"

"Almost fifty years," Evelyn said.

She and Paula invited Dylan and Rebecca to join them for dessert. They took turns sharing their life stories over plates of Mexican tiramisu.

Paula and Evelyn were like walking pieces of history. They had witnessed everything from the McCarthy trials to the moon landing to the dawn of the twenty-first century. The love they shared was so tangible Rebecca could practically hold it in her hands. She could have listened to them all night, but they called it a day after the dessert dishes were cleared.

"We've kept you long enough," Paula said. "You've got a prom to scamper off to."

Evelyn shook her head in wonder. "What I wouldn't give for the opportunities you two have."

"Thank you for paving the way," Dylan said. "We'll dedicate our first dance to you."

"As long as you save the last one for each other."

"It's a deal."

❖

Willie greeted Rebecca with a kiss on the cheek. "I was beginning to think you had stood us up. You look hot, teach."

"Really?" Rebecca placed her hand on her forehead. "I don't feel hot."

"She means you look sexy," Dylan said.

"Oh, right. Remember, I speak English, but I don't always understand *English*."

Dylan couldn't remember Rebecca ever having a laugh at their cultural differences. Perhaps the trip to Lolita had helped her relax a bit. Their encounter with Paula and Evelyn definitely seemed to have opened her eyes. She had gushed about the couple the whole way back from Philadelphia. Had she finally realized it was possible for two women to make a life together with no regrets and no repercussions? Dylan hoped they would have the same luxury.

Dylan introduced Rebecca to Willie's date Danielle and her friends Brendan and James. The couples, like the ones at the surrounding tables, sat twiddling their thumbs until someone finally broke the ice.

Dylan pushed her chair away from the table and extended her hand. "May I have this dance?"

"I thought you'd never ask."

Dylan led Rebecca to the empty dance floor. Willie and Danielle and Brendan and James followed them. The three couples had the floor to themselves for only a few seconds before the large rectangular space quickly filled with people.

"Leave it to the gays to lead the way," Dylan said.

Two songs later, the student body president walked onstage and announced it was time to reveal the names of the couple who had been voted Prom King and Queen.

Dylan used the respite to hit the punch bowl. She poured two cups and handed Rebecca one. "The most popular couples have been campaigning for weeks."

"Who do you think will win?"

"The usual suspects. The jock and the head cheerleader. I would love to be surprised, but I don't think that's going to happen. If anyone else won, there would probably be a mutiny."

"And the winners are…Dylan Mahoney and Rebecca Lapp!"

Dylan blinked when someone from the AV Committee turned a klieg light on her and Rebecca.

"Is this a joke?" Rebecca asked.

Dylan looked on in horror as the confidence Rebecca had gained that night quickly faded away. "I don't think so." Despite her reassuring words, she couldn't prevent her eyes from drifting skyward.

"Stop looking for the pig blood, you goober," Willie said. "This isn't a scene out of *Carrie*."

"Then how—"

Willie grinned. "Can you say write-in candidates?" She gently pushed Dylan and Rebecca toward the stage.

The crowd, which had lapsed into silence, roared its approval when the student body president placed felt-covered crowns on Dylan and Rebecca's heads. The band played something slow and romantic. A spotlight followed the couple as they moved across the empty dance floor.

The theme the prom committee had chosen was "Make it Last Forever." When Dylan twirled Rebecca in a languid circle and pulled her into her arms, she wished she could do exactly that.

CHAPTER SEVEN

Rebecca had seen it time and time again, but the fact that the men in her community were able to build a barn in one day never ceased to amaze her.

The work began early. As soon as the sun rose—if not before—dozens of men would descend on the owners' property. An Amish man with an extensive carpentry background would be in charge of the project. He would divide the men into teams, assign them tasks, and oversee their progress. If everything went according to plan, the framing would be complete by noon when everyone would break for lunch. The midday meal would be like a giant potluck as the wives of all the men working on the construction project brought out their best dishes. The men would sit at one table, the women at another. Both sides would laugh and talk until it was time for the work to resume.

Children were not excluded from the events. They made themselves available to run errands if need be, but they spent most of their time playing with and getting to know their neighbors.

Rebecca loved a good barn raising. It felt like a picnic everyone was invited to. Like Christmas come early, Sarah and Joshua's barn raising gave her a chance to spend time with friends and family, some she hadn't seen in months. It gave her a chance to put work and chores aside and just enjoy herself. It gave her a chance to see Dylan.

When she saw Dylan and Mr. and Mrs. Mahoney spill out of

Mr. Mahoney's truck, Rebecca couldn't hold back her smile. Mr. Mahoney volunteered his services at each barn raising even if he didn't know the family he was helping. Though he wasn't one of their people, Rebecca couldn't think of a time when Mr. Mahoney showed up to help and he was not made to feel welcome.

Rebecca waved at the Mahoneys. When they waved back, she began to head in their direction. Tobias Hershberger blocked her path.

"You're looking lovely today, Rebecca." He removed his hat and ran a hand over his hair in a futile attempt to tame his unruly cowlick. His body was a solid mass of muscle, thanks to years spent working on his parents' farm. His face, however, still bore the angelic countenance of a child. He was truly a boy in a man's body.

"Thank you, Tobias. And thank you for helping with the barn raising today. Joshua and Sarah will be most appreciative."

"I would do anything for your family. Or any of my neighbors."

Service and humility were two of the primary tenets of Rebecca's faith. Rebecca thought Tobias exemplified both.

"I haven't seen very much of you lately," Tobias said. "How have you been keeping yourself?"

"Well, thank you. And you?"

"Like my father says, 'I could complain, but who would listen?' Are you being treated well at the bakery?"

"Mrs. Dunham is a wonderful boss. She makes work seem more like play. The workday passes very quickly."

"Esther tells me you have moved to town."

"Yes. Marian Schlabach and I have rented an apartment. We moved in a couple of weeks ago."

"Will I continue to see you at services?"

Rebecca suspected Tobias was really asking if she would still allow him to court her after the Sunday sings.

"You will see me at services, though perhaps not at the sings. The walk into town is too long and treacherous to make at night."

"I'm not fond of town, but I could drive you home if you like."

Tobias shuffled his feet. Rebecca could feel nervousness emanating from him. His anxiety put her on edge as well. What was he working up the courage to say?

"I know you're curious about the world, Rebecca. I want you to know that I will wait for you until you satisfy your curiosity."

Was that what she was doing with Dylan, satisfying her curiosity? Surely not. The journey she was on was too complex to be summed up by so simple a phrase.

"Are there no other girls that interest you, Tobias?"

"There are no other girls like you."

Rebecca looked over at Dylan. "Yes, there are."

Dylan watched Sarah's son break up Rebecca and Tobias's tête-à-tête. "Way to go, kid." She tossed the truck keys to her father, who tossed them right back.

"You'll need them more than I will." He cinched his tool belt around his waist. "Aren't you the designated errand girl today?"

"Huh?" Focused like a laser beam on Rebecca and Tobias, Dylan had to force herself to concentrate on what her father was saying. "Oh, yeah, sorry." She shoved the keys into the front pocket of her jeans. "See ya, Dad."

"Hold up."

Dylan nearly groaned in frustration. She didn't have time for a pep talk. She needed to see what sweet nothings Tobias had whispered in Rebecca's ear. "Yes, Dad?"

"Do you have your head in the game?"

"You should ask Mom that question. I'm not the one who brought a slow cooker to a barn raising."

Dylan's mom cradled a large bowl of tossed salad in her arms. "That was years ago."

"Yeah, but the story gets better every time I tell it."

Rebecca struggled to keep up with her two-year-old nephew. He had figured out how to climb and was anxious to get into everything that had previously been tantalizingly out of his reach.

"Are you the designated child wrangler today?" Dylan asked.

Rebecca picked up Isaiah before he could overturn a bucket of finishing nails. "Sarah has her hands full with Moses, so I said I'd look after this wiggle worm for a while."

Moses was Sarah's younger son, born just three weeks prior. Unlike Isaiah, he was the spitting image of his father. Everyone said so.

Dylan put her hands in front of her face and quickly removed them. "Boo!" Isaiah giggled and clapped his hands until Dylan did it again. She played peek-a-boo with him until he tired of the game. Then she pressed a finger to his button nose. "He's a cutie."

"He's going to be a real heartbreaker one day."

Dylan lowered her voice. "Just like his aunt."

Rebecca pressed a kiss to the top of Isaiah's head to hide her reddening cheeks.

"You're so cute when you blush."

"Is that why you try so hard to make me do it?"

"That's just it. I don't have to try hard. You make it easy for me." Dylan pulled an envelope out of her back pocket and handed it to Rebecca. "This is for you."

"What is it?" Rebecca fingered the embossed initials—DKM—on the cream-colored stationery. She rarely received letters and when she did, they were from family.

"An invitation to my graduation next month. I'd love it if you could come, but even if you can't you're still obligated to buy me an expensive gift. I'm kidding about the gift. The expensive part, at least. I'm low maintenance. I don't need much to make me happy. Will you come?"

"And miss out on a chance to see you in a dress? Not on your life."

"Sorry to disappoint you, but I'm going to be wearing shorts under my cap and gown. Unless it's really hot. Then I might go commando."

Rebecca looked down at the formally worded invitation in her hands. "You're graduating. That means you'll be moving to Philadelphia. I knew this day would come, but I didn't think it would be this soon."

"It's only eighty miles," Dylan said reassuringly. "And I promise I'll come home every weekend. If you're not working, I can take you back with me. We can see the Phillies. We can spend all day at the Museum of Art. Or"—she lowered her voice even more—"if you like, we won't even have to leave my room."

"I'd like that." Rebecca blushed again, but this time she didn't try to hide it. She liked it when Dylan looked at her. When Dylan's eyes were on her, she felt awake. She felt alive. She felt like she—like they—could do anything. "Maybe I could show you *my* room later."

Dylan did a double take. "The one in your apartment?"

"You can be my first official visitor."

"What would your roommate say?"

"She has friends over all the time. Why can't I?"

Dylan searched the sea of faces. "Where is she, anyway?"

Rebecca didn't want to admit Marian was nursing yet another hangover. "She isn't feeling well. She says she's going to sleep in and come over after lunch. So if you need help running errands this afternoon, I'll be happy to pitch in. Maybe we can make a pit stop along the way."

"Will you be done babysitting by then?"

"I'm sure I won't have a problem finding someone to fill in for me." Rebecca indicated the crowd of women who were lining up to watch the men begin framing the barn.

Dylan grinned. "I'll be sure to come find you."

"Where are you going?"

"I'm organizing a softball game to give the children something to do while their parents are working. I could use a coach for the losing—I mean *opposing* team."

"Give me a few minutes and I'll be there to show you how it's done."

"Bring it on."

They parted ways when Dylan left to scout a good location for the softball game and Rebecca went in the house to put Isaiah down for a nap.

❖

The kitchen was as much a whirlwind of activity as the construction site while the women tried to calculate cooking times for their dishes and schedule use of the oven. Rebecca quickly moved out of the way. She headed to Sarah and Joshua's room, which was just off the kitchen but far enough away from the hustle and bustle to give her some semblance of privacy.

She sat in the rocking chair by the window and cradled Isaiah in her arms, intending to sing him to sleep. Rubbing his eyes with one hand and twisting the other in his soft brown curls, he was already halfway to LaLa Land. Rebecca tried to think of a lullaby to send him the rest of the way. She chose the one Dylan had used on her the first night of her *rumspringa*. The one Dylan's grandmother had brought with her from Ireland.

Ireland. The name sounded like Our Land. A magical place made just for her and Dylan. Did such a place really exist?

"You're better at it than I am," Sarah said.

Rebecca, who had been watching Dylan place bases on a makeshift diamond, drew her attention away from the window. "At what?"

Sarah placed one sleeping son in his crib and reached for the other. "Getting this one to quiet down." She gently took Isaiah out of Rebecca's arms and placed him on his back in the crib opposite Moses's. "He always puts up a fight with me. He's the same way you were at his age: scared to go to sleep because he's afraid he might miss something." Sarah looked from Isaiah to Rebecca. "Then again, I guess not much has changed."

Rebecca tried not to wither from Sarah's pointed stare. "How are things with you?"

Sarah cocked her head. "I was just about to ask you the same thing."

"You first."

"Joshua is beside himself. He is the head of a steadily growing family and he has finally found us a place to call our own."

"That's Joshua. What about you?"

Sarah's sigh sounded like a balloon deflating.

"The farm is small, the house is even smaller, and the work never ends. I know I'm expected to smile and make the most of it, but sometimes I wish I could throw it all away and start over."

Rebecca had suspected Sarah was unhappy, but she hadn't realized the extent of her discontent.

"I've always wanted to be a wife and mother. When I was a little girl, I dreamed of being married to a prosperous man with many acres to his name. Joshua isn't that man. Limited to a scant five acres of farmland and burdened with two young children, we're barely able to make ends meet. This isn't the life I imagined living for myself. I expected more."

Sarah sat on the side of the bed and ran her hands over the quilt that covered it. The quilt Rebecca had crafted as a wedding gift. "Have you given yourself to Tobias yet?"

Rebecca reeled back in shock. "Sarah. Such a question."

"I'm not supposed to ask and you're not supposed to answer. I can tell by looking at Tobias that the answer is no. He still walks with the hesitancy of a boy, not the confidence of a man. Looking at you, I can't help but wonder if you have found another. You are becoming a woman before my eyes. If not Tobias, who is the reason for the change I see in you?"

"I have not changed. I'm the same person I always was."

"So you *have* found another."

"I never said—"

"You didn't have to. I can see it in your eyes."

Rebecca wondered what else her eyes had to say.

"Just tell me one thing: are you and Marian getting along?"

Rebecca shrugged. "She's a good roommate. We don't get in each other's way."

"But you don't have anything in common. What do you talk about?"

"You know Marian as well as I do. She does most of the talking. I don't have to say much. All I have to do is listen and nod every once in a while so she'll know I'm paying attention."

"What are you going to do when she joins church next year? You can't live on your own."

"Why can't I?"

"Living in the world might not be so bad if I had someone to share my fears with. I can't imagine doing it alone. You would do that?"

"The rent isn't so bad. I could pay it on my own if I cut down on other expenses."

Sarah arched an eyebrow. "Expenses?"

Rebecca laughed, realizing she must sound like she was putting on airs. "I have another year to save up. Even if I keep giving Papa money to help with the farm's expenses, I still should have enough to live on my own. Or I could always find another roommate. I know lots of girls who are thinking of living in the city, so it shouldn't be hard to find one to move in with me."

"Papa allowed you to move in with Marian because she's my friend. He won't permit you to live with just anyone."

Sarah caught Rebecca staring out the window at Dylan, who had rounded up enough children to field two teams and was helping them choose sides. "You can't depend on her. She's going to be gone soon. She's just like the rest of the English—she'll get bored and she'll leave."

"She'll be back."

"How do you know?"

Because she loves me, Rebecca almost said. "Because she said she would."

Sarah snorted. "Do you believe everything the English tell you? If you do, you're even more gullible than I thought you were. She's going to go to college, she's going to meet someone, and she's going to forget all about you."

Rebecca thought the same thing at least once a day. But did Sarah have to compound her misery? And did she have to look so gleeful about it? "Why do you hate the English so much?"

"I don't hate them. I'm just trying to look after you. I don't want to see you get hurt the way I did."

"What do you mean?"

Rebecca had hoped marrying Joshua would put a smile on Sarah's face and, if not that, then the births of her children. None of those things seemed to have worked. If anything, Sarah seemed more despondent than ever. It hadn't always been that way. Sarah had been bright and bubbly when she was younger, and when she had started her *rumspringa*, she had been positively ecstatic. Sarah's whole demeanor had changed when she found out she was pregnant. After that, she had become jumpy and nervous. She had seemed to shrink into herself. She had acted like a child who had been caught doing something she shouldn't and was afraid of being reprimanded. What could Sarah have done that could cause her so much pain?

Rebecca sat next to her on the bed. "Is there something you want to tell me?" She said the words as gently as she could, but Sarah's eyes widened in alarm.

"Something like what?"

"Like anything." Rebecca rested a hand on Sarah's arm. "If you ever want to talk, I'm here for you."

Sarah shook off Rebecca's attempt at comfort. "That's just it. You aren't here. You're out there." She pointed out the window, through which Rebecca could see Dylan cheering on the youthful players. "You're becoming one of them."

"I'll never be one of them. I'll always be one of us."

No matter how much the Mahoneys tried to make her feel included, Rebecca sometimes felt more like an object of curiosity than an equal. Not to the Mahoneys, but to their friends and acquaintances. Mrs. Ziegenfus was a prime example. Rebecca still remembered the teacher's ill-conceived attempt at levity at Dylan's birthday party. The painful reminder that her culture, which seemed so normal to her, was considered strange by nearly everyone else.

Torn between two worlds, Rebecca couldn't seem to find a place in either.

"Go play with your friend," Sarah said, waving Rebecca away. "She's waiting for you."

❖

The little girl chattered away in Pennsylvania Dutch. Dylan nodded as if she understood what she was saying, but Rebecca could tell Dylan had no idea what the girl was trying to tell her. Dylan had probably been able to follow along for a while, but the more excited the girl became, the less Dylan was able to keep up with what she was saying. Now she looked completely lost.

"Need some help?"

"Rebecca." Palpable relief flooded Dylan's voice. "I need all the help I can get." She took the little girl by the shoulders and turned her to face Rebecca. "She's saying what?"

Rebecca knelt in front of the girl, an adorable moppet who was the spitting image of a Raggedy Ann doll. The rag doll in her arms, though, like all the other dolls Amish children played with, had no face. Children were taught from an early age to strictly adhere to the Second Commandment. Idols and graven images of any kind were forbidden. That rule was applied to everything from photographs to dolls.

Rebecca recognized the girl as the youngest daughter of her former schoolteacher. Her name was Rachel like her mother and her grandmother. Rebecca looked into Rachel's big blue eyes and listened to her talk about how much she was looking forward to starting school the next year so she could learn to speak English and be more like Dylan.

Rebecca looked up at Dylan and grinned. "It looks like someone has a crush on you."

As if on cue, Rachel reached out and closed her small hand around two of Dylan's fingers. Dylan's ears turned bright red.

"Who's blushing now?"

Dylan draped an arm across Rebecca's shoulders and dragged her toward the field. "Just help me with the game, will ya?"

Every boy who was old enough to swing a hammer was helping with the barn, so most of the players were girls. They ranged in age from six to sixteen, with the older ones and the younger ones equally distributed between both teams.

Though she longed to play, Rebecca remained on the sidelines with Dylan. They kept score and acted as glorified cheerleaders, making sure to root with equal enthusiasm for both teams so they couldn't be accused of playing favorites. Some of the mothers wandered over after a while, but their support wasn't nearly as impartial.

The game was close and high-scoring, highlighted by even more laughs than home runs. Rebecca couldn't remember the last time she'd had so much fun. She always enjoyed doing things in Dylan's world. She was glad to see Dylan enjoying herself in hers.

During the midday meal, some time was spent in discussions about the progress of the barn, but most of the hour-long break was devoted to less serious subjects. Most of the smiles around the table disappeared when Marian and a couple of her friends staggered onto the scene.

"What's with all the surprised looks?" Marian plunked a container of store-bought potato salad on the table. A bright red sticker affixed to the plastic tub boldly declared the contents had been reduced for quick sale. "Didn't Rebecca tell you I was coming?"

Rebecca, who was sitting next to her mother and across from Dylan and Mrs. Mahoney, tried to make herself invisible. It was one thing for Marian and her friends to be drunk at a hoedown or behind closed doors. For them to be that way at a barn raising was unacceptable. They had gone from embarrassing themselves to embarrassing everyone else as well. The girls' mothers looked mortified, their fathers visibly angry.

Eyes downcast, Sarah excused herself to check on Moses, who had not stirred from his nap.

Hermann Yoder was in charge of the project, but Rebecca's father took the lead during the awkward silence that followed Marian's arrival. "Let's get back to it," he said quietly.

The men didn't need to be told a second time. Rising as one, they prepared to return to the construction site. Some grabbed extra pieces of bread or meat for fortification for the work that remained.

The girls' mothers sprang into action, too. After guiding their daughters to the women's table, they piled food on plates and placed them in front of their wayward children.

"Eat something," Annie Schlabach said, obviously hoping Marian would sober up before she caused even more of a scene. "You'll feel better."

Marian pushed the plate away. "I want a Big Mac and a rum and Coke, not a pile of other people's leftovers."

Rebecca was tired of watching Marian make a fool out of herself even if Marian had not yet reached that point. When Mr. Yoder signaled he needed Dylan to run her first errand of the day, Rebecca nearly burst into a dance of joy.

"Give this list to Mr. Grunewald at the hardware store and he'll take care of everything." Mr. Yoder's accent was so thick he almost sounded like a parody of himself. "Some of the things are pretty heavy. I can't spare any of the men, but I can send a couple of the boys with you to help load." He turned to signal for a couple of teenage boys to come down off the roof, but Dylan stopped him.

"No, don't bother. I don't think I'll have a problem finding help." She walked away before he could try to convince her to change her mind. She found Rebecca bouncing Isaiah on her knee on the front porch. Dylan's mother sat next to them. The rest of the women were inside. Some were washing the dishes from lunch. Others, Dylan could hear, were giving Marian and her friends an earful about their behavior. "I'm up." Dylan brandished the shopping list. "Can you get away?"

Rebecca nodded. "Your mother said she'd watch Isaiah if we had to leave."

Dylan thanked her lucky stars for having understanding parents.

"See you in a bit, Mom," she said when her mother took Isaiah from Rebecca's arms. Too busy cooing to the baby, her mother didn't respond. "Mother?"

"Oh, I'm sorry. He's just so cute. His impish little smile reminds me of you at his age."

"We're going to go now, okay?"

"Take your time, honey." She lifted a warning eyebrow. "Just don't take too long."

"You got it."

Dylan and Rebecca scampered off to the Silverado, climbed in, and slammed the doors.

"Finally."

Dylan turned the key in the ignition, put the truck in gear, and drove off, resisting the urge to floor it once she hit the highway. She wanted to pick up the items from the list as quickly as possible so she could have more alone time with Rebecca.

Downtown Lutz was a mix of old and new. Mom-and-Pop stores that had been owned by the same families for generations operated next to national chains owned by faceless corporations. Parking spots for SUVs, compacts, and hybrid vehicles sat alongside hitching posts for horses and buggies. Depending on where she was, Dylan had a hard time determining if she was in the twenty-first century or the nineteenth.

She parked in front of Art Grunewald's hardware store, which had sat in the same spot for nearly eighty years. Dozens of competitors had come and gone over the years, but Grunewald's had managed to outlast them all. An additional store in Lancaster had been open for going on twenty years, but its hold on the market was slowly being squeezed out by the large home improvement chains. Loyal customers continued to visit, but Dylan didn't know how much longer Mr. Grunewald could afford to keep the doors in the Lancaster store open.

"I have good news and bad news." Mr. Grunewald ran a hand through his thinning gray hair as he regarded the list. "I've got everything in stock but the tin. I've got it, too, but it's at the Lancaster store."

"Do you want me to go pick it up?" Dylan asked.

"That would just take longer, and I know how anxious Hermann is to get this job done on time. I'll have a couple of the stock boys drive it down. It'll take at least forty-five minutes for them to load it up and get it here. Longer if they fiddly fart around like I expect them to."

Dylan suppressed a smile. Mr. Grunewald's colorful language always amused her, but that wasn't what had struck her fancy. The delay might throw the men off schedule, but it worked to her advantage. It would give her and Rebecca extra time together. "That's fine. We'll run some errands and swing back here in a few."

"I'll gather the other stuff Hermann wants and the boys will load everything up when you get back. I'll see you back here in about an hour, then."

Dylan and Rebecca headed out to the truck. Dylan used her cell phone to inform her mother of the unforeseen holdup so she could tell the men not to expect her and Rebecca back any time soon.

"Dylan, if—"

Dylan anticipated her mother's argument. "I'm not making this up, Mom. Mr. Grunewald's right here if you want to ask him."

"I'm not going to make you go that far, but you couldn't have planned it any better if you'd tried, could you?"

"I could have, but I'll take what I can get." Dylan ended the call and turned to Rebecca, who was trying to find a good song on the radio. "Is there something you want to show me?"

"There are lots of things I want to show you." Rebecca settled on a station that specialized in '90s alternative rock. She bobbed her head to Nirvana's "Smells Like Teen Spirit." She didn't know all the words yet, but the ones she did know she sang as loud as she could. "What do you want to see first?" she asked when the song ended.

Dylan was fascinated by Rebecca's ability to seem innocent

one moment and coquettish the next. Like Forrest Gump's box of chocolates, she never knew what she was going to get. She was looking forward to the day when she would finally be able to unwrap all the pieces.

❖

The apartment was a fourth-floor walk-up a few blocks from the center of town. Dylan could see the signs for Grunewald's and the diner from the fire escape outside the living room window. With a clear view of Grunewald's parking lot, she would be able to see when the delivery truck arrived. Sweet.

The living room looked like a stereotypical college apartment or frat house—filled with mismatched furniture, half-empty pizza boxes, and crushed beer cans. A small TV sat atop a card table that did double duty as a TV stand and a catch-all.

"I know you probably think the room looks frightful, but I got tired of picking up after Marian and her friends. I'm supposed to be her roommate, not her maid. No matter how much time I spent straightening things up during the week, it took them only two seconds to mess everything up last night."

"Marian never cleans up?" Dylan tried to determine if the furry brown object under the trash-laden coffee table was a discarded sock or an old banana peel.

"When she can't find something she's looking for, I give her about a week before she pulls out a trash bag and tosses all this stuff out."

Dylan followed Rebecca into the kitchen. She could tell Marian didn't hang out there because the room was spotless. The laminated counters were clean enough to eat off of. The cabinets were filled with canned goods and were well organized, everything in its place. The refrigerator, surprisingly, was empty. Rebecca had an explanation for that, too.

"If I put anything in there that doesn't need to be cooked, it tends to disappear before I can have any. I keep a secret stash of fresh fruit and snacks in my room. Maybe you'll have better luck with your roommate than I do with mine. Do you know who she is yet?"

"No, it's too early. I don't even know which dorm I've been assigned to yet. I suppose I'll get something in the mail this summer unless the administration decides to wait and spring it on me during freshman orientation."

"My room's this way."

Rebecca led Dylan to her bedroom, then closed and locked the door behind them.

Dylan took in the small room. It seemed similar to Rebecca's room at the Lapps' but was more open and relaxed, the mood brightened by a vase of flowers that sat on the window sill. The sun beat down on the colorful tulips, teasing them to open their blooms wider. A row of books lined the writing desk opposite the window. The titles were all over the place. Rebecca had everything from mysteries to true-life adventures to historical fiction to autobiographies. A dog-eared copy of John Krakauer's *Under the Banner of Heaven*, the true story of two Mormon brothers who had committed murder on what they said were orders from God, rested on the end table next to the bed. *Talk about your difficult reads.*

Dylan was glad to see Rebecca was able to indulge her love of reading again. With her formal schooling complete and Mr. Lapp in charge of any additional education she received, her reading material had been limited to the Bible and religious tracts.

"Maybe you'll have time to convince Willie to change her mind," Rebecca said. "You could go to the same school and be roommates."

Dylan returned *For Whom the Bell Tolls* to its place on the desk. "Not a chance. Willie has had her heart set on going to Bryn Mawr since she found out Katharine Hepburn went there. Surrounded by that many women, I probably won't even see her until she graduates four years from now. If, that is, she doesn't get her heart broken and flunk out first. Whoever I'm paired up with, I'm sure it will be an adventure."

"Are you looking forward to it?"

"The adventure, yes, but not being away from you. Though I may have found a way to make it easier."

"How?"

Dylan reached into her pocket and pulled out a small key. She presented the key to Rebecca.

"What's this?" Rebecca turned the key over and over in her hands.

"I got you a post office box in town. It's in your name, so what goes in and out of it is your business and no one else's. I already paid the first year's rent so you won't have to worry about that. Write me as often as you can. I'll write back. This way, you won't have to worry about anyone opening my letters by accident or intercepting your mail."

Rebecca continued to stare at the key. A tiny object, to be sure, but one that held great promise. More than just the key to a box, it represented the key to a whole new life. It would provide a way to bring the world to Rebecca's front door.

"Will you write me?" Dylan's left hand rested on Rebecca's waist. Her right brushed across Rebecca's cheek.

"Every day." Rebecca leaned into Dylan's hand, enjoying the warmth and pressure of her touch. She removed her bonnet and unpinned her hair, letting the long locks fall in a free-flowing cascade. The wondrous sight never failed to take Dylan's breath away.

Swallowing hard, Dylan ran her hands through Rebecca's hair, then cupped her face in her hands. Rebecca was even more striking in her everyday clothes than she was in her weekend ones. She seemed more relaxed. More at ease. She didn't have to check to see what everyone else was doing and mimic their actions. She could be herself. She could do what came naturally. "Do you have any idea how beautiful you are?"

Rebecca shook her head. "I'm not—"

"Yes, you are."

Dylan silenced Rebecca's protests with a kiss. She initiated the contact, but Rebecca surprised her by being the aggressor. Before she knew it, she was on her back on the bed with Rebecca on top of her. She tried to slow things down when what she wanted to do was move forward. Their weekly make-out sessions left her simultaneously frustrated and hungry for more.

"We can't," she said, returning to what was becoming a constant refrain.

"Yes, we can." Rebecca touched her lips to the side of Dylan's neck. Her hands slipped under Dylan's shirt and touched her bare skin. Dylan gasped and pulled Rebecca closer. Rebecca's hips pressed down and Dylan's rose to meet them. "Don't you want to?"

Rebecca's leg slipped between Dylan's. Dylan found herself moving against it before she forced herself to stop. "You know I do." Dylan fought to regain control of her emotions while her body sought to give in to sensation. "But we can't."

"Why not? It's perfect. There's no one here. We don't have to be back for a while. Why not now?"

"Because I don't want my first time with you to be spent waiting for the phone to ring or hoping we don't hear footsteps coming up the stairs. For your birthday, I've booked us a two-night stay in one of Philadelphia's best hotels. We can have dinner, go for a carriage ride, then go back to the room and—"

Rebecca placed her fingers over Dylan's lips. "Do me a favor. Stop planning everything and just let it happen."

"But—"

"My birthday is four months from now. Four months is a long time." Rebecca reached up and unbuttoned her dress. "Do you really want to wait that long?"

Dylan watched wordlessly as Rebecca pulled her dress over her head. When Rebecca removed her slip as well, she let out a low moan. "Four months isn't a long time," she whispered. "It's an eternity."

Smiling, Rebecca lay back and watched Dylan undress. Dylan's T-shirt and jeans joined the growing pile of clothes on the floor. Their underwear came next.

"Are you sure?" Dylan asked, giving Rebecca one more chance to change her mind.

Rebecca pushed a stray lock of hair behind Dylan's left ear. Then she put her hand on the back of Dylan's neck and pulled her in for a kiss. "We're wasting time."

Dylan lay on top of Rebecca, letting her get used to the feel of her weight and the idea of what they were about to do. She kept telling herself not to rush but, in the back of her mind, she knew they didn't have much time. Her phone could ring at any second.

"Touch me."

Hearing the longing in Rebecca's voice, Dylan let go of the last strands of her uncertainty. She slowly slid her hands over Rebecca's skin, feeling goose bumps trail in their wake. With her tongue, she carefully navigated each curve, committing each turn to memory. She intended to travel the route many more times.

Rebecca gasped when Dylan's tongue curled around an erect nipple and she arched her back. Dylan sucked one breast for several minutes before turning to give the other equal attention. Then she reached down and touched the apex of Rebecca's need.

"May I?" Dylan whispered, asking for permission to go further.

"Please." Rebecca buried her face against the side of Dylan's neck, her teeth nipping at the soft skin.

"Harder." Dylan leaned into the pressure of Rebecca's mouth. When she slipped her fingers into Rebecca's center, Rebecca's nails raked across her back and she cried out. Then Rebecca was touching her, too. Filling all the spaces that had once been hollow.

Rebecca whined when Dylan took her hand away.

"I want to taste you."

Dylan replaced her fingers with her tongue. When her mouth closed around Rebecca's sensitive center, Rebecca's body torqued at the foreign sensation. She wrapped her legs around Dylan's waist so Dylan couldn't get away.

Dylan lapped at Rebecca's juices, drinking as greedily from her as someone who had stumbled upon an oasis after being lost in the desert. She moved her tongue faster and faster as Rebecca's cries became higher pitched. Rebecca was close. So close. So was she.

She covered Rebecca's body with hers, then parted Rebecca's

legs with one of her own and slipped it in between. They rode each other's thighs until they were both screaming.

When it was over, they lay sprawled across the tangled sheets, chests heaving as they gasped for air.

Dylan pushed herself up on one elbow. "You're rather persuasive when you want to be."

Rebecca grinned. "Do you wish I weren't?"

Dylan shook her head and trailed her finger down the center of Rebecca's chest. "I love you."

She wished she could shout the words from the nearest rooftop but she didn't dare. No one could know what had just happened between her and Rebecca. Their lovemaking would have to remain a closely guarded secret. Their friendship was accepted—for now. The same could never be said for their love.

"Have you ever done this before?"

"No, this was my first time."

"Was it—I mean, was I...any good?"

Dylan traced a finger over Rebecca's lips. "You were perfect. No one is going to be able to wipe this smile off my face for a long time. If ever."

Rebecca lay with her head on Dylan's chest. "Can we do this again tomorrow?"

"And the day after and the day after that."

They kissed. Idly, at first. Then with mounting passion. Dylan groaned in frustration when her cell phone rang. She reached for the phone. And nearly dropped it when Rebecca placed a warm hand on her breast.

"Don't answer it."

Dylan reluctantly removed Rebecca's hand. "I have to. It's probably Mr. Grunewald calling to tell us the order's ready." She reached for the phone and pressed it to her ear. "What's up, Mr. G?"

"Where are you?"

"Dad?" Dylan sat bolt upright in bed as if her father were in the same room instead of on the other end of the line.

"Where are you?" he repeated.

"At Rebecca's." Dylan could hear loud voices in the background but assumed her father was calling from the work site. The men must really be anxious to receive the order. She frantically motioned for Rebecca to gather their clothes. "We're waiting for Mr. Grunewald to call. Didn't Mom tell you?"

"Yeah, she did, but that doesn't matter now. Just get back here as soon as you can."

Dylan didn't like the way her father sounded. It reminded her of the night he'd told her about TJ. An icicle of fear chilled her heart. "What's wrong?" She hurriedly put on her bra and panties as Rebecca did the same. "Where's Mom?"

"She's here. She's fine. Everything's fine. Just get back here as soon as you can, okay?"

Dylan climbed out of bed and held the phone to her ear with her shoulder while she stepped into her jeans. "Bullshit, Dad. You know I can always tell when something's up with you."

"Dylan, I don't have time to get into it now. For once, just do what I say and don't ask me any questions, okay?"

"Yes, sir." Dylan ended the call.

Rebecca's face was ashen. "What's wrong?"

Dylan shrugged and slipped her arms through the sleeves of her T-shirt. "He wouldn't tell me. But whatever it is, it can't be good."

Rebecca pinned her hair up and covered it with her bonnet. "I don't like the sound of this."

"You and me both."

CHAPTER EIGHT

Dylan accelerated, urging the truck past the caravan of buggies clogging the road.

"Do you think there's been an accident?" Rebecca reached for something to hold on to when Dylan made the turn onto Sarah and Joshua's road on two wheels.

"If there had been an accident, everyone would be heading *to* Sarah and Joshua's place instead of away from it."

"What do you think is wrong?"

"Anything I could come up with is probably ten times worse than the real thing so I don't want to speculate." Dylan put a hand on Rebecca's arm. "No matter what happens, never forget I love you."

"I love you, too."

Hearing—and saying—the words brought Rebecca great comfort. She hoped this wouldn't be the last time she and Dylan would be able to share such sentiments.

"Is that my dad on the porch?"

Rebecca peered at the lone figure pacing in front of Sarah and Joshua's front door. "I think so."

"Damn. He looks pissed."

Dylan sped up the driveway and stomped on the brakes. She and Rebecca climbed out after the truck lurched to a stop.

"We're here. What's going on, Dad?"

"Come inside." Mr. Mahoney held the front door open. "This concerns you, too. Both of you."

Rebecca, anxiety gnawing at her insides, slowly approached the door. The only thing she feared more than losing Dylan was having her love for Dylan become public knowledge. Had someone found out what she and Dylan had been up to that afternoon? Had someone seen or heard something they shouldn't? If so, the consequences could be devastating. For both of them.

Most of Sarah and Joshua's guests had left. The ones who remained were gathered in the living room. Marian and Sarah stood in the middle of the room. Both were visibly upset. They looked like they could—or already had—come to blows. They were surrounded by several groups of people. Her parents and Uncle Amos. Joshua, Moses, and Mr. and Mrs. King. Mr. and Mrs. Schlabach. Cousin Peterli. Mr. and Mrs. Mahoney.

Isaiah sat in Mrs. Mahoney's lap. Squirming and crying, he stretched his arms for his mother. Why didn't Sarah take him out of Mrs. Mahoney's arms when he so clearly wanted her to hold him?

"Sit down."

Her father's deep voice sounded stern. Rebecca didn't know if she was being asked to choose sides or have judgment passed upon her. She wanted to sit next to Dylan but the lines had clearly been drawn. She sat next to her mother, who continually dabbed her moist eyes with a handkerchief. Dylan sat next to Mrs. Mahoney.

"Begin again," her father said.

Marian spoke first. "I apologize for disrupting the frolic, Mr. Lapp. It was not my intention."

"We will discuss your behavior at a later time. We will begin with the charges you have leveled. You have accused Sarah of consorting with an Englishman and allowing that man to father her child."

Rebecca looked from Sarah to Joshua. Neither could meet her eyes—or each other's.

"She's lying, Papa," Sarah said.

"You are the one who's lying," Marian said. "Isaiah is not the son of Joshua King but Matthew Mahoney."

Rebecca heard Dylan's gasp of surprise. If she had been able to breathe, she might have managed one of her own. Was it true? Was

Isaiah Dylan's nephew? And if he was, would he be allowed to stay? Would Sarah?

Papa had been elected *Volliger Diener* because he was considered one of the wisest and most compassionate men in the community. Sarah appealed to the judgment that had served him so well in the past.

"Are you going to believe the word of a drunkard over mine?"

"You don't have to believe what I say. Let your eyes show you the truth."

Marian reached into the back pocket of her jeans and pulled out a photograph. She handed the photograph to Rebecca's father. Her mother averted her eyes from the image in accordance with the *Ordnung*.

Rebecca lowered her gaze from her father's stricken face to the photograph in his shaking hands.

The snapshot was of Sarah and Matthew Mahoney. It had apparently been taken during Sarah's *rumspringa*. Sarah was dressed in jeans and a printed blouse. She had a bottle of beer in one hand and a lit cigarette in the other. She was sitting on the lap of a shirtless Matthew Mahoney. He was kissing her—and touching her in a familiar way.

Her father covered the photograph with his hands as if he wanted to crumple it up or tear it to pieces. Then he held it up for the others to see.

Rebecca watched their reactions. Mr. and Mrs. Mahoney clenched their teeth and remained silent. Dylan, her lower lip trembling, said the one word that surely everyone else was thinking: "No."

Seeing the photo, Sarah turned as white as a sheet. It was obvious she didn't know it existed. Until it was too late.

"The charges Marian has made are true," she said.

Joshua buried his head in his hands. Mr. and Mrs. King comforted him when he began to cry. Sarah's tears flowed just as freely as she began to confess her sins.

"I dated Matthew Mahoney during my *rumspringa*. I can count on one hand the number of times I was with him. He left me after he got what he wanted."

"When you realized you were with child, did you know the child might not be mine?" Joshua asked.

Sarah, beyond words, could only nod.

"Did you share your suspicions with anyone?" her father asked.

"Only Marian. She was my friend. I thought she would keep my secret."

"And so she did."

"Surely you must have known that because you are his mother, I would have loved him as my own whether or not I was his father," Joshua said. "Why didn't you tell me?"

"I thought you would leave me," Sarah said. "I wanted to wait until after we were married because I knew we could not be divorced. When the time came, I could not bring myself to destroy your happiness."

Her father held up one hand. "Say no more. I have heard enough." He pushed himself out of his seat, a task that seemed to take more effort than normal. "Amos, gather the members of the council and tell them we must meet. Thomas Mahoney, take the child with you until his fate has been decided."

"No," Sarah wailed in despair. "You cannot take my child from me."

"All actions have consequences. You would be wise to remember that."

His shoulders sagging from the weight of the responsibility heaped upon them, he walked out the door. Peterli, Uncle Amos, and Mr. King trailed behind him. The Schlabachs soon followed. Her mother and Mrs. King remained behind to comfort Sarah and Joshua.

Mr. Mahoney, despite her father's dismissal, looked like he didn't know if he should stay or go. Then he abruptly stood. "No offense, Mrs. Lapp, but your husband cannot decide the course of so many people's lives based on the word of a couple of kids barely out of their teens. There's only one way to settle this." He pulled Isaiah from Mrs. Mahoney's arms. "Ask Samuel to do nothing until he hears from me."

Mr. Mahoney headed for the door, Dylan hot on his heels. "Dad, where are you going?"

"To see your brother."

"I'm coming with you." Dylan looked back at Rebecca. *Wait for me*, her eyes seemed to plead.

Unsure if she would be able to heed the silent command, Rebecca projected a one-word reply: *Hurry*.

❖

It had been years since Dylan had seen her father so upset. "Do you want me to drive?" she asked after he nearly missed the on-ramp to the Pennsylvania Turnpike. She peered into the backseat to check on Isaiah. He was sleeping peacefully in the ancient car seat that hadn't been used since the last time she was strapped into it.

"I can handle the driving. I need you to read the instructions on that test kit so we don't screw this up. I don't want to make the situation any worse than it already is."

Dylan read the instruction sheet inside the paternity test collection kit her father had bought from the pharmacy in Lancaster. "It shouldn't be too hard. We swab the inside of Matt's cheek with one of these giant Q-tips, do the same to Isaiah, and mail the swabs to the processing center to be tested. In three to five business days, we'll know if Matt really is Isaiah's father."

"There has to be a faster way."

"Do you want it done fast or do you want it done right?"

"I just want it done." He weaved in and out of traffic, passing cars at will.

"What will you do if Matt is Isaiah's father? Matt can barely take care of himself, let alone a kid."

"Isaiah would stay with us, obviously, even though I thought your mother and I were done raising children. If Sarah leaves the church and decides to assert her parental rights, we wouldn't stand in her way. He is her son, after all. But what about you? What will you do if it turns out Isaiah is your nephew?"

"I already love the little rug rat, so that's not going to change. Rebecca is reluctant to commit to a future with me. She can't imagine not being with her family. I understand that, so I'm not pressuring her. At least, I hope I'm not. We have fun when we're together, but each time I take her home, I feel like she's saying, *That was a nice place to visit, but I wouldn't want to live there.* If she's looking for an excuse to walk away, this could be the one she needs. If she takes it, it would feel like she's rejecting more than the English world. It would feel like she's rejecting me, too."

❖

It had been three days since the barn raising. Three days since Sarah's world had been torn apart. Three days since Sarah had seen Isaiah. Three days since Rebecca had seen Dylan.

When Dylan and Mr. Mahoney had returned from Reading and told everyone about the waiting period for the test results, Rebecca feared Sarah might collapse from the strain. Her fears seemed to have come to fruition. Her sister was wasting away in front of her eyes.

Rebecca placed a tray of food in front of Sarah and tried to get her to eat.

Sarah stirred the potato soup but didn't lift the spoon to her mouth. Her carefully crafted web of deceit lay in tatters at her feet. "Have I been shunned?"

Rebecca placed a hand on Sarah's back. She could feel Sarah's bones poking through the thick material of her dress. Sarah had lost so much weight. And so quickly. Her grief was total and overwhelming. Rebecca felt her pain and longed to take it away. "The council has not met," she said gently. "No decision has been made."

"And yet Joshua treats me as if I have been shunned. He will not speak to me or share a table with me."

"He is hurt and confused. What would you have him do?"

"Forgive me."

"You broke the *Ordnung*, Sarah."

Rebecca wondered if Sarah's torment would become her own one day. She had romantic feelings for Dylan Mahoney. By acting on those feelings, she, too, had broken the *Ordnung*. She, too, risked punishment.

"I broke the *Ordnung* before I made a vow to uphold it."

"And you continued to break it each day you remained silent about what you had done. That's how the council will see it."

"But that's not how I see it. I paid the price for my silence every day. I paid it every time I looked at my husband. I paid it every time I looked at my son. Have you never done something you regret?"

Rebecca was in love with Dylan Mahoney. She grew to love her a little more each day. She was certain she would never regret loving Dylan or acting on that love. But would she—like Sarah—be forced to pay for her actions?

❖

Dylan opened the web browser and logged on to the family's e-mail account.

"You've got mail," a computer-generated voice said.

Dylan checked the unread messages. She quickly located an e-mail from the lab that had processed the paternity test.

"The results are back."

She clicked on the link in the secure e-mail and input the provided user ID and password. Her father watched over her shoulder. Her mother, saying she was too afraid to look, remained on the couch with a sleeping Isaiah stretched across her lap.

Her mother ran a hand over the toddler's curls. "Even though I would love it if Isaiah were part of this family, I hope Sarah got her dates wrong. I know she must be eager to see him. I can't believe Samuel would even think of keeping them apart, let alone follow through with it."

"The rules are the rules," Dylan said, wondering if those same rules would soon force her and Rebecca to part as well.

"Being separated has to be as hard on Sarah as it is on Isaiah," her mother said. "If it were me, I would fall apart. Then I would tear down every obstacle in my path until we were reunited. Give me good news, Dylan, so we can take this little one home where he belongs."

"Fingers crossed, Mom." A multipage document appeared on the screen. Dylan silently read the disclosures.

"Well?" her father said anxiously.

"I'm getting there." She scrolled through the complex medical jargon and skipped to the last page. "Here we are. 'Test results indicate a ninety-nine point nine percent probability that there is a paternal relation between Sample A and Sample B.'"

"So he is Matt's son."

"Congratulations, Grandpa. It's a boy."

"Not funny, Dylan."

"That's why they call it gallows humor, Dad."

She looked at the test results again to see if, by some miracle, she had read them wrong the first time. Nothing had changed. Then again, everything had changed. Or was about to. If Isaiah's father wasn't Amish, that meant Isaiah wasn't Amish. Chances were he would not be allowed to stay with the only family he had ever known. Would he be allowed to stay with Sarah, or would Dylan's home become his permanent one?

"Do you think they'll take him away?" Her mother covered Isaiah's ears with her hand as if she didn't want him to overhear their conversation.

Dylan printed the test results and handed them to her father. "That piece of paper makes him English, which means he can't live with the Lapps. He can stay with Sarah if they kick her out of the church or if she chooses to leave on her own, but with no job and only an eighth-grade education, she would have to fight one uphill battle after another."

"She could stay with us until she gets on her feet. They both can. We have plenty of room. What do you think, Tom?"

"I think she'll see it as charity and she'll say no, but we can certainly make the offer."

❖

Rebecca's heartbeat quickened when she saw Mrs. Mahoney standing on the front porch with Isaiah in her arms. Then her heart nearly stopped when she saw Dylan's face. She didn't need to read what was on the paper in Mr. Mahoney's hand to know what it said. The look in Dylan's eyes said it all.

Mr. Mahoney handed the piece of paper to Rebecca's father. "It's true," was all he said. It was all that needed to be said.

Sarah began to cry.

Rebecca watched as her father's face colored with emotion. Sadness. Fear. Disappointment. All three seemed to play across his features at the same time. He cleared his throat and shoved the piece of paper into the pocket of his work shirt. Then he shook Mr. Mahoney's hand and tipped his hat to Mrs. Mahoney. "Thank you for coming all this way. If you will excuse me, I must gather the council."

"Can't it wait?" Mrs. Mahoney asked as she tried to soothe a disgruntled Isaiah. He looked as if he had just woken from a nap or needed to take one.

"It cannot. We have waited long enough. Come, Amos."

After their father and Uncle Amos walked away, Sarah's quiet sobs turned into wails. Isaiah soon joined her. Rebecca flinched when their keening grew louder.

Mrs. Mahoney placed Isaiah in Sarah's arms, giving mother and son a chance to comfort one another. Each held on to the other for dear life.

Rebecca looked at Dylan. She wanted to run to her and cling to her the way Sarah was grasping Isaiah, but she knew she could not. If she did, she would surely give herself away. To keep her secrets safe, they would have to maintain their distance. But for how long? How long would she be able to go without seeing Dylan? Without touching her. Kissing her. Holding her hand. A week? A month?

Forever? Rebecca didn't think she'd be able to last a day. Never had she needed someone so much. And she saw the same longing she felt reflected in Dylan's face.

"If things don't go well for you with the council, Sarah," Mrs. Mahoney said, "Tom and I may have a solution. You and Isaiah can stay with us for as long as you like."

Sarah looked up, her eyes flooded with tears. "Thank you, Mrs. Mahoney, but I would not be able to bear the shame. To have everyone look at me and know— To have everyone look at him and say—" She shook her head fiercely. "I would not be able to stay here, but I could not take him with me. I don't have the money." She began to cry even harder.

Rebecca's heart broke a little more with each tear that fell from Sarah's and Isaiah's eyes.

Sarah pulled Isaiah's arms from around her neck and returned the squalling child to Mrs. Mahoney. "Keep him. Care for him as you would your own. He is your own. I will visit as often as I can. And when he is old enough, he can decide for himself if he would rather live in your world or mine."

Sarah turned and walked into the house, her mother close behind. Their departure left Rebecca alone with the Mahoneys. She didn't know what to say to them. She was too stunned to think, let alone speak. How could Sarah turn her back on her own flesh and blood? Was her pride so great that she would rather sacrifice her relationship with her son in order to save face? If Sarah left, the whispers about her would not stop. She simply would be too far away to hear them. But what about Isaiah? If he were left behind, he would hear everything that was said. About his mother and himself.

"Rebecca—" Dylan began.

Rebecca couldn't bear to hear what Dylan had to say. Words of comfort—no matter how heartfelt—were the last things she wanted or needed. She brushed past Dylan, hurried down the steps, and began to run.

She ran to escape the pain. She ran to escape the past. She ran to escape the future. She ran until she could run no more. Then she sank to her knees and cried.

Dylan started after Rebecca but her father grabbed her by the arm. "Not now, honey."

"I have to talk to her. I have to make sure she's okay."

"I'm sure she's just as confused as you are. More even. Give her the time she needs to figure things out. She needs some space right now. Don't crowd her."

"But, Dad, I have to make her understand."

"Understand what? Whatever happened—whatever's going to happen is beyond our control. And hers."

Dylan looked off into the distance, hoping she would see Rebecca heading back. She felt torn in two. Where did her loyalties lie? With her brother? With Rebecca? Whose side was she supposed to take?

If none of this is my fault, why do I feel so guilty?

CHAPTER NINE

The council gathered on Friday. They met for less than an hour. They said they considered the case from all angles, but how could they have done that in such a brief amount of time? The punishment was swift and harsh. Too harsh, Rebecca thought as she waited for her father to inform the congregation during Sunday services. But with no written rules or covenants, each congregation was able to pass its own judgments in order to discipline wayward members.

Rebecca lowered her eyes as she listened to her father pronounce the sentences. His deep voice was steady and emotionless. It seemed as if he had never met the people involved, let alone fathered one of them.

A few days before, Rebecca was happier than she had ever been. The plans she and Dylan had made had started to come true, and they had finally been able to express their love physically. Now her life was shattered and she had no idea how to make the pieces fit.

"In Exodus 20:4, we find these words," her father said. "'Thou shalt not make unto thee any graven image, or any likeness of anything that is in heaven above, or that is in the earth beneath, or that is in the water under the earth.' By possessing a photograph, Marian Schlabach has broken the *Ordnung* against such things. Because the offense occurred before she became a church member, she cannot be punished for this transgression, but she has been counseled that future incidents will not be so easily dismissed.

"Let me remind you photographs are evidence of pride. They tempt people to look at a likeness of themselves with self-admiration. Pictures represent the outward appearance, which is temporary. By paying too much attention to the passing, you risk losing sight of the eternal. Despite her methods, Marian is to be commended for helping to bring the truth to light. She was baptized this morning and is a welcome member of this congregation."

Rebecca flinched involuntarily. She didn't consider herself a vengeful person, but she didn't believe Marian should be able to destroy people's lives and get away scot-free. The last thing she would ever do was congratulate Marian for it, no matter what Papa said.

She thought Marian should feel more like a pariah than a hero. Because of her, there was a division in the church. A schism that wouldn't have existed if she had remained loyal to someone who was supposed to be her friend. Talk had already begun that her father should step down as *Volliger Diener* and make way for Micah King. If he couldn't control his own children, the naysayers said, how could he lead the congregation? And weren't his frequent Bible quotations evidence of pride?

If it came to a vote, Mr. King could probably ride a wave of sympathy into an office he had never professed a desire to inhabit.

Her father had devoted his life to the church. He and Uncle Amos both. When they were ordained, it was supposed to be for life. Why should they be made to pay for something that wasn't their fault? The blame, if there was blame to be cast, was Sarah's. And she was being forced to pay the price.

"First Corinthians 5:11 advises us this."

The moment had arrived. The other congregants leaned forward in their seats. Rebecca continued to examine the floor. She hated this part of Sunday services. Her father was about to perform a duty she had witnessed only a few times in her life. Knowing what was coming didn't make it any easier to hear.

"We are not to keep company or share a table with anyone determined to be a fornicator, an idolater, a railer, a drunkard, or an extortioner. Romans 16:17 says this: 'Now I beseech you, brethren, mark them which cause divisions and offenses contrary to the doctrine with ye have learned; and avoid them.'"

Rebecca looked up when she heard her father pause. Part of her expected him to break down. He had to at some point, didn't he? He was only human, after all. Sarah was his firstborn and Isaiah, even if an Englishman was his father, was still his grandson. Nothing could change that.

He closed his Bible and continued his sermon as if he were dictating a grocery list instead of sealing someone's fate.

"Sarah King has broken the *Ordnung* against consorting with the English. This union has produced a child whose paternity prevents him from becoming a member of this congregation. Sarah King lied to hide her actions, which goes against the *Ordnung* about concealing the truth. For these transgressions, Sarah King has been excommunicated. If she chooses to join another congregation, she must be shunned for a period of one year before being allowed to become a member in good standing. Her son Moses King will remain with his father Joshua King. For the time being, the child presently known as Isaiah will join his father's family and will be raised by them according to their traditions. If Sarah decides against joining another congregation, she will be free to seek custody of Isaiah King if she so desires."

He paused again, then surged forward as if he were anxious to get the unpleasant chore over with.

"A marriage built on a foundation of lies cannot thrive. Because of this, though it is not our way, a divorce has been requested by and granted to Joshua King. He is free to take another wife at the time of his choosing."

Hearing the murmurs spread through the room as the words of condemnation spilled from her father's lips, Rebecca tried not to cry. She wanted to run to her room and bury her head under the covers, but she forced herself to remain in her seat. She had to set an example. She had to be above reproach in order to make up for Sarah's fall from grace. To make up for her own.

Making love with Dylan had felt so right at the time. After everything that had happened, it felt just as wrong. She felt such guilt for what she and Dylan had done. God seemed to be punishing her by hurting Sarah. Could that be? Had her actions helped to drive Sarah away?

Sarah had looked so scared when she had boarded the bus to Oregon that morning. She was about to venture into the world alone. The Mahoneys had offered to bring Isaiah to see her off, but Sarah had turned them down. "I don't want to subject him to the trauma of another parting. He has been through enough already."

When the time had come for her to say good-bye to the rest of her family, Sarah's brave exterior had crumbled.

"Don't forget about me," she had begged, knowing that none present could respond to her entreaty. If she had been shunned, they would simply have been forbidden to share a meal with her. But she had been excommunicated, a punishment normally reserved for only the most unrepentant sinners. Anyone who saw Sarah knew she was mightily sorry for what she had done. But the council's decision was irreversible. Now none of the members of the congregation, her family included, were allowed to have anything to do with her unless she was reinstated by another church. Until then, church members were forbidden to communicate with Sarah in any way. Rebecca was not part of that group, but she was encouraged to follow the edict nevertheless.

She had used most of her savings to buy the ticket that would help Sarah begin her new life. Some of their cousins on their mother's side of the family had agreed to take Sarah in. Followers of the less strict Mennonite faith, they had been the only ones willing to give her a second chance. They didn't believe in shunning and did not practice it themselves but, understanding the seriousness of Sarah's offenses, they had agreed to mete out the punishment at her father's request. Abraham was a logger who lived just outside Eugene. His wife Barbie ran a small school in the same town. Sarah had seen them so few times that they were practically strangers, but she'd had no choice but to accept their offer. She had nowhere else to go.

In less than a week, Rebecca had lost her sister and both her nephews. She had also lost the ability to come and go as she pleased. After Marian was persuaded to end her *rumspringa* and return to her parents' home, no one else had volunteered to move into her half of the apartment. Rebecca felt as if she had been shunned along with Sarah. Most of the people she thought were her friends now seemed to want nothing to do with her. She often caught them staring at her out of the corner of her eye, but when she turned to face them—to confront them head-on—they would hurriedly look the other way.

With her savings depleted, Rebecca would not be able to remain in the apartment. Instead of moving back into her parents' home, however, she decided to move in with Uncle Amos.

"You and Mama can lean on each other to help you through this," she had told her father when she explained her decision. "Uncle Amos is hurting just as much as the rest of us, but he has no one to share his sorrow."

"That was a choice he made many years ago," her father had replied, his thin lips pressed into a firm line. "The burden he now bears is his own. It is not yours to share."

Her mother had placed a hand on his arm, seeking to blunt his simmering anger. "Let her be," she had urged in a rare display of resistance to her husband's wishes. "There is no harm in it."

Rebecca felt a hand grip her own. Esther's hand. She wished the hand belonged to Dylan. She had not spent time with Dylan since the day of the barn raising. Rebecca needed to see her. To talk to her. To tell her—What, exactly? If she continued to see Dylan, she would suffer the same fate as Sarah. Wasn't she already guilty of some of the same crimes?

Esther put her arm around Rebecca's shoulders. "Tobias and I are here for you. I will be the sister you have lost. He will give you the strength you need. Together, we will see you through this ordeal."

Rebecca could not stop the tears that coursed down her cheeks. She knew what she must do. She had to let Dylan go before Dylan's hold on her heart became impossible to break. But she would not need Tobias to give her strength. She would need to find it within herself.

CHAPTER TEN

The bell over the front door tinkled. Both Rebecca and her boss were busy. Rebecca was frosting an Italian cream cake and Jessica Dunham was up to her elbows decorating a SpongeBob SquarePants–themed birthday cake for an order that was due to be picked up in half an hour.

"Will you take care of whoever that is?" Mrs. Dunham asked. "If I stop now, I'll never get this design right."

"Not a problem." Rebecca wiped her hands on her apron and went to check on the customer. "May I help—" She stopped when she saw Dylan and Isaiah. She had heard the Mahoneys were going to change Isaiah's name. He would soon be known as Michael Thomas Mahoney. A new name for a new life. Rebecca didn't think she would ever get used to calling him Michael. To her, he would always be Isaiah. Whatever his name, both he and Dylan were a sight for sore eyes. She hadn't seen either of them for two weeks.

"I miss you," Dylan said.

Rebecca missed her, too. So much the hurt was nearly unbearable at times, but she had to be strong for both their sakes. If they remained together, the union would cost Rebecca her family. She and Dylan would end up blaming themselves for the loss.

"Dad thought it would be best if I gave you some time to come to terms with all the changes that have taken place in your life since the day of the barn raising. I tried, but I couldn't stay away. I had to see you. To talk to you. To know if you're feeling as crappy about all this as I am. Do you want—"

"We can't talk about this here." Rebecca looked over her shoulder to see if Mrs. Dunham might have overheard. "Not here and not now."

"When can we talk? Name the place and I'll take you there."

"I get off work at five. Can you come back in an hour?"

"Of course. Maybe we could go for a drive." Dylan flashed a shy smile.

Rebecca's body said yes, but her head said no. "I can't. I have to get home. I have extra chores now that…Sarah's not here."

Dylan's smile disappeared. A concerned frown took its place. "I heard she was sent away. I'm so sorry for your loss. How is she doing?"

Rebecca shook her head, fighting back the wave of emotion that hit her like a tidal wave whenever she thought of her sister. "I haven't heard from her. No one has."

"I'm so sorry, Rebecca. I can't imagine how difficult this whole situation must be for you and your family. If you need me at any time—day or night—I'm here for you."

Dylan's sympathetic words—and the obvious sincerity behind them—brought fresh tears to Rebecca's eyes.

"I almost forgot the other reason I came. I'd like to place an order."

Rebecca reached for the notepad next to the cash register and prepared to take down the details of Dylan's order. She hoped she seemed calmer than she felt. Seeing Dylan—and Isaiah—had shaken her to her core. "What would you like?"

"I'd like to lick this bit of butter cream frosting off your cheek."

Dylan brushed her thumb across Rebecca's face. Her touch was electric. Rebecca reeled from the shock.

"But I'll settle for two dozen German chocolate cupcakes. My manager is being transferred to one of our sister theaters in Pittsburgh and his last day is tomorrow. We're having a going-away party for him tomorrow night. Do you think you can have the order ready by then?"

"I don't see why not." Rebecca wiped her hand across her face to remove the remnants of the frosting—and the reminder of Dylan's touch. Then she noted the expected delivery date on the order pad. "Are you going to take the job?"

"I'd like to—the extra money would be great—but I'm not going to be here long enough. If I applied for the job and got it, management would just have to replace me in a few months. I'll get another job when I get to Philadelphia."

Rebecca wanted to kick herself. Dylan was leaving for college in three months. How could she have forgotten something like that? "What time tomorrow would you like to pick these up?"

"My shift starts at six so I'll swing by around five thirty. Is that okay?"

Rebecca would be on her way home at five thirty. Mrs. Dunham would have to fill Dylan's order.

"Five thirty's fine." Rebecca made a final note on the order pad and stuck her pen behind her ear.

Isaiah, happily dangling from a baby carrier strapped around Dylan's shoulders, reached out and grabbed the pen. He gnawed on the writing instrument as if it were a teething ring. "Becca," he gurgled as drool dribbled down his chin.

Rebecca gasped. "Did he just say my name?"

"I think he did." Dylan smoothed his hair.

Rebecca tickled the bottom of one of his bare feet. "What's my name?"

"Becca." He stretched his arms toward her.

Rebecca reached for him, but pulled back. "Can I?"

"Of course you can hold him. You don't need my permission." Dylan pulled Isaiah out of the carrier and handed him to Rebecca.

Isaiah pulled the strings of Rebecca's bonnet and tried to draw them into his mouth. Then he squeezed her cheeks in his pudgy hands and smiled, flashing the beginnings of pearly white teeth.

"He remembers me," Rebecca said in a voice filled with wonder.

"Good. I don't want him to forget. You're his family, too."

"He's getting so big."

"Yeah, he's growing like a weed. He should be. His appetite's as big as my dad's. He's eating us out of house and home. He's starting to pick up some English, but Willie and I are making sure he doesn't forget any of his Pennsylvania Dutch. Thank you again for giving us all those lessons. Who knew they'd prove so beneficial?"

"It was my pleasure. Thank you for this." Rebecca kissed Isaiah on both plump cheeks and helped Dylan strap him into his carrier.

Dylan's scent—her green apple shampoo and citrus body wash—brought back pleasant but unwanted memories. Slow dancing at the prom, sharing a bowl of popcorn while they watched old movies, making love the afternoon everything changed. The day their future ended and their past began.

When Rebecca kissed Isaiah's cheek again, a lock of Dylan's auburn hair brushed against her face. She wondered if she would ever feel that exquisite sensation again.

"You can see him any time you want. I can bring him here or you can spend time with him when you come to the house. This doesn't have to be good-bye, Rebecca. Not yet."

Was Dylan talking about Isaiah or herself?

"It's probably better if I say good-bye now. The longer I wait, the more it will hurt when I do have to walk away."

Walk away. The words began to haunt Dylan the instant they fell from Rebecca's lips. Had Rebecca meant what she had or were the words simply a slip of the tongue? Dylan was still trying to read between the lines when she parked in front of the Sunrise Bakery at four forty-five. She watched as Rebecca and Mrs. Dunham waited on a slew of last-minute customers. The bakery didn't close until six, but Rebecca's workday ended an hour before that so she could make her way home before dark.

A few minutes before five, Tobias Hershberger parked next to Dylan's car. Muscles rippled in Tobias's broad back and tree trunk–sized legs as he climbed down from the buggy. He tied his horse to a hitching post and leaned against a nearby lamp post as if he were waiting for something. Or someone. Dylan's gut told her Tobias was waiting for Rebecca.

"Please, God, let me be wrong. I can't lose her now." Dylan gripped the steering wheel so hard her knuckles turned white. "Not when we've come this far."

❖

Rebecca saw Tobias Hershberger standing a few feet from Dylan's car. Tobias came by promptly at five every afternoon to pick her up. He'd park his buggy right outside the door and wait for her to come out. Seeing him staring through the glass made her feel like a condemned prisoner waiting for the moment of her execution to arrive. The moment had come.

After making sure all the counters were prepped for the next day, Rebecca loaded the dirty cake pans and mixing bowls into the dishwasher, selected the SaniWash setting, and started it up. She wrapped the unsold pastries in plastic wrap and moved them from the display window to the small wicker basket next to the cash register so they could be sold for a discount the next day. Then she headed to the storeroom to clock out.

She pulled her time card out of the metal holder above the machine and slid it through the reader. The machine beeped, indicating it had captured her time. She tried to think of a reason to postpone the unpleasant task that lay before her, but she was out of excuses. She had to set Dylan free. Wasn't that what you were supposed to do to someone you loved?

"Are you okay?" Mrs. Dunham asked. "You look like someone just walked over your grave."

"I'll be fine."

Rebecca mustered a smile that disappeared as soon as she walked out the door. Dylan and Tobias were walking toward her. Both began speaking at once.

"Are you ready to go?"

"Are you ready to talk?"

Rebecca looked from Dylan to Tobias and back again. How was she supposed to choose one without hurting the other? And how was she supposed to be with the one she wanted without hurting herself?

She laid a hand on Tobias's arm. "I need to talk to Dylan about something. I won't be long."

"I'll wait for you in the buggy."

"Now are you ready to talk?" Dylan asked after Tobias ambled away.

Rebecca suggested they sit in Dylan's car so they could have some privacy. The raised windows would muffle their voices, the tinted windows would shield their faces from prying eyes.

Dylan sat in the driver's seat and turned to face Rebecca. Her face was pale, her eyes guarded but anxious. "Tell me what's going on. What is Tobias doing here?"

"He offered to drive me home and I accepted."

"I can drive you home, Rebecca. Or anywhere else you want to go."

"That won't be necessary. I don't need you to do things for me any longer. I have Tobias to—"

"What are you saying? Are you...*with* him?"

Rebecca turned away. "That is a private matter I do not wish to discuss."

Dylan cupped Rebecca's face in her hands. "Baby, please don't shut me out. Talk to me. What's going on?"

Rebecca gently removed Dylan's hands. Instead of settling them on her breasts where she wanted them, she placed them in Dylan's lap. "We must go our separate ways."

"Why?"

Dylan looked pained. As if Rebecca had stuck a dagger in her heart. Rebecca bore the same wound.

"I can deny the truth no longer," she said, unable to stop the tears that flowed down her cheeks. "I have committed as many offenses as Sarah."

"Loving me is an offense?"

"To some. But I have seen the error of my ways. I forgot to be humble and put others' needs before mine. Now I must repent for my actions."

"Rebecca, you—*we* didn't do anything wrong."

"We might think it's right, but the *Ordnung* says otherwise. I don't want what happened to Sarah to happen to me. I don't want to force Papa to stand in church and condemn another daughter." Rebecca's tears turned into sobs. She backed away when Dylan moved to comfort her. "If I stay with you, I would gain the world but I would lose my family. Losing Sarah was difficult. Losing Isaiah was difficult. Losing Mama, Papa, and Uncle Amos would be a burden impossible to bear."

"You don't have to lose them. Any of them. We could find a way."

"There is no way for me to have all of you in my life. Not the way you want. In your world, perhaps, but not in mine. We would have had to stop seeing each other in two years anyway, so why wait? Perhaps this way, we can work through the hurt and find our way back to being friends."

Dylan looked incredulous. She looked like she doubted the words Rebecca desperately needed her to believe.

"Do you honestly expect me to watch you spend the rest of your life with someone you don't love when I know that I'm the one you should be with? The one you want to be with?"

"Dylan, if you love me as much as you say you do, you will respect my decision and you will move on. You will find someone else and you will love her as you once loved me. I wish I could be that person, but I can't."

Rebecca reached for the door but Dylan grabbed her arm to prevent her from leaving. Her grip was so strong Rebecca was sure it would leave a bruise to match the one on her heart.

"Look me in the eye and tell me you never loved me."

"You know I can't do that."

"Then be with me."

"I cannot."

"If you can't—if you *won't* be with me, at least be true to yourself and who you are."

"That's what I am doing. Above all else, I am Amish."

"And you're a lesbian."

There was that word again. The one Rebecca could not say.

"My faith defines me more than anything else can. This is who I am. This is who I will remain. Be happy for me, Dylan. As I will be for you."

Rebecca dried her eyes and let herself out of the car. She expected Dylan to run after her. To try one more time to convince her to change her mind. But Dylan remained where she was, crying as if her soul had been torn in two. Rebecca hoped she would find comfort soon.

Tobias offered his hand when Rebecca began to climb into the buggy. "Did you say everything you wished to say?"

"Yes," Rebecca said with one last look back. "Let's go home."

CHAPTER ELEVEN

Dylan looked out at the audience as she prepared to deliver her valedictory speech. A sea of familiar faces stared back at her. Her parents and grandparents sat in the front row. Her mother, Grandma Joan, and Grandma Siobhan all dabbed at their eyes. Her father's chest was so puffed with pride Dylan was surprised he didn't pop the buttons on his shirt. Her nephew—damn, that still took some getting used to—was perched on her mother's lap. Michael clapped his hands as enthusiastically as the rest of the crowd when Dylan strode to the podium.

She smiled at her family and the dozens of teachers, present and past, who had helped her reach the precipice on which she stood. But there was one face she didn't see. One face she wanted to see more than anyone else's. Rebecca's face.

She understood Rebecca's reasons for breaking up with her, but she never stopped believing they would work things out. She never stopped believing they would find a way to be together. Until Rebecca didn't come to her high school graduation after she had promised to be there, no matter what. Then she realized Rebecca was gone for good.

Had she really expected Rebecca to attend the ceremony? Obviously, she had. Otherwise, she wouldn't be so disappointed that Rebecca didn't show up.

She had seen Rebecca around town a few times, but Tobias was always with her so Dylan had not had a chance to talk to her alone since that awful day in her car. What was left to say? Rebecca had made her position perfectly clear. She had chosen the church over Dylan. She had chosen to live in the shadows instead of being open and honest.

Dylan had to admit her Catholic faith didn't have the greatest track record when it came to gays and lesbians, but she thought the tide was slowly beginning to turn. Her parish priest, for one, was incredibly understanding and accepting. Perhaps the pope would eventually share his progressive views.

Even though Dylan understood Rebecca's dilemma, she couldn't relate to it. Not completely. It was easy to *say* she wouldn't deny who she was in order to comply with a set of archaic rules because she would never be faced with the choice. She tried to put herself in Rebecca's shoes. If she were told she could be with the woman she loved only if she never spoke to her family again, what choice would she make? Would she be able to forgo sharing hours of late-night girl talk with her mother or listening to her father crack one of his (many) corny jokes in order to live her life with the woman who made her feel complete? What would she really do if push came to shove?

"There's my valedictorian," Grandpa Richard said after Dylan and her fellow graduates tossed their mortarboards into the air. "Come here and give the old man a hug." He wrapped his arms around her and lifted her off the ground. "You were wonderful, sweetie."

"Thanks, Grandpa."

"You make me so proud."

"Thank you, Grandma Joan."

"How did you get so smart having this big lug for a father?" Grandpa Richard lightly punched her father on the arm.

"The big lug picked the right woman to marry." Grandpa Malcolm wrapped his arm around her mother's shoulders.

Her mother had Grandma Siobhan's auburn hair and emerald eyes, but she had Grandpa Malcolm's height. Dylan had all three plus the trademark Mahoney dimple in her chin.

Grandma Siobhan steered Dylan away from the crowd of well-wishers. Her lilting Irish accent had not faded despite the fact she had lived in the States for decades. "The summer between high school and college is the longest of your life. How are you going to spend yours? Are you going to go to summer camp with Willie and get out of the city for a while?"

"No, she's taking her girlfriend so I won't have to worry about putting on a happy face for six weeks."

"Willie has a girlfriend?"

"She took Danielle Kim to the prom and they've been inseparable ever since. They're going to be bunkmates at summer camp. If all goes well, they plan to room together when they get to Bryn Mawr. If I tagged along, I'd feel like I was interrupting their honeymoon."

Willie had been a counselor at Camp Wannamuck (Camp Run Amok to those on the inside) for the past three years. Each year she came back raving about what a blast she'd had. Each year she would try to convince Dylan to go with her. Dylan hadn't been to summer camp since she was ten years old. She'd gotten homesick after the first couple of days and had spent the next five weeks miserable and covered in bug bites. The experience was not one she cared to repeat.

"Why don't you spend the summer in Albany with me and Grandpa Malcolm? We have a spare room with your name on it."

"Thanks for the offer, Grandma, but I've decided to enroll in summer school. I'm going to take a few classes and get my feet wet before the real work begins this fall."

"What are you taking?"

"A couple of film classes, a journalism class, and a class on Irish politics. I start next week and finish in August."

Grandma Siobhan's eyebrows shot up. "It sounds like you intend to do much more than get your feet wet. Are you even going to have time to see the sun?"

"I'll have a couple of weeks off between the end of the second summer session and the beginning of fall semester."

"You're going to spend your last summer of freedom tied to a desk."

"What else would you have me do?"

"Break a few hearts? That's what your mom did when she was your age."

"I'd rather heal my own heart than break someone else's."

❖

Dylan could have commuted from home or taken her courses online, but she thought a change of scenery might do her good. There were too many memories in Lancaster. Too many reminders of what she had lost. Then again, Philadelphia wasn't much different. Each time she passed the Liberty Bell, the ballpark, or the museum, she knew she would think of the times she and Rebecca had spent at each site.

She sat on the twin bed and looked around the room that would be her home for the next two months. She had brought four of her favorite film posters from home and hung them on "her" side of the room, but the artwork couldn't completely dispel the institutional feel of the space.

Summer session wasn't very busy—fewer than four thousand students took part—but the dorm teemed with activity as new and returning students hooked up, introduced themselves, and shared their life stories. Dylan didn't feel like sharing. She pulled out a scrapbook and flipped through it. When she got to the pictures of her and Rebecca at senior prom, she wistfully fingered the souvenirs affixed to the pages. A takeout menu from Lolita, a jewel from her prom king crown, the boutonniere she had worn in her lapel. She picked up the spray of flowers Rebecca had worn in her hair and held it to her nose. Though the flowers had dried, she could still smell their scent.

"Bad breakup?"

Dylan had been so caught up in the scrapbook that she hadn't heard the door open. She snapped the book shut and turned around.

The new arrival was tall and loose-limbed. Athletic without being intimidating. Her white tank top and camouflage cargo shorts showed off the well-defined muscles in her arms, legs, and abs. Her straight dark hair was cut short like Demi Moore's in 1990's *Ghost*. Her blue eyes were piercing, even from ten feet away. Her voice was a sexy contralto that would have been equally at home onstage in a smoky jazz club or across a shared pillow.

"I'm Erin." She dropped two large duffel bags on the floor and extended her hand. "I'm going to be your roommate this summer. You must be Dylan."

Dylan wiped her sweaty palm on her jeans and shook Erin's hand. "Pleased to meet you."

"I'm going to be honest with you, Dylan. This whole Unabomber look isn't working for me." She indicated Dylan's outfit—Doc Martens, jeans, and a hooded T-shirt. "The way I see it, you have two options: change into something else or be prepared to spend the rest of the afternoon telling me all about the girl in the scrapbook."

"You don't mince words, do you?" Erin's bluntness was going to take some getting used to.

"Nice women don't make history. If I'm going to make some, I can't afford to spare anyone's feelings. So which is it to be, costume change or sob story?"

Dylan wasn't up for pouring her heart out to a complete stranger. "Is there any particular outfit you'd like to see me in?" she asked with what she hoped was the right amount of sarcasm.

"Given a choice, I'd say a thong and a peek-a-boo bra, but we can save that for next week." Erin stood in front of Dylan's closet and pulled out a pair of khaki shorts and a T-shirt that asked *How many licks does it take?* "These will do. Get changed." She tossed Dylan the clothes. "We can split a pizza while you tell me about Mystery Girl."

"I thought it was either/or. *Either* I change clothes *or* I tell you about...Mystery Girl."

"There's something you should know about me, roomie: with me, it's always and. It's never either/or."

Dylan kicked off her boots and unbuckled her belt. She cleared her throat when Erin continued to stare at her.

"So you're the shy, retiring type. Remind me to fix that before summer ends."

Dylan waited for Erin to turn and face the wall before she continued to undress.

"So where are you from?"

"Lancaster. What about you?"

"I grew up in Pittsburgh but my family is from Charlottesville."

"What's your major?"

"Journalism."

"Mine, too. Print or broadcast?" Dylan pulled off her thick cotton socks and slid her jeans over her hips.

"Broadcast. Nice tush, Lancaster."

Dylan looked up and saw Erin staring at her reflection in the floor-length mirror. Erin wiggled her fingers and cheekily waved hello.

Dylan pulled on her shorts and zipped them up. "I would tell you to kiss my ass but I'm afraid you might do it."

Erin flashed a wicked grin. "Now you're learning."

They walked to a popular hangout a few blocks away and ordered a pizza with the works.

"Relax, Lancaster. You don't have to tell me about Mystery Girl until you're ready. And I'm not going to try to get into your pants until *I'm* ready."

"I don't get a say?"

"I'll think about it and get back to you. Thought about it. No, you don't."

Dylan laughed for the first time in weeks. "You're unbelievable."

"So I've heard. And you're really cute."

"Thanks. So are you." Even though Rebecca had told her to move on, the admission felt like a betrayal. Was it too soon?

"Come here."

"Excuse me?"

"Come here." Erin's eyes were half-lidded, her tone sultry.

"No."

"Okay, then I'll come to you." Erin slid to Dylan's side of the booth. "I'm not going to bite you, Lancaster. I'm just going to kiss you."

Dylan froze, uncertain if she should relent or resist. She wasn't up for a one-night stand, but she had to know if she could feel something—anything—for someone other than Rebecca. If she could, she could do as Rebecca asked and move on. If she couldn't, all was lost.

When Erin leaned forward, Dylan met her halfway. Their lips pressed against each other. Gently at first, then with increasing purpose. Erin's tongue caressed Dylan's. Dylan vaguely registered the comments from diners at surrounding tables, but she was more concerned with what her body had to say.

Erin pulled away. The corner of her mouth lifted into a half-smile. "That was…"

"Awful."

Erin sighed with apparent relief. "I'm so glad you agree." She stuck out her hand. "Friends?"

"Yes, please. I think I'm going to need one."

Chapter Twelve

W"rite to me," Rebecca had said the night before Sarah left town. "Write to let me know you're all right. Write before I won't be allowed to read what you have to say."

Sarah had promised to write, but each time Rebecca went to the post office, unlocked the little door, and peeked inside, the box was empty. Had Sarah received the many letters she had sent? If she had, why hadn't she responded in kind? Rebecca was almost ready to give up hope when one day she checked the box and found not one letter but two. One was from Sarah, the other from Dylan. Clutching the prizes to her chest, she hurried back to the bakery so she could read them in private.

The bakery's storage room was filled with dozens of industrial-sized containers of flour, sugar, baking soda, and other ingredients, but Rebecca had managed to carve out a bit of space for herself. An area she could escape to when she needed some time away—to have lunch, to read or just to sit and think. She called it her office. It wasn't as nice as Mrs. Dunham's office, but she didn't care. It was hers. That was all that mattered.

She turned on the bright fluorescent overhead light and closed the door. Then she examined both envelopes. The postmark on Sarah's letter was a week old, the one on Dylan's only a couple of days. Anxious for news of her sister's new life, she decided to open Sarah's letter first.

Her hands were shaking when she slid her finger under the flap. She took a deep breath, ripped the envelope open, and pulled out several sheets of lined, wide-ruled paper. The kind she and Sarah used to use to complete their assignments when they were in school. She unfolded the pages and began to read.

My dearest Rebecca,

It was a joy to receive your letters. I am sorry I have not written before now, but it has taken me this long to adjust to the many changes that have come to pass since the last time I saw you.

I have so much to say I hardly know where to begin. First, I hope this letter finds you well. I am sure these past few months have been nearly as difficult for you as they have been for me. I find it hard to believe it took something this drastic to make me appreciate you as much as I do now. It is true what they say: you don't know what you've got until it's gone. If I had only known before now how kind and generous you are, life might have turned out different for me and for you. We could have been as close as sisters instead of feeling like distant relatives.

There was a chasm between us even before we ended up on separate coasts. I felt it but I was powerless to do anything about it. No, I made a vow to be honest from now on so I must be honest with you no matter how much it hurts or how awful it makes me seem. The truth is I never tried to establish a relationship with you. I intentionally kept you at a distance because I thought we didn't have anything in common. I see now I should have celebrated those differences instead of allowing them to come between us. I will regret that for the rest of my life.

It may be too little, too late, but I feel I should take the time to thank you for all you have done for me and what you continue to do for our family. I wish I could be there to help you—all of you—through this difficult time. The knowledge that I cannot weighs heavily upon me each day. I will continue to keep you in my prayers. I hope you will keep me in yours.

How are my boys? Are they growing big and strong? Are they being well looked after? I miss them so much that it is all I can do to get out of bed most days but I tell myself it is for the best. After all, I cannot undo the past. I cannot change what has happened no matter how much I might want to. I have made my mistakes and now I must pay for them.

I wish I had confided in you instead of Marian. If I had, the result might have been the same—I don't know if you would have been able to convince yourself to keep the news from Papa—but I feel certain you would have found a better time and place to reveal the truth to him than she did. Marian did what she did in order to hurt me. I only wish I knew the reason she feels such spite for me. I have never done anything to harm her. I have never done anything but be her friend. I thought she was mine but I guess I was wrong. I hold no malice for her. It is my hope she will be able to find peace—as I have.

Because it doesn't do any good to dwell on what took place, I won't speak of it again after today. Just know I regret my actions but not the result. Isaiah is a part of me and always will be. I will love him no matter what name he is called or in whose family he is raised. When you see him, please tell him that for me. Tell him I remain his mother and I love him and Moses more than I can express in words. I hope you are and will continue to be a part of both their lives. Please don't let them forget about me. I am counting on you to keep me alive in their memories until the glorious day arrives when I will be able to perform the task myself.

Are you still spending time with Dylan Mahoney? I hope this situation, as awkward as it is, has not damaged your friendship. I know how much your relationship with her means to you. If anything, what happened should have made your bond even stronger. In a way, you two are like family now.

Does Matthew know he is a father? I hope his reaction to the news was one of pleasant surprise instead of outrage or denial. Perhaps one day he will find himself in a position to assume his rightful place in Isaiah's life. I loved him in my own way—he lived life to the fullest every second of every day and I adored my time with him, as brief as it was—but I never made plans for a future with him. Why plan for the impossible? You know as well as I that an English and an Amish cannot join their lives in marriage. It goes against everything we hold dear. I went with him because it was forbidden but I never intended to stay. Such a life isn't for me. I only wanted to visit it for a while so I would be able to say I had. So no one could say I didn't know what I was missing. Don't make the same mistake I did. Don't let anyone try to tell you what is best for you. Only you know what it is in your own heart. Always be true to yourself. Don't let anyone keep you from fulfilling your dreams. Not even you.

Life here is so different than it is back home. (You might think it strange but I still consider Lutz my home, even though I am no longer welcome there.) It rains nearly every day here, so all the foliage is lush and green. Abraham will certainly never lack for trees to cut. If he were in the business of selling umbrellas or raincoats, he would be a millionaire many times over. Though he and Barbie cannot share meals with me while I'm being shunned, they have gone out of their way to make me feel welcome. They have assured me time and time again that I am not imposing on them and insist I can stay with them as long as I like. Despite the restrictions placed upon them by the council's decision, I don't know if I've ever felt such support. It's overwhelming at times.

Working with Barbie is a joy. She is a wonderful

teacher and her students are so eager to learn. In many ways, they remind me of you. When you were in school, you soaked up knowledge like a sponge. I was more like a sieve. Better late than never. Isn't that how the saying goes?

Are you enjoying living with Uncle Amos? He seemed out of sorts when Joshua and I lived with him. It was like he put himself on his best behavior for us and couldn't afford to let his guard down. He acted like we were guests he felt the need to impress. It was almost as if he had a secret that our presence would help to uncover. Joshua kept telling me it was just my imagination. That Uncle Amos is simply a private man not accustomed to having company. I know Uncle Amos has always been different from most men, but I can't rid myself of the feeling there is a part of his life we, his family, are not privy to. During your time with him, have you also found that to be true?

Speaking of Joshua, has he found another wife yet? I am sure he isn't lacking for candidates. He is a good man. I hope he finds someone who will make him happy instead of causing him more pain. Someone who is willing to treat Moses as her own child instead of a burden she must carry.

As for me, there are many suitable men here. I don't think I could go wrong with any of them but, even if I were allowed to seek a new lifemate right now, I am nowhere near ready to spend time with anyone yet. Perhaps in a few more months. If then. When I am no longer shunned, I will content myself going to Sunday sings and getting to know the people in my new community. Kind of makes me sound like a simmie, doesn't it? I used to make fun of them for being so uncool, but I guess they had the right idea after all. There is something to be said for living the simple life. Things tend to go wrong when life gets too complicated.

I have an early day tomorrow. Growing up the way

we did with chores that began well before dawn, we're certainly no strangers to those. Tomorrow will bring a different kind of chore. Barbie and I will be taking the children to Portland for a field trip. We're going to take them to the Oregon Zoo so they can see the animals we've been studying about in person instead of in a textbook. I think I am even more excited than the children. I will probably be awake all night thinking about it, but I had better try to get some rest. Tomorrow's bus ride will take only a couple of hours but I will need to be alert to watch over the children. You know the kind of mischief students their age can get into.

I will write again as soon as I can. Kiss my boys for me. Mama and Papa, too. I love you—all of you—with all my heart.

Sarah

Rebecca read the letter once, then twice. Instead of providing answers, Sarah had raised more questions. Some questions Rebecca didn't know how to respond to. How was she supposed to tell Sarah that not only was Joshua seeing someone, but the person he was seeing was Marian? That they seemed happy when no reasonable person could expect them to be? How was she supposed to tell Sarah that the woman who ruined her life, who tore her family apart might be the woman who would help raise her son? The news could be a lesson in forgiveness Sarah might not be ready to learn. Rebecca prayed Marian's apparent redemption was complete.

Rebecca glanced at the clock over the door. Her lunch hour was almost over. Dylan's letter would have to wait until after supper. When she had washed the dishes, put them away, and finished the rest of her chores, then she would have the time to read what was on Dylan's mind. She slipped both envelopes into the pocket of her flour-dusted apron, giving herself something to look forward to at the end of the day.

She wanted to be able to mention Sarah's letter to her family, especially her father. Sometimes he seemed as lost without Sarah as Sarah did without her boys. He busied himself with work and church, but how long could he keep up his frenetic pace before it proved to be too much?

Her mother and Uncle Amos were just as bad. They said they were happy, but Rebecca sensed such sadness in them. She thought she would bring a measure of joy to their lives when she joined church, but she couldn't do that until Sarah had finished serving her sentence. If she joined church now, she would lose contact with her sister. Rebecca couldn't sever ties with her now that she and Sarah were finally beginning to connect.

Sarah had told her not to stand in the way of her dreams, but those dreams were beginning to seem more like nightmares. The price for making them come true was more than she could afford to pay. Her family was her first and only priority. Nothing else mattered. Not even her own happiness.

Rebecca closed the book she was reading and pronounced herself ready for bed.

Uncle Amos removed his reading glasses and looked across the room at the clock that rested on the mantel of the stone fireplace. The antique timepiece had been in the family for generations, passed down to each firstborn son.

"So soon?"

Barely thirty minutes had passed since they had sat down. They usually read for an hour after dinner, Uncle Amos interpreting passages from the Bible while Rebecca devoured the latest popular novel by the flickering light of the gas lantern positioned on the side table between them.

Esther and Tobias visited upon occasion. They would play games and sit and talk for hours. Well, Rebecca and Esther would talk; Tobias and Uncle Amos would simply listen. Rebecca enjoyed their visits, but she preferred the quiet nights she and her uncle spent alone with only books and companionable silence to keep them company.

"I have letters I need to write."

She kissed Uncle Amos on the top of his balding head and retired to her room. As in the apartment she once shared with Marian, the room was sparsely decorated, nearly all of the available storage space filled with books.

Books and the endless variety of stories within them fascinated her. Moved her. Made her think. She lived vicariously through the characters, imagining herself living a life far different from her own. It felt like torture sometimes. Other times it felt like bliss as she got to live the happily-ever-after ending that had been denied her in real life. She read her favorite tales over and over again, trying to commit them to memory. Once she was baptized, memories would be all she would have left.

When she joined church, she would have to renounce all outside influences, including the books she loved so dearly. The thought of living without them distressed her nearly as much as the reality of living without Dylan. She was trying to wean herself off them so she wouldn't miss them as much. Lately she had been spending more time quilting and less time reading, increasing both her income and her peace of mind.

When she quilted, she could empty her mind of all extraneous thoughts. She didn't have to think about anything but the next stitch and how it fit into the overall design. Hours passed in the span of what seemed like only a few minutes.

When the time came, she planned to donate her books to the local library so other people could gain as much pleasure from them as she had. She wasn't looking forward to the day when she would no longer be allowed to read worldly books. Reading was one of the things she would miss most. Dylan and Isaiah were the others.

If she was to be in Isaiah's life, however briefly, she needed to forget she was ever Dylan's lover and return to being her friend. The task was easier said than done. Rebecca wasn't able to relax around Dylan. Her feelings were always just below the surface waiting to bubble up again. She couldn't see Dylan without wanting to kiss her. To throw her arms around her neck and tell her how much she loved her. To feel her warm skin yielding and compliant beneath her. To look into those green eyes and feel the love in them wash over her. To shout that love to the world instead of hiding it away.

She dashed off a quick response to Sarah's letter and carefully read it over to make sure her mixed feelings didn't appear on the page. Then she turned to Dylan's letter.

The envelope—butterscotch yellow with Dylan's initials embossed on the back flap—was so pretty Rebecca almost didn't want to open it. She ran her finger over the raised letters, remembering the last time Dylan had given her such a fancy envelope. That one had contained an invitation to Dylan's high school graduation. Dylan had given her that envelope on the day of the barn raising. The day their lives had changed forever.

Rebecca remembered the excitement she had felt holding the invitation in her hands. She remembered how special she had felt knowing Dylan had wanted her to share such a momentous occasion in her life. She remembered the crushing disappointment that had followed. She had missed the graduation. She had missed hearing Dylan deliver her valedictory speech. She had missed her chance to tell Dylan how proud she was of her accomplishments. And now Dylan was gone.

How she missed her. She missed going out with her. She missed teasing her about The List. She missed doing things with her. She even missed doing nothing with her. The times when they used to sit quietly holding hands with nowhere to go and nothing to do. Those were some of Rebecca's fondest memories. "This is what love feels like," she used to whisper in the silence. "Unhurried and unfettered." Because Dylan always seemed to have something planned for them to do—some grand experience she wanted to share—those moments had been rare, which made them even more precious. What Rebecca wouldn't give to have one of them back.

Steeling herself, she opened the envelope, hoping what was inside would confirm that letting Dylan go was the right decision instead of convincing her it was the wrong one.

She pressed the letter to her chest. "If she's happy, everything I have done will be worth it."

Rebecca,

I promised you once I would write you as often as I could. No matter what we are to each other and no matter where we are in life, I intend to keep every promise I ever made to you. I love you and I always will. I hope that's something you will never tire of hearing because I will never tire of saying it.

College is everything I had expected it to be and more. Every day is a challenge, one I have managed to meet (so far). My grades are right where I want them to be. Woo hoo! Because my high school was so small and public instead of prep, I feared the education I received might not be up to par with my classmates here, but I am glad to report that it was. In fact, it might even have been better. Willie is doing well, too. Both personally and academically. We don't see or hear from each other as much as we used to. We had to grow apart sometime. I guess the time has finally come. Surrounded by intelligent, socially aware, and politically active women, I think it's safe to say she has finally found her niche. She's still seeing Danielle. Even though it's two years away, they're already planning to spend part of their junior year abroad. Bryn Mawr offers a six-week summer session at the Institute of French Studies in Avignon, France. I can picture Willie and Dani rolling out of bed in a tiny apartment overlooking the Rhone, grabbing a cup of café Americain and a croissant, and catching the train to school. I'm already envious.

It looks like the U-Haul is packed and running. Our little girl is growing up (sniff!).

Villanova offers a study abroad program, too. One of our sister schools is in Ireland. If I keep my grades up and save enough money to cover expenses, I'll be able to spend a year at the National University of Ireland in Galway. The school is a short train ride from the village where Grandma Siobhan grew up. Remember how we used to talk about visiting there one day? I may actually get the chance to check item number five off The List. Okay, half a check. The trip won't be the same without you. You won't be able to receive picture postcards by then so I'll try my best to put all the beauty I see into words and share it with you.

We were friends before we were lovers. I hope we can be friends again. I'm ready to try if you are. We can cross a few more items off The List or we can just hang out. It's up to you. I would like to have you in my life even if you can't be my life. Do you feel the same way?

I hope I get to see you when I come home for Christmas break. I know you celebrate the holiday a different way than I do. For you, Christmas Day is a solemn occasion instead of the raucous secular celebration of mass consumption it is at my house, but perhaps you can find the time to pay us a visit. I would love it if you could be there when Michael opens his presents. If you can't, I'll understand, but at the very least, when you visit friends and family on "second Christmas," please add my house to your list of stops. My parents and I still consider you and your family our friends. Nothing will ever change that.

I thought writing this letter would be easy, but it's one of the hardest things I have ever done. We used to be so free with each other, but I no longer know what I'm supposed to say to you. What is allowed and what isn't? I don't know if you're still reading at this point or if you even opened the envelope in the first place. If you are still with me, I won't waste your time and mine reminding you of what we used to have or begging you to give me—us— another chance. You know how I feel about you. I've been very clear about that. I won't pressure you. I just want to be with you in whatever way possible.

This summer, I tried doing what you asked me to do. I tried to move on. Her name is Erin. She's a wonderful friend and roommate, but she isn't you. She and I shared a kiss, but we're better at sharing laughs. If you're up for a visit, I would love to introduce you. I must warn you, though, that Erin makes Willie look tame, a feat I didn't know was possible.

I have a biology test to study for and I'm sure you're busy as well so I won't keep you any longer than I already have.

I hope to hear from you soon.
Your friend,
Dylan

Dylan still wanted to be friends. She had accepted the reasons they could not be together and was willing to amend her role in Rebecca's life. A life she would always be a part of.

Tears of joy clouded Rebecca's vision. She had done the right thing.

❖

When Tobias kissed her, Rebecca knew she had made a mistake.

Tobias slowed his horse to a walk and put his arm around Rebecca. She didn't offer any resistance. He had been courting her for months without attempting to get closer. When he finally made his move, she waited to see how she would react. Even though her heart belonged to Dylan, could her body belong to Tobias? After they were married, would she be able to give herself to him and perform her wifely duties or would the act become something she would dread instead of anticipate?

He pressed his lips against hers and she placed a hand on his chest as if to ward him off. His thin lips weren't full like Dylan's. His hard pectoral muscles weren't Dylan's soft, supple breasts.

His hands, hesitant and unsure, didn't set her body aflame the way Dylan's did. Rebecca pushed him away.

"I'm sorry, Tobias. I cannot do this."

His eyes were wide and apologetic. "Did I move too fast?"

"Fast or slow, it would not matter. I cannot be with you."

"Is there another who interests you more than I do? Someone in the world?"

Rebecca knew many assumed she would follow Sarah's lead and live her life among the English. She nearly had.

"There is no one. I will devote myself to the church and remain celibate like Uncle Amos."

"Your uncle is old and worn out. You are young and vibrant. You have your whole life ahead of you. You would deny yourself marriage and children?"

"I would deny subjecting you to a lifetime of unhappiness. I see you as a brother and a friend, not a husband. I have my family and the church. I have no need for a husband. I am not the one for you, Tobias, but you have time to find another."

"Will you do the same?"

"I do not intend to look."

Because I already found her.

CHAPTER THIRTEEN

Dylan hummed "We Wish You a Merry Christmas" as she finished getting dressed. She couldn't get the song out of her head. She didn't know why. It wasn't like it was her favorite Christmas carol or anything. "Silent Night" was. But she was infected with an earworm she couldn't rid herself of. It could have been worse. She could have had "It's a Small World" running through her brain instead.

Thankful she had finally outgrown the gaudy holiday-themed sweater her mother used to insist she wear every Christmas Eve, she tucked her black button-down shirt into her jeans and buckled her black leather belt. She was standing in front of her closet trying to decide what shoes to wear when her father called her name.

"Almost ready!" she yelled out of the open doorway, hoping her voice would carry all the way down the stairs.

It was weird being back home, sleeping in her old room after so many months away, but it was good to see some things never changed. Her mother was still the keeper of the family traditions and her father was still in charge of keeping everyone on schedule. Her role was still the same, too. Whenever they went somewhere as a family, she was always the last one out the door.

Her parents were waiting for her so they could begin their annual Christmas Eve activities. First, they would have a leisurely dinner at Cillian's, an Irish restaurant owned by a couple of old family friends. After a cursory round of window shopping, they would slowly drive around town to see all the Christmas lights. They would end the evening by attending midnight Mass at their church.

It was a date they had kept every year for as long as Dylan could remember. It was a date she never intended to break even after she moved into a place of her own.

"Dylan!" her father called again.

"I'm coming!" Choosing comfort over fashion, she reached for her trusty black high-top Chuck Taylors.

"You have a visitor!"

Dylan paused as she laced up her tennis shoes. A visitor? She first thought it might be Willie, but Willie knew better than to ask her to make plans on Christmas Eve. Willie also wouldn't need to have her presence announced. She'd just come bounding up the stairs and burst into Dylan's room without warning. Besides, Willie had tickets to the Flyers game. She and Danielle were probably standing in the concession line or settling into their seats.

Watching Willie relate to someone in a romantic way had taken some getting used to, but Dylan thought Willie and Dani were a perfect match. They had so much in common and they were obviously crazy about each other. It was too soon to take bets on how long they would last, but Dylan was happy for them. And a little envious, too. She wanted what they had. The unassailable bond. The easy camaraderie. The palpable connection.

She had had that with Rebecca.

Rebecca.

Dylan's heart skipped a beat. Could Rebecca be downstairs? She had invited Rebecca to drop by during the holidays but she hadn't really expected her to show up. Rebecca hadn't responded to any of her letters, but Dylan continued to send more once a week without fail. A promise was a promise. *We're just friends*, she told herself every time she put pen to paper.

Feeling the adrenaline course through her body at the thought of Rebecca coming to see her, she realized none of the conversations she'd had with herself had done any good. She was just as in love with Rebecca as she ever was.

She kept trying to convince herself to move on, but maybe she didn't have to.

She ran down the stairs and found Rebecca sitting on the

couch. Michael was standing on her lap. His short arms were locked around her neck. Her parents, their arms wrapped around each other's waists, stood watching the happy reunion. Everyone had huge smiles on their faces.

Yes, Virginia, there is a Santa Claus.

Dylan was afraid the wonderful tableau might disappear if she spoke. Rebecca broke the spell.

"Hello, Dylan."

"Hello, Rebecca."

Dylan struggled to put her thoughts into words. She needed a pen in her hand or a computer keyboard under her fingers to kick her brain into gear.

Her mother covered for Dylan's uncharacteristic silence. "We were about to head to dinner, Rebecca, but why don't you two stay and talk?"

"Are you sure?" Dylan asked. When she began dating, her mother made her the same promise she had made Matt and TJ—she would not involve herself in Dylan's relationships. Dylan appreciated the change in protocol.

"You can meet us at the restaurant when you're done. Or you can stay here and babysit the little guy. Take your pick."

"Thanks, Mom."

"It's good to see you again, Rebecca."

Her mother gave Rebecca a hug. Her father followed suit.

"Don't be a stranger."

"I won't, Mr. Mahoney."

Her parents headed out and closed the door behind them.

Dylan sat on the ottoman across from Rebecca and Michael. "I didn't expect to see you."

Rebecca bounced Michael on her lap. He giggled in delight and thrust his arms in the air as if he were a superhero preparing to take flight. "I'm sorry I didn't write, Dylan. I didn't want to say I was coming unless I was sure I could make it. Mrs. Dunham closed the bakery early today and dropped me off on her way home."

"No worries." Dylan placed a hand on Rebecca's knee, then quickly drew back. The brief contact caused a rush of liquid warmth to gather in her center. She withdrew physically and emotionally. *We're just friends*, she reminded herself. "How have you been?"

"Between the farm, the bakery, and quilting, I have a lot to keep me busy."

"Mom tells me you're quilting up a storm."

"I've been inspired lately."

"May I ask why?"

"I received encouraging words from a friend."

Based on Rebecca's Mona Lisa smile, Dylan assumed Rebecca was referring to her letters. "A good friend?"

"The best."

Dylan bit her lip to temper her excitement. Rebecca was back in her life. Maybe not exactly like before, but she was back nevertheless. "Have you heard from Sarah?"

"Yes, she writes me nearly as much as you do. We're three thousand miles apart, but she and I are closer now than we were when we shared a room. She misses Isai—*Michael* and Moses, but she's doing well. She plans to join Abraham and Barbie's church as soon as she's allowed."

"Have you joined church yet?"

"No, I'm waiting until Sarah is no longer shunned. Then I'll join."

"And then you'll get married and have lots of little Rebeccas." Dylan regarded Rebecca's traditional clothes and demure manner. Rebecca's *rumspringa* had not ended, but she seemed to be preparing for its conclusion. An end that would find her bound to Tobias for the rest of her life.

Rebecca shook her head. "I won't be getting married."

"But I thought you and Tobias were—"

"I asked him to stop courting me."

"You did?" Dylan held her breath and waited for Rebecca to elaborate.

"I can't love him the way he wants me to. I have a job I love and a family that loves me. Physical love is something I can learn to live without."

"Will you be able to do that?"

"With God's help. Tobias will make someone a good husband, but I'm not that someone."

And you'll make someone a good wife, Dylan almost said. *Be mine.*

Dylan indicated the brightly wrapped package resting next to Rebecca on the couch. "Is that for Michael?"

"Something to put under the tree for tomorrow."

"Why wait?" Dylan picked up the package and set it on the floor. Rebecca and Michael joined her. "Michael, would you like to see what Aunt Rebecca brought you?"

Michael tore into the present, prompting laughter from his aunts.

"I guess that means yes."

When Michael got to the container underneath the wrapping paper, he was more interested in the discarded paper than the contents of the box. Dylan unfolded the handmade coverlet while Michael busied himself turning the wrapping paper into confetti. The patchwork quilt was covered with cloth palm prints. Michael's name and birth date were stitched into the material.

"This is beautiful, Rebecca. It looks like the one in the museum."

"The exhibit was my inspiration. Thank you for taking me there. It was an experience I'll never forget."

"We could have more of those experiences if you like. What would you like to do?"

"When I was in school, my classmates and I used to spend hours standing next to the globe at the front of the room. 'If you could go anywhere in the world,' we would ask each other, 'where would you go?' Some of my classmates took the easy way out—they spun the globe, closed their eyes, and pointed to a spot—but my answer would depend on what we had studied that week. One day I would say Australia, the next day Germany, the next Hawaii. I never thought I would actually get to visit any of those places. Or stop learning about them."

"You don't have to. Not yet. Where do you want to go?"

Rebecca was silent for several minutes. "I've never seen the ocean," she said at length. "Can we go to the beach?"

Dylan pointed to the snow-covered ground outside the picture window. "It's a little cold right now, but if you can wait until it's warmer, I would love to take you. I have a week off in April for Easter recess. We can go then."

"How would we pay for it? Aren't hotels expensive?"

"My high school graduation present from my parents was an I.O.U. for an all-expense-paid trip to the destination of my choice. We could have a luau in Honolulu, collect seashells in Cancun, or check out the view from the top of a lighthouse in Maine."

Rebecca grinned. For Dylan, the sight was like the sun breaking through the clouds after a storm.

"All of the above."

"I'm afraid you'll have to settle for one. But spring's not for a few months. What do you want to do tonight? We could ride around and look at the Christmas lights, listen to the carolers downtown, or meet my parents for dinner."

"I'd like to sit here with you and our nephew."

Our nephew. The words hit Dylan with unexpected force. She and Rebecca were joined by blood. They were family. Even if they couldn't be together, they would always be in each other's lives. The question Dylan had to ask herself was would that be enough? The answer was yes—for now—but would it continue to be when nights like this were a thing of the past?

When Rebecca concluded her visit, Dylan drove her to Lutz and parked outside her uncle Amos's house. She gripped the steering wheel with both hands, afraid to let go.

Rebecca turned around to look into the backseat. Michael was strapped in his car seat, a half-eaten candy cane in his hands. Rebecca rubbed his round belly. "Merry Christmas, nephew."

"Mewwy Kwismas, Becca."

Rebecca turned back to Dylan. "I was wrong. He isn't going to be a heartbreaker one day. He's one now."

Just like his aunt.

Rebecca leaned and pressed a kiss to Dylan's cheek. Dylan had to use every ounce of her willpower to stop herself from turning her head and meeting Rebecca's lips with her own.

"Merry Christmas, Dylan. If I don't see you before you go back to school, have a safe trip."

"You're going to see plenty of me. I'll be at the bakery bright and early Monday morning for two of your famous German chocolate cupcakes."

Rebecca blushed. "I'll be sure to sprinkle an extra helping of coconut on them just for you."

Dylan waited until Rebecca was safely inside the house before she drove away. She didn't know whether to laugh or cry. How could she be so happy and so miserable at the same time?

It was too late to meet up with her parents for dinner so she headed to church instead, hoping to catch the parish priest before he began his final preparations for midnight Mass. She parked in front of Saint Peter's and strapped Michael into his stroller.

"Come on, big guy. Let's go see Father Liam."

Inside the cathedral, she walked up the aisle, kneeled at the transept, and quickly crossed herself. Then she headed to the vestry.

Father Liam ruffled Michael's hair and welcomed Dylan into his office with a warm hug. "How is my favorite undergrad?"

"Conflicted."

Father Liam looked concerned as he directed Dylan to sit in one of the chairs in front of his desk. He sat opposite her and took one of her hands in his. "Are you having a crisis of conscience or faith?"

"Conscience. I need some advice."

"That's why they pay me the big bucks."

Father Liam was only a few years removed from the seminary. His youth endeared him to the younger members of his congregation but distanced him from the older ones. Dylan had been a fan of his since the day he took the helm of Saint Peter's. She had sought his opinion before, but not his advice. She usually turned to her parents for that. But this time, she needed an unbiased opinion.

"How can I help you?"

"I need to know how you subjugate your desires."

"How do I or how do you?"

"I should probably explain myself."

"That would help."

"I'm in love with someone. She loves me, too, but her faith won't allow us to be together."

"And she has chosen to remain celibate rather than express her sexuality?"

"Yes. How did you know?"

"Lucky guess."

"I respect her wishes and I'm trying not to take her decision as a personal affront, but I don't know how I'm supposed to act when I'm around her. I still want…the same things I used to want. My feelings for her haven't changed."

"Most likely, her feelings for you haven't changed, either. She's probably feeling the same confusion you are if not more. The decision to remain celibate is not one that is taken lightly. Don't think of it as a denial of her love for you. Think of it as confirmation."

"So what do I do? And don't tell me I should pray about it, because I already have and it obviously didn't work. If it did, I wouldn't be here."

"As you well know, love takes many forms. Romantic, platonic, fraternal. None of them are any better or worse than the others. They're equally worthy in God's eyes. You don't have to stop loving her, Dylan."

"I know, but how do I stop wanting her?"

"Short answer? You have to want to. You have to learn to separate love from desire. It takes time. It takes practice. It's not something you can do overnight. But it can be done. If you truly want to see it through. Is that what you want?"

Dylan examined her heart. Would friendship be enough or would she always long for something she couldn't have?

"I guess I'm going to have plenty of cold showers in my future."

❖

December 26, second Christmas, was a day set aside for family dinners and visits with friends. Dinner wouldn't be the same without Sarah, Joshua, Michael, and Moses at the table, but Rebecca was determined to make the most of it.

She and Uncle Amos made the short walk to her parents' house, where they climbed into the large buggy her father saved for family trips. Her parents sat in the front, Rebecca and Uncle Amos in the back. Her father and Uncle Amos sat on the right side, her mother and Rebecca on the left. When a man and woman rode together, the man always rode on the right and the woman to his left. Rebecca smiled as she remembered the times she and Sarah used to fight about who would have to ride on the "boy" side. Her parents made sure they had the same number of turns on each side. That was her parents in a nutshell. Firm but fair.

Her father drove to the Hershbergers' farm first. Rebecca played Scrabble with Esther while her parents and Uncle Amos talked with Mr. and Mrs. Hershberger.

Esther totaled the scores. "You win again, Rebecca. That's three games in a row. You should be teacher's assistant instead of me."

Rebecca packed the tiles and game board and put them away. "You're doing a fine job at the school, Esther. All the students love you and Mrs. Knepp wouldn't trade you for the world."

"Everything I learned, I learned from you. Except how to beat you at Scrabble." Esther warmed her feet next to the gas heater. "Tobias is to be baptized next Sunday. Did he tell you?"

"No, we haven't seen much of each other lately."

"I wish things could have worked out for the two of you. Now it's too late. He's spending all his time with Naomi Rader."

"Is he serious about her?"

Esther lowered her voice as if she were revealing a state secret. "I think they are to be wed. Why does that make you smile?"

"I am happy for him. When he's published, I will tell him so."

Rebecca felt as if a weight had been lifted off her shoulders. Tobias, who had claimed to have no interest in other girls, had managed to find love. Perhaps Dylan would be able to do the same. The thought didn't hold as much appeal as Rebecca thought it would. She wanted Dylan to be happy, but part of her longed to share that happiness. Though she had relinquished her rights to Dylan's heart, her heart would always belong to Dylan. Whether Dylan knew it or not.

After leaving the Hershbergers', Rebecca and her family traveled to Joshua King's farm. Joshua and Marian, who had gotten married the previous month, seemed surprised but pleased to see them.

"Come in out of the cold," Joshua said warmly.

The house was as Rebecca remembered it. Small and cozy. Marian sat by the fireplace. She was feeding eight-month-old Moses, who sucked greedily from a bottle of fresh milk.

Her father gazed fondly at Moses. "That looks like thirsty work."

"Would you like to take over, Mr. Lapp?"

"It's been years since I held a baby. I might not remember how."

Her mother gave him a gentle push. "It's like riding a bicycle. Once you learn, you never forget."

Marian stood and waited for her father to sit down before she placed Moses in his arms. He cradled Moses in the crook of his left arm. Moses wrapped his tiny hand around one of her father's work-calloused fingers and drew the bottle to his mouth.

"He has his—he has a good appetite."

The room quieted at the near mention of Sarah. Before the silence stretched on too long, Joshua cleared his throat. "Marian and I have an announcement. We are expecting a child." He placed a hand on Marian's stomach.

Marian covered Joshua's hand with hers. "If the child is a girl, we will name her Sarah."

Her mother dabbed at her eyes. Her father looked as if he were fighting back tears of his own. "That is a fine name," he said.

Christmas was a time for forgiveness and fellowship. Rebecca, who usually strived to make every day like Christmas, had not been able to forgive Marian for her role in Sarah's downfall. Seeing Marian's apparent contrition compelled her to make amends.

"I am glad Moses will have a little sister or brother to play with." She wrapped her arms around Marian and drew her into a hug. "Congratulations, sister."

"I look forward to being able to say the same to you in a year or two. The love of a good man can change your life."

So can the love of a good woman. It certainly changed mine.

❖

"There you are. Two German chocolate cupcakes with extra coconut."

Rebecca pushed the bag of sweets and a cup of hot chocolate across the counter. Dylan handed her a ten-dollar bill and waited for her change.

"Do you have time to share the fruits of your labors with me?" Dylan asked, dropping a pair of ones into a nearby tip jar.

Rebecca looked around the bakery. The morning rush had not quite ended. She didn't want to leave Mrs. Dunham shorthanded.

"I can handle this unruly mob for fifteen minutes," Mrs. Dunham said. "Take a break."

"Thank you."

She and Dylan sat at a small round bistro table by the window. Rebecca drew doodles in the condensation on the glass but stopped when she realized the doodles looked suspiciously like the hearts lovesick boys carved into trees. She erased the artwork with her hand and folded her arms on the table.

Dylan ate her cupcake with a fork instead of pinching it with her fingers like she used to. "Mmm. These are so much better than the stale bagels in the school cafeteria."

Dylan's smile stopped Rebecca's heart. She seemed so different after only seven months away. Her hair was longer, her energy still vibrant but far less animated. A sweet tomboy had left for college and a sophisticated woman had returned in her place. And yet her effect on Rebecca was the same. Attempting to break the connection, Rebecca turned her attention to her cupcake.

"How were your holidays?" she asked, dipping her finger into the thick coconut-pecan icing.

"Enlightening."

"Mine, too. Did you get everything you wanted for Christmas?"

"Almost. Santa didn't bring me the Harley I asked for, but maybe next year. How about you?"

Their knees brushed under the table. Rebecca, enjoying the contact, didn't pull away.

"I got everything I wanted and more. I got my friend back."

Dylan smiled. "And she's glad to be back."

"Will friendship be enough for you?"

"It will have to be."

"I don't want to make you uncomfortable, but I want you in my life."

Dylan covered Rebecca's hand with her own. "And I want you in mine. Don't worry about me. I'll deal. Don't I always?"

Rebecca nodded. She longed to link her fingers with Dylan's but resisted the urge. Dylan seemed to be doing a much better job than she was separating who they were now from who they used to be. "Have a safe trip back to school," she said after Dylan pulled her hand away.

"I'll try." Dylan pushed her chair away from the table and zipped up her jacket. "I'll see you next spring."

"I can't wait."

They parted with a hug that left Rebecca wanting more.

"You two make a cute couple," Mrs. Dunham said after Dylan left.

The statement shocked Rebecca. Not the statement itself but its implications. Were her feelings for Dylan that obvious?

"We're not a couple."

"You could have fooled me." Mrs. Dunham put a caramel cake in a box and taped the original order form to the back of the box.

Then she looked up at Rebecca and smiled. "I guess it's safe to say your parents don't know you're gay."

Rebecca didn't know what to say. Lutz was a small town. Admitting the truth could cost her her job or, more importantly, her friendship with Mrs. Dunham. Swallowing hard, she decided to take a chance. "No," she said. "No, they don't."

"They won't hear it from me." Mrs. Dunham's hug provided much-needed reassurance. "Thank you for sharing your secret with me."

Relief washed over Rebecca like a wave. She felt like crying. "How did you know?"

"I may be straight but I'm not narrow. My gaydar's always been pretty good. Is Dylan your girlfriend?"

Rebecca's gaze dropped to the floor. "She was for a time. We're just friends now."

"Those are important, too."

"She's taking me to the beach this spring."

"Which one?"

"We haven't decided yet. Atlantic City is closest."

"You don't want to go there. It's like Vegas without The Strip. Why don't you go to Provincetown? It's the largest gay and lesbian resort in the country if not the world. You'll love it there. It's small, quiet, and close enough to be accessible but far enough away to be liberating."

"How do you know so much about it?"

Mrs. Dunham grinned. "Like I said, I may be straight but I'm not narrow. If you go to Provincetown, there are four things you're going to need for your trip: sunscreen, a swimsuit for the days, a sweater for the nights, and courage for everything else. You can get most of those things at the mall, but you're going to have to find the courage within yourself."

"Why would I need courage?"

"As I'm sure you're beginning to find out, it takes guts to be yourself. Use them on your trip. Don't stand in your own way. Go for it. Don't be afraid to let whatever happens happen. Don't force it. Don't run away from it. Just follow it to its natural progression. If you do that, you'll have an experience you'll remember for the rest of your life."

Rebecca absorbed the advice, but didn't know if she should follow it. If she did what Mrs. Dunham said, would she have an experience to remember or one she longed to forget?

No matter how great the temptation, she had to keep telling herself that she and Dylan were just friends. She had made her decision. Now she had to live with the consequences. She suspected the trip with Dylan would test her resolve as never before. Would she pass the test?

CHAPTER FOURTEEN

Rebecca counted the days until spring. Until she could see Dylan again. Until they could go away together. Even though she and Dylan were no longer a couple, Rebecca missed spending time with her. She missed talking to her. Exchanging letters was okay, but it wasn't as good as hearing Dylan's voice. As seeing her face. Sharing a room with her was bound to be awkward after everything they had experienced, but Rebecca thought she was up for the challenge. When the day of their departure finally arrived, she was so excited she felt like she was jumping out of her skin.

The ferry pulled into the dock at MacMillan Wharf. Rebecca gathered her bags and, like she had been doing all day, followed Dylan's lead. Dylan looked around to get her bearings before she consulted the map she had bought in the ferry station in Boston. They had left her car in the station's secure parking lot. Mrs. Dunham said Provincetown was so small and its streets so narrow that cars weren't necessary. She suggested they walk or rent bikes instead.

"According to the map, we need to find Commercial Street and head west."

Commercial Street was the main road through town. Spanning the length of the village, the thoroughfare was dotted with dozens of hotels, restaurants, souvenir shops, bars, and art galleries. The outdoor cafés were overflowing as patrons competed for the best spots to watch the crowds of new arrivals stream past.

Rebecca's eyes bugged in amazement. Everywhere she looked,

same-sex couples were being openly affectionate. Some were holding hands. Some were kissing. Some were practically going at it right there in the street. She had never seen anything like it.

Nine men dressed in nuns' habits whizzed by on rented bicycles. One wore a placard around his neck that read, "The Sisters of (No) Mercy. Prepare to be Disciplined." One of the men at the back of the pack, an older man with a silver goatee, a white wimple, and a long string of rainbow-colored beads tied around his waist, looked right at her as he passed. Laughing, he turned to his identically dressed companion and said, "Looks like someone forgot to tell Dorothy she isn't in Kansas anymore."

Stung, Rebecca quickly shifted her eyes away from the men and turned back to Dylan. Their hotel was located on Bradford Street, which ran parallel to Commercial. If they had calculated correctly, their destination should be only a few blocks ahead.

Dylan slowed down, carefully regarding the street signs. Rebecca followed her as she turned right on Gosnold, then left on Bradford. They walked another block, then stopped in front of The Sand and The Sea, a restored eighteenth-century ship captain's house that had been converted into one of the few women-only hotels in town.

A set of wide plank pine stairs led to a wraparound porch. White rockers and weathered Adirondack chairs lined the bright yellow banister.

Inside, Dylan and Rebecca headed to the reception desk.

"May I help you?" the spiky-haired clerk asked.

"We'd like to check in, please. I made a reservation for two. Last name Mahoney. First name Dylan."

While the clerk clicked through screens on her computer in search of the reservation, Rebecca looked around the lobby.

True to its seafaring origins, the area had a nautical theme. The walls were covered with vintage photos of men and women who made their living in, on or around the sea. Models of ancient sailing ships lined the mantel of a huge stone fireplace flanked by two floor-to-ceiling bookcases. The bookcases contained works written by area authors—Emily Dickinson, Nathaniel Hawthorne, Herman Melville, and the like.

I may never leave the hotel. I have everything I want right here.

"There you are." The clerk tapped a few more keys. "You're in the Crow's Nest," she said, pointing to a diagram of the hotel's layout. "It's on the top floor. It's our smallest room and, I'll admit, one of our least popular. If something else becomes available, I'll see if we can move you."

Dylan showed Rebecca a copy of the drawing. Based on the listed measurements, the room was much smaller than the others and sported a sharply angled roof that could make maneuvering in the dark something of a challenge. Maneuvering around each other was going to be even more of one.

"I'm sure it will be fine," Rebecca said.

"You haven't seen it yet."

"I don't have to. It's in Provincetown. Nothing else matters."

Dylan turned back to the clerk. "We'll keep this room."

The clerk tapped more buttons on her computer. "Is this your first time here?"

"Yes," Dylan said.

"Then I'm sure you're anxious to do a little exploring. Here's a map of the village. Ptown's only three miles long, so the chances of you getting lost are pretty slim, but if your sense of direction is as bad as mine, just aim for Commercial Street and you'll get back on track in no time. If you don't want to risk venturing out on your own, there are several escorted walking tours that are really good. The dunes tour is excellent, and I'm not just saying that because my girlfriend's one of the guides. Anything that includes a barbecue on the beach is automatically tops in my book."

"Where do we sign up?"

"The departure point is on Standish Street near the wharf. The first group leaves at ten and they drive you over to National Seashore Park. The group's not too big—at least four people and not more than eight—so everyone really gets to know each other. It's a three-hour trip altogether. You walk the dunes for a couple of hours, learn about the area, have lunch, and come back. If you're interested, I can give Tracy a call and get you hooked up."

Dylan turned to Rebecca. "Do you want to?"

Rebecca nodded enthusiastically.

"Hook us up."

"You got it." The clerk pulled several sheets of paper off the printer behind the desk and gave the forms to Dylan to sign. "This is your receipt for the room."

Dylan signed where indicated, then slipped the duplicate copies and a list of the week's scheduled events into the side of her suitcase.

During the ferry ride from Boston, Rebecca had not been able to wipe the smile off her face. Unable to sit, she had stood near the railing for the ninety-minute trip. As the ferry chugged across the harbor, she had dreamed of a life on the water. A life filled with opportunities as vast as the ocean that beckoned her. The wind whipping off the water had chilled her to the bone, but she had refused to seek shelter inside the warm cabin. Why would she watch the beautiful views through thick, weatherproof glass when she could see them as God intended? The experience was magnificent. Even better than she had imagined. Having Dylan to share it with made it even more special.

She had watched, fascinated, as the mainland disappeared. When the Cape had come into view, she had felt as if the ties that bound her to her home had been severed. She was free. Free to be whoever she wanted. Free to be herself.

When they finished checking into their hotel, she and Dylan climbed two flights of stairs and headed to the door in the middle of the third-floor hall. Because the area was so small, there was only one room on the entire floor. Rebecca already thought of it as theirs—hers and Dylan's.

Dylan unlocked the door and they headed inside.

The room *was* small—cramped, even—but it had a certain charm. Like the rest of the inn, the room was designed with a nautical theme. Framed portraits of female pirates lined the wall, creating a veritable rogue's gallery. A wooden carving of a topless mermaid hung above the double bed. The nightstand was an authentic lobster trap, the coffee table a brown leather footlocker with brass hardware.

Two small porthole windows were on the ends of the room. One looked out over Bradford Street. Its mate offered a bird's-eye view of the entertainment area on the back of the property. Nearly a dozen women were frolicking in the pool, soaking up the sun on the patio, or having a drink in the bar.

Rebecca's eyes drifted from the window to the bed. One bed, not two. She and Dylan had not slept together since they had *slept* together. Sharing a room would be hard enough. Sharing a bed might be too much to ask. How was she supposed to lie next to Dylan every night without wanting to curl her body around hers? *Wanting isn't the same as doing. You can do this. You have to. It's too late to change your mind.*

"We made it." Dylan held up her hand. Rebecca gave her a high five. "What do you want to do first?"

The smell of burgers sizzling on the communal grill made Rebecca's stomach growl. Mrs. Dunham had given her the day off so she and Dylan could get an early start. Rebecca had been so excited about her journey she had not been able to eat breakfast. Eight hours later, she had finally regained her appetite. In spades.

"Let's get something to eat."

"It's too early for dinner, so let's have a snack somewhere and spend the rest of the afternoon wandering in and out of the shops on Commercial Street. That will give us time to decide what to do tonight. We should have seafood for dinner, obviously. We can't visit Massachusetts without sampling one of the world-famous steam pots."

"What about afterward? What will we do then?"

Dylan shrugged. "The options are endless. We could take a dip in the heated pool downstairs, check out the view from the pier, or go for a walk on the beach."

Rebecca's mind reeled. How was she supposed to pick just one? Dylan called dibs on the shower. She emerged wearing a gray Villanova sweatshirt and a pair of navy blue shorts. After her shower, Rebecca pulled on a pair of khaki Capri pants and a white cap-sleeved T-shirt. On her feet, she wore thick-soled flip-flops.

The thermometer outside the inn read sixty-five degrees. Temperatures were unseasonably warm, but not warm enough for T-shirts and shorts. Rebecca grabbed a yellow cardigan sweater to guard against the chill. She regarded her reflection in the mirror above the dresser. She hadn't worn English clothes in months. She was going to have to get used to them all over again. Her T-shirt and short pants revealed more skin than she had ever shown in public. To wear the swimsuit that rested in the bottom of her suitcase, she would need to employ the courage Mrs. Dunham had urged her to find.

At Spiritus, a local landmark famous for its extravagant design as well as its late-night cruising, Dylan limited herself to an espresso milkshake while Rebecca inhaled a slice of pepperoni pizza in about two seconds flat. Rebecca was tempted to go for seconds but she wanted to save room for dinner. The steam pot sounded too good to miss.

On the street, Rebecca walked briskly. Her head swiveled from side to side as she tried to soak in all the new sights and sounds.

Dylan grabbed Rebecca by the elbow, forcing her to ease her frenetic pace. "We have all week. We don't have to do everything the first day." Her hand slowly slid down Rebecca's arm. Then she wrapped her fingers around Rebecca's. The gesture seemed companionable, not romantic.

Rebecca squeezed the hand she held in hers. "It seems odd that you're the one slowing me down for once."

"There's a first time for everything."

They visited a couple of souvenir shops. At one of them, Dylan bought a water globe with figurines of a tiny whale and mermaid inside. The inscription on the outside read, *Provincetown—Having a Whale of a Time.* Then they headed to The Write Stuff, a bookstore that doubled as an art gallery. Rebecca picked out a postcard for Mrs. Dunham and another for Sarah—one card was slightly risqué, the other benign. She prayed the cards wouldn't get crossed in the mail when she posted them the next day.

After paying for her purchases, she spent several minutes leafing through the books and magazines. The bookstore at the mall had a tiny GLBT section that she had seen from a distance but had never visited for fear of discovery. Here was an entire store devoted to such themes. And she had all week to wander the aisles.

"Why don't you buy a couple of books to read while we're hanging out at the hotel?" Dylan said.

"But I couldn't possibly take them home with me."

"Give them to me. I'll take them back to school with me next week. A nice lesbian romance would make a refreshing change from Ethics in Journalism."

Rebecca couldn't resist teasing her. "These are books, not movies."

Dylan pursed her lips. "I do know how to read, you know."

"Oh, yeah? Prove it to me." Rebecca picked up the closest title, a book from the Men's Erotica section, and flipped it open to a random page.

"See Spot. See Spot run."

Rebecca snapped the book shut. "That's not what that says."

"You don't want me to read what that says. But seriously, pick out as many books as you like. I'll be in the movie section if you need me."

"I never would have guessed."

Dylan laughed, obviously enjoying the teasing banter. "You're a funny lady, Rebecca Lapp."

Rebecca picked up a romance, an action adventure, and a historical epic. All written by and for lesbians. Books in hand, she turned to head to the cash register when a title in the Spirituality section caught her eye. She felt drawn to it. As if the book were a magnet and she was a pile of metal shavings. The book's title was *Amish and Gay: Is it Possible to Be Both?*

Heart racing, palms sweaty, she picked up the book, which the introduction said had been written under a pseudonym in order to protect the author's identity since he was still an active member of his congregation.

"I'm not alone," Rebecca said under her breath. "There are more like me."

She turned to the first chapter, expecting to find the guidance she would need to live her life openly. The first paragraph took that hope away.

"The Amish faith is one of the most conservative in the world. It is a religion that stresses forgiveness, yet its views on homosexuality are unforgiving. Its followers believe sexual orientation can be changed. Gay and lesbian members are urged to reject their natural urges or risk being shunned. As a result, there are many more closeted gay and lesbian members of Amish congregations than there are openly gay ones. I am one of those people."

The writer went on to describe a life eerily similar to Rebecca's—an existence filled with secret trysts, guilt, indecision, and a constant fear of discovery. She felt like she was reading her own story.

The answer to the question posed by the book's secondary title—*Is it Possible to Be Both?*—appeared to be yes and no. But the answer to the question that mattered to her most—was it possible to be Amish and *openly* gay—appeared to still be a resounding no.

Disheartened, she put the book back on the shelf. And came face-to-face with the man who had laughed at her earlier. He had changed out of his nun's habit into a Hawaiian shirt and a pair of jeans, but she recognized him nevertheless. She could never forget that cruel smile.

"How's the weather in Kansas today, Dorothy?" he asked.

With a start, Rebecca realized the man was only joking with her. She had misjudged him. His seemingly cutting comments weren't meant to be hurtful. They were just his way of making fun. She decided to play along.

"The skies were clear when I left, but I hear there's a chance of tornadoes later so I would hold on to your broomstick if I were you."

"It's more fun when I have someone else do it," he replied with a playful swat to Rebecca's arm. "So where are you really from, Dorothy?"

"Pennsylvania."

"Really? Which part?"

"You've probably never heard of it. It's a small town called Lutz."

He perked up. "Ooh, Amish country. I used to live there a hundred years ago. I froze my twigs and berries off each winter until I wised up and moved to Florida to thaw out. My husband Alan and I come up here for a couple of weeks each summer." He pointed to the man standing next to Dylan in the DVD section. Both Alan and Dylan looked up and waved. "So what's your name?"

"Rebecca. Rebecca Lapp."

"Lewis Conrad. It's a—" The man's smile faltered. "Wait. Did you say Lapp? I know there are hundreds of Lapps in Lancaster County, but you wouldn't be related to Amos Lapp, would you?"

"He's my uncle."

"Then I guess it really does run in the family," Lewis said. "Is Samuel Lapp your father?"

"Yes, sir."

"Honey, we're all friends here. Don't call me *sir*. It's *ma'am*. How is your uncle? Is he still as handsome as ever?"

"Yes, s—" She caught herself just before the offending word could escape her lips. "How do you know my uncle?"

"Let's just say you two have more in common than you might think."

Rebecca pondered what he might mean by that but decided the answer couldn't be as obvious as it seemed. Or could it? If it were true, it would explain so much—why Uncle Amos had never started a family, why he had not sought a higher position in the church, why he preferred to live alone, why she felt closer to him than she did to the other members of her family. It all made sense.

"Did he ever let Samuel talk him into finding a wife?"

"No, Uncle Amos can be pretty stubborn when he wants to be."

"Yes, I know," Lewis said wistfully. He looked off in the distance as if he were remembering old times.

Rebecca longed to hear about those times but she knew it wasn't Lewis's place to tell her about them. It was Uncle Amos's.

Alan beckoned Lewis to join him. "I'd better see what Her Majesty wants. When you get back to Lutz, tell Amos I said hello."

"I will."

Watching Lewis and Alan interact with each other, Rebecca wished some of the happiness they had obviously found could have been passed on to her uncle. She didn't know how he would react when she gave him Lewis's message. Would he be grateful to receive news of a long-lost friend or would he be devastated to realize the secret he had worked so hard to maintain had been exposed?

She tried to put herself in his shoes. She tried to imagine what she would do if she were in his position. She didn't have to try very hard. She was already in his position. The question was, could she keep her secret as long as he had or would she eventually tire of the charade? Could she live without Dylan? Could she live without love?

Dylan and Rebecca had dinner at the Lobster Pot, where the seafood was as good as advertised. Better, even. Unfortunately, Rebecca seemed to be too preoccupied with other matters to enjoy her meal.

"Penny for your thoughts."

Rebecca pushed aside her half-eaten plate of blackened tuna. "What do you mean?"

Dylan had told herself not to expect too much from the trip. The voyage was supposed to be mindless fun, not a search for self-discovery. There would be plenty of sightseeing but no earth-shattering revelations or romantic *From Here to Eternity*–style rolls in the surf. So why didn't Rebecca seem to be having fun?

"You've been quiet since we left the bookstore. You haven't even touched the novels you bought. Is something wrong?"

"I'm not sure. Do you remember that man I was talking to?"

"The one in the Hawaiian shirt? What about him?"

"He used to live in Lutz. He says he knows Uncle Amos."

"What's wrong with that?"

"He said he *knows* Uncle Amos."

"Ah," Dylan said as recognition slowly dawned on her. No wonder Rebecca was so quiet. Her brain was probably working overtime as she tried to determine how the revelation about her uncle's secret would affect her ability to keep her own. Would it make it more or less likely for her to come out? "So is Lewis the reason your uncle never married? Is he the one your uncle tried to build a life with?"

"Tried and failed."

"You aren't your uncle, Rebecca. You can do anything you set your mind to. I've always told you that. If you tried to live a life different from the one you've chosen—"

"My decision is made, Dylan."

Dylan felt as if she were butting her head against the same brick wall. But she was going to keep slamming into that wall until she broke through—or died trying. "I'm not asking you to change your mind, Rebecca. But if I were you, I wouldn't make any more decisions until I talked to my uncle." She left enough money on the table to cover the bill and the tip. "Are you ready to go back to the hotel?"

"If we do that, I'll spend the rest of the night trying to come up with answers to problems I can't solve on my own. Take me dancing. I want to get lost in the music."

And I want to get lost in you.

"Unfortunately, we're too young to get into most of the clubs in town. Even though we won't drink anything alcoholic, we still have to be twenty-one to go inside."

Dylan watched Rebecca's face fall. Running her hands through her hair, she tried to think of a way to lift Rebecca's sinking spirits. She snapped her fingers. "I've got an idea." She grabbed Rebecca's hand and pulled her to her feet. They walked through the narrow streets, squeezing past pedestrians and snarled traffic until they reached their hotel.

"Why did you bring me back here?" Rebecca asked.

Dylan turned to Rebecca and smiled. "Just trust me."

She led them to the communal area next to the pool, where employees in the hotel's snack bar were dishing out veggie burgers, nachos, and tofu hot dogs to a half-dozen women huddled around three outdoor heaters. The in-house DJ was playing a mixture of dance music, ballads, and disco.

Dylan bought a couple of Cokes and steered Rebecca to an empty table. Instead of sitting down, she walked over to the DJ and made a request.

"What are you up to?" Rebecca asked after Dylan returned to the table.

Dylan grinned. "You said you wanted to dance, didn't you?"

"Yes," Rebecca said slowly. Warily.

An Indigo Girls song ended and a new tune began.

"Come on," Dylan said. "They're playing our song."

❖

Rebecca cocked her head and listened to the music. She didn't recognize the song, but she did recognize the dance the other women were performing on the makeshift dance floor. They were doing the Electric Slide, one of the dances Dylan had taught her the night she learned to dance.

Rebecca rushed to join the crowd. Dylan was right. Doing the Electric Slide was more fun with more people participating. Even though Rebecca didn't know the women who surrounded her, she felt a kinship with them. She felt like she was part of something bigger than herself.

When the music slowed, she hesitated only briefly before she settled into Dylan's arms. She liked the way Dylan's arms felt wrapped around her. She rested her head on Dylan's shoulder and sighed deeply. She felt safe. And loved.

When the song ended, Rebecca looked up at the stars, dazzling pinpricks of light that glittered overhead. "I can't believe we're here," she whispered.

"Neither can I."

Rebecca pulled her eyes away from the night sky. Dylan wasn't looking at the breathtaking view. She was looking at her. Rebecca felt her face flush.

"I don't know how to thank you," she said.

"For?"

Loving me.

"Everything."

"You don't have to thank me. It was my pleasure."

"No," Rebecca thought, "the pleasure was all mine."

Upstairs, Dylan changed into her pajamas and climbed into bed. She lay with her back to Rebecca, her face toward the opposite wall. Rebecca assumed an identical position on the other side of the bed. A chasm that felt as wide as the Grand Canyon lay between them. Rebecca wanted to lay with her body pressed against Dylan's, but she knew she could not—*should* not bridge the gap.

Dylan fell asleep as soon as her head hit the pillow. Rebecca thought she should have been equally exhausted after their long day but she was too excited to sleep. She lay in bed staring at the ceiling waiting for the sun to come up so she could do it all over again.

Rebecca listened to the tour guide's narration with one ear. The other was tuned to the sound of the waves crashing in the distance.

"Coming up on your left," the guide said, "you will see some of Provincetown's famous 'dune shacks,' structures originally built by the Life Saving Service, an early version of the Coast Guard, as shelters for shipwrecked seamen. Provincetown is home to seventeen of these shacks. Built within the dunes themselves, they have no electricity, running water, or modern conveniences, but that didn't stop them from serving as inspiration for artists and writers such as Eugene O'Neill, John Dos Passos, Edmund Wilson, Susan Glaspell, Harry Kemp, and Hazel Hawthorne-Werner."

Rebecca craned her neck to get a better look at the desolate structures. Next to her, Dylan snapped picture after picture with her digital camera.

After they passed the Peaked Hill Life Saving Station, the tour guide parked the SUV in the shadow of a wind-gnarled pine tree and shut off the engine. Rebecca stepped down, her feet sinking into the sand. Wispy beach grass brushed her legs as she walked.

"For you." Dylan pulled a plum from her jacket pocket and handed Rebecca the prize. The fruit's dark red flesh was sweet and ripe. When Rebecca bit into it, juice trickled down her chin. She reached to wipe it off but Dylan beat her to it. She brushed the pulpy liquid off Rebecca's chin with her thumb and stuck her thumb in her mouth. "Delicious," she said, licking her lips. "Lunch will pale in comparison after that."

Rebecca's heart was beating so hard she could barely breathe. Dylan said she wanted to be friends, but sometimes it seemed like she wanted more. Sometimes Rebecca felt like she did, too. The feelings she thought would fade with time had only grown stronger. Whenever Dylan took her hand and gave it a gentle squeeze, friendship was the last thing on Rebecca's mind. But she had made her choice. Both she and Dylan had accepted it. Both had moved on. Hadn't they?

The tour guides set up a portable grill and stoked it with charcoal briquettes. When the charcoal reached the proper temperature, they added marinated salmon filets and seasoned T-bones to the grill. While they waited for the food to be prepared, Rebecca and Dylan walked down to the shoreline. Rebecca dipped her fingers in the water, pulling back in shock when she felt how cold it was. A flock of hungry water birds circled overhead, occasionally diving into the water in search of food.

"Look!" Rebecca pointed to a colorful bird with a writhing fish clutched between its claws.

Dylan raised her camera and quickly snapped a picture. "You don't get out much, do you?" she said lightly.

Rebecca felt comfortable enough to make a joke at her own expense. "I can't be trusted in towns with populations greater than a couple thousand."

Dylan draped her arm across Rebecca's shoulder. "Then I'd better be sure to keep my eye on you so you don't get into trouble."

Rebecca hesitantly slipped her arm around Dylan's waist. When Dylan didn't protest, she left it there. "How do you plan to do that?"

"Don't worry. I'll think of something."

"You always do."

They spent the rest of the week relaxing at their hotel, either hanging out near the snack bar or sitting in the oversized chairs on the front porch. Then Dylan discovered the Jacuzzi on the back deck. She released a loud moan as she submerged herself up to her neck in the heated water.

Rebecca, a blanket thrown over her legs, lay on a lounge chair. She was grateful for the cool temperatures. If the weather were warmer, she would be expected to strip down to a swimsuit. She didn't think she'd feel comfortable doing that with so many people around.

"You wouldn't believe how good this feels," Dylan said.

"I'll take your word for it."

"You don't know what you're missing."

"We'll see if you still feel that way when you get out."

Dylan's smile disappeared. "I hadn't thought about that." She shrugged and dipped lower into the swirling water. "All the more reason to stay in."

Rebecca couldn't remember the last time she had laughed so much. Yes, she could. The last time she had been with Dylan. When the two of them had sat and watched Michael play with his Christmas presents. When they had felt like something much deeper than friends or lovers. When they had felt like a family.

Rebecca shook herself out of her reverie and returned to her book. She couldn't dwell on the past. Not when the future was staring her in the face. It was Friday. The last day of their trip. In less than twenty-four hours, they would have to catch the ferry to Boston and begin the journey home. The journey back to reality.

Rebecca jerked her head up when Dylan let out a high-pitched squeal. "Oh, God, that's cold." Water dripping off her lithe frame, Dylan stood quaking on the pool deck. Her mottled skin was covered in goose bumps. A complimentary beach towel was within arm's reach, but she seemed—literally—frozen in place.

"Let me help." Rebecca tossed her blanket over her shoulder and ran toward Dylan. She grabbed a towel and dried Dylan's hair. Then she vigorously rubbed the towel over Dylan's arms and legs. Dylan shivered violently, her teeth chattering so loud Rebecca feared they might shatter.

"G-go ahead. S-say 'I told you so.'"

Rebecca shook her head. Dylan looked too miserable to make fun of. "Maybe later." She had heard the best treatment for hypothermia was body heat. She wrapped the blanket around Dylan and pulled her into her arms. "Is that better?" she asked, rubbing Dylan's back through the thick blanket. Dylan didn't say anything, but she moved closer. She buried her face in the curve of Rebecca's neck. Her skin felt like ice. "I'll take that as a yes."

Rebecca continued to rub Dylan's arms and back. She stopped when Dylan's shivers subsided, but she didn't let go.

"Thank you," Dylan said after she freed herself from Rebecca's arms.

"That's what friends are for."

Dylan glanced at the Jacuzzi and shook her head. "That was definitely not one of my better ideas."

With her hair standing straight up on her head and her cheeks bright red from the cold, Dylan looked so cute Rebecca wanted to kiss her. Like a lover, not a friend. She had been fighting her feelings for Dylan all week. All week? Try all year. Should she keep fighting those feelings or give into them? Desire surged through her. "Do you—Do you want to go inside and warm up?"

"No, that's okay. I'm much better now." Dylan sat on a lounge chair and wrapped herself in the blanket. She lifted her face to the sun. "And I can't go back home without a tan."

"You're crazy."

"So I've been told."

"If you're not going inside, I am. There's a hot shower with my name on it." Rebecca gathered her things. She hoped—and feared— Dylan would follow her.

"Enjoy."

Dylan watched Rebecca walk away. Then she sighed in frustration. She didn't know what else she was supposed to do. She had tried being serious. She had tried being nonchalant. Neither strategy seemed to work. Every time she drew closer, Rebecca pulled away. How many times would Rebecca have to run out on her before she finally took the hint?

Give her a break. This situation is harder for her than it is for you. She has a hell of a lot more to lose. So stop trying to be the girlfriend she doesn't want and concentrate on being the friend she needs.

She headed inside.

Upstairs, Rebecca undressed and stepped into the shower. She spun the temperature controls to their warmest setting and turned on the water. She immediately regretted her decision. The water was too warm. Too sensual. The shower spray's gentle caress increased the ache between her legs instead of easing it.

Rebecca's senses were on overdrive, flooding her mind with memories of her hands sliding sensually over Dylan's body, filling her nose with the smell of Dylan's apple-scented skin. She pressed a hand against the side of her neck, where Dylan's face had briefly rested. Before Dylan had done what Rebecca hadn't been able to do—pull away.

Thank God this is the last day, because I don't know how much more of this I can take.

She turned off the shower when the hot water began to grow tepid. Then she dried off and tied a towel around her body. When she opened the bathroom door, she saw Dylan waiting for her in the room. Just like the first weekend of her *rumspringa*. Her life with

Dylan had come full circle. The revolution was complete. From the beginning to— Was this the end, or had she and Dylan been granted a new start?

Dylan's eyes crawled up Rebecca's body. When they reached Rebecca's thighs, Dylan mumbled, "I'm sorry," and averted her gaze. She began to shiver again but, this time, Rebecca didn't think it was from the cold.

"Don't be sorry. What did you tell me once? You don't have to hide how you feel. Not with me."

Rebecca waited for Dylan to meet her gaze, then she opened the towel and let it fall to the floor.

Dylan's eyes darkened and her breathing quickened. Rebecca recognized the signs. Dylan wanted her. Still.

Dylan took a tentative step forward but didn't move any closer. "Are you sure?" In the quiet room, her whisper reverberated as loudly as a scream.

Rebecca's head said no but her mouth said, "Yes." Her voice was calm, betraying none of her inner turmoil. As soon as she got the word out, Dylan's mouth met hers. The only sound Rebecca could hear was the beating of her heart. Its rhythm matched the one provided by Dylan's exploring tongue as it danced with hers.

She put her arms around Dylan's neck as the kiss continued. Her skin tingled when Dylan's fingers slowly slid across the bare skin of her back. The blood rushing in her ears sounded like waves crashing on the shore.

Dylan swept Rebecca into her arms and carried her to the bed, where she gently lay her down. She cupped Rebecca's breasts in her hands and kissed them slowly. Reverently.

Rebecca arched her back when Dylan took one of her nipples into her mouth and gently sucked. "Yes," she hissed. "Yes."

Dylan covered Rebecca's body with kisses, each one stoking Rebecca's arousal to an even higher level. Dylan glided her fingers over Rebecca's calves and up the insides of her thighs. Rebecca shivered as the delicate touch sent waves of pleasure rippling throughout her body.

"I need you, Dylan."

"Where?"

"Everywhere." She peeled off Dylan's sweatshirt, shorts, and the damp swimsuit underneath.

Dylan lay on top of her again, their bodies touching up and down. Nothing came between them. Dylan put her hands on Rebecca's knees and urged her legs apart.

Their hips ground against each other, moving in slow, deliberate circles.

"I love you, Rebecca."

"I love you, too."

Rebecca sucked on Dylan's lower lip, drawing it into her mouth. Dylan whimpered and raised herself to her knees. She gripped Rebecca's hips with both hands, increasing the pressure. Her movements, once smooth, grew jerky as her body tried to find the release it so desperately sought.

Her back arching, her hips moving as if on their accord, Rebecca clutched at Dylan, trying to pull her closer. She was almost there. She guided Dylan's mouth to her nipple and her eyes slammed shut as her body exploded.

Dylan fell over the edge, too, her cries mingling with Rebecca's as they tumbled back to earth. Then they repeated the journey.

"Are you okay?" Dylan asked some time later.

Rebecca nodded that she was, but her feelings were all over the board. Though her body was satisfied, her mind was troubled.

Dylan wrapped a lock of Rebecca's hair around her finger. "What are you thinking?"

"I don't want to miss this. I don't want to miss you."

"You don't have to."

"Dylan, don't."

"So this was the last time?"

"It has to be."

Dylan pulled Rebecca into her arms and held on tight. "I can't let you go."

"Everything ends, my love. Including us."

❖

"You look different," Uncle Amos said as soon as Rebecca walked in the door.

"Do I? I hadn't noticed."

Did she bear Dylan's mark? Had Dylan's touch been burned into her skin? Rebecca put her things away and returned to the living room with a book under her arm. This one was from her old collection, though she would have preferred one of the books she had bought in Provincetown. Those were on the way to Philadelphia with Dylan. Rebecca had read them all during her vacation and longed to read more like them, but she didn't know when or if she would be able to. Dylan's offer of friendship was made before they had given in to temptation. Did her offer still stand?

Uncle Amos wrote something in the notebook on his lap and returned to the Bible in his hands. "Did you enjoy your time away?" he asked almost as an aside.

"I did, thank you." Rebecca was surprised Uncle Amos asked about her trip. When she had told him she would be gone for a week, he hadn't displayed even the mildest curiosity. He hadn't asked where she was headed or when she would be back. She loved how he respected her privacy. She hoped he was able to say the same about her—especially after she told him about meeting Lewis. "Did I miss anything?"

"Your mother received a letter from Sarah. She has joined Abraham and Barbie's church. Samuel went to the council and had the strictures against Sarah removed, which means she is able to communicate with her family once more. Even though she is welcome to come home if she wishes, she says she had no intentions of moving back. She intends to visit Michael as often as she can, but her life is in Oregon now. She is happy there in a way I do not think she could be if she were to return."

Rebecca tried to absorb all that Uncle Amos had said. Now that Sarah had joined church, Rebecca was free to do so as well. But if she did, there would be no more private time with Dylan. No more weeks like the one they had just spent. No more days like the day before. Did she still want days like that? Yes. A thousand times yes.

But those days were over. They had to be. But she and Dylan could still be friends. If they could only remember how.

"Sarah said to tell you hello," Uncle Amos said, giving Rebecca the opening she needed.

"While I was away, I ran into someone who told me to give you the same message."

"Really? Who?"

Rebecca tried to act nonchalant, even though she knew what she was about to say would have long-lasting repercussions. "Lewis Conrad."

Uncle Amos didn't say anything for a full minute. When he finally spoke, his face was closed off, not open like it usually was. He removed his reading glasses and pinched the bridge of his nose as if he were trying to alleviate the pain of a severe headache. "Was that the entire message?"

"Yes."

"Was he well? Did he seem…happy?"

Afraid of what she might see, Rebecca could barely bring herself to look at him. Always small, he seemed like he was shrinking right before her eyes. "Yes. He has someone and they're very happy together."

Uncle Amos seemed surprised—and vaguely disappointed. "He is married?"

"Yes. His husband's name is Alan." Rebecca let that sink in before she continued. "I asked Mr. Conrad how he knew you, but he said I should ask you. How well did you know each other?"

"As well as two men can, I suppose," Uncle Amos replied with a wan smile. "On this earth anyway."

"How did you…begin?"

Uncle Amos's smile grew wistful. "I was young and I knew my desires weren't the same as everyone else's. When I looked at Lewis, I knew he felt the same things I did. When I was with him—" He shook his head. "You're asking me to remember things I've tried my best to forget. I am not ashamed of the way I am." He looked at her. "The way *we* are, but—"

Rebecca finished the sentence for him. "Family comes first."

Uncle Amos nodded resolutely. "Family comes first."

"How did you know about me?"

"I've seen the way you look at Dylan Mahoney. I've seen the way she looks at you. I know love when I see it."

"Does Papa know about me?"

"I suspect not. He knows about me and he doesn't approve. He has made his opinions on the matter quite clear. Like most of our brethren, he is convinced I can change, and I am certain I cannot. I will not."

Rebecca had intended to ask Uncle Amos if he had loved Lewis, but she didn't have to. The answer was as plain as the look on his face.

"Have you decided what you will do when your *rumspringa* ends?"

"I will be as I am now: like you."

Uncle Amos dropped his head. "Perhaps you should aspire to something greater."

"Are you saying I should leave the church?"

"The decision is not mine to make. It is yours solely. You have not been baptized yet. Before you are, make certain the decision you make is the right one. This is the one time I would preach it is all right to be selfish. When you make this decision, make it for you and no one else. Don't think of me. Don't think of your father. Don't think of Dylan Mahoney. Think of yourself. Don't ask me what you should do. Ask yourself what it is you want."

"I want what I've always wanted: Dylan."

"Then tell her so."

Rebecca opened her mouth to reply but quickly closed it again. Her old reasons for staying were no longer valid. She could no longer say half of her belonged in the English world and the other half in her own. Something had changed in Provincetown.

Dylan had always had Rebecca's heart. A year ago, Rebecca had given Dylan her body as well. When they were together on that last night in Provincetown, Rebecca had given her everything that was left.

She was Dylan's. Mind, body, and soul. There was no denying it—and no reason to try.

She borrowed a pen and a piece of paper and began to write. She had to get in touch with Sarah. She had to tell her how she felt. Other than Uncle Amos, Sarah was the only one who could understand what she was going through. She and Sarah were closer than they had ever been. Now it was time to put that bond to the test.

CHAPTER FIFTEEN

Dylan stared at the envelope, afraid to even pick it up let alone open it. "I can't." She snatched the envelope off the counter and pressed it into Erin's hands. "You do it."

"I can't believe you're being such a chicken about this."

While Erin searched for the letter opener, Dylan paced the way she always did when she was nervous. "Why shouldn't I be chicken? It's only my entire future we're talking about here."

Erin slipped the cutter under the envelope's flap and slit it open. She pulled out the letter, unfolded it, and began to read. "'Dear Ms.—'"

"Not out loud."

Erin dutifully began to read silently, her eyes skimming over the words.

Unable to stand the wait, Dylan stopped pacing and turned around. "What does it say?"

"Hold on. I'm getting there. Received your application. Thank you for your interest. Blah blah blah. One of many worthy candidates. Gobbledygook gobbledygook. Okay, here it is. 'Based on your stellar academic record, your admission to the University of Albany's summer session has been accepted.'"

"I got in?"

"You got in."

"I don't believe it." Dylan grabbed the letter so she could read the words herself. Seeing them didn't lessen her shock. "I got in."

During its summer session, the University at Albany offered a couple of courses Dylan thought would be beneficial to honing her journalistic skills. The first class was devoted to information literacy, the other class to narrative and descriptive journalism. The second class was the one Dylan really wanted to take. The weekly writing assignments and in-depth critiques of her work would give her a chance to see if she had a real future as a journalist or if she was just a small-town girl who knew how to concoct a witty headline and string a couple of sentences together.

Even though the summer session was limited to students who were enrolled at the University of Albany, Dylan had written an impassioned but (she thought) well-reasoned letter to the university asking for permission to audit the classes. She had included several writing samples and a letter of recommendation from her academic advisor to strengthen her argument. Then the interminable wait had begun. It had ended with an unexpected but incredibly pleasant surprise. Her letter-writing campaign had worked.

"I'm proud of you, Lancaster. Have you told Mystery Girl you're not coming home this summer?"

"I told you all about Rebecca when I got back from Ptown."

"When you cried on my shoulder for a week?"

"Whatever. You can stop calling her Mystery Girl now."

"Mystery Girl sounds cooler, but okay. Have you told *Rebecca* you'd rather hide out at your grandparents' house than try to work things out?"

"I'm not hiding out."

"Then how would you describe it?"

"I'm…laying low. But seriously, there's nothing to work out. We're just friends now."

"Friends with benefits."

"That was one time and she made it very clear it was the last time. Rebecca and I are done. I get it. I've finally seen the light. So I'm going to do what she asked me to. I'm going to move on and stop hanging around waiting for her to change her mind. Because that isn't going to happen."

Dylan glanced at the leather-bound journal on her desk. The List she had worked so hard to compile had remained static since April, but it took an act of will for her to allow it to remain that way. She often found herself reaching for it in order to add another entry before remembering there was no need to continue cataloging all the experiences she wanted to share with Rebecca. In a few months, Rebecca would no longer be allowed to have such experiences. But if she and Rebecca were over, why did the situation between them feel so incomplete?

Dylan told herself she was a sucker for punishment but she knew the reality was much worse. She was a sucker all right. A sucker for love.

Because she was still in love with Rebecca.

"We should celebrate your big news, Lancaster. How about Lolita? My treat."

Lolita was one of Dylan's favorite restaurants, but every time she ate there, she was reminded of the night she took Rebecca there. The night she thought Rebecca had allowed herself to envision a future with her. But Rebecca's future—and her present—would be in her family's arms instead of Dylan's.

"Lolita works for me."

"I'll call and reserve us a table. Why don't you get your parents on the horn and ask them if they want to join us?"

"It might be short notice, but I'll give it a shot." Dylan picked up her cell phone and hit speed dial. "You know if Dad comes, he's going to insist on picking up the tab," she said while she waited for someone to answer. "Or is that what you were counting on?"

Erin grinned as she held her hand over the receiver on her own phone. "I don't know what you're talking about."

At the end of the semester, Dylan and Erin were moving into an apartment in Conshohocken, a small mill town fifteen miles from campus. The city had a population of a little less than eight thousand, most of them Villanova students who couldn't find affordable housing in Philadelphia. Erin was going to summer school at Villanova again. If Dylan hadn't been able to get into Albany—she had waited until the last minute to apply and the school had waited until the last minute to respond—she had planned to work in Philadelphia until classes resumed in the fall.

Dylan's parents had shown some initial resistance to the move, saying the commute might cut into her study time. The deciding factor had been the cost savings. Because Dylan and Erin split the rent and expenses, their parents no longer had to pay expensive dorm fees, saving each of them five figures a year. Now Erin was going to have to find someone else to share the load for three months. As full as Erin's social calendar was, Dylan didn't expect Erin to lack for a roommate for very long.

"Mom, I got in." Dylan held the phone away from her ear as her mother's piercing scream made the speakers vibrate. "Can you and Dad do dinner tonight?"

"Name the time and the place."

"Lolita at eight." Dylan held up four fingers, indicating Erin should reserve a table for four.

"Yes!" Erin pumped her fist and made the reservation.

After Erin left the room, Dylan devoted all of her attention to her conversation with her mother.

"Your grandma and grandpa are going to be so happy to have you stay with them this summer. Have you told them yet?"

"They're my next call."

Dylan toyed with the water globe she had bought in Provincetown. No matter how much she tried to put Rebecca out of her mind, memories of her always came flooding back. Their first kiss. Their first date. Their first time. The stolen moments and the ones they had shared with friends. All the things that hadn't seemed like much at the time but had combined to form a rich tapestry Dylan would do anything to be able to continue weaving.

Dylan shook the water globe and watched the plastic mermaid and whale frolic in the artificial water.

"I've been thinking."

"Uh-oh. Should I be sitting down?"

"No, it's nothing like that. I'm thinking of upping my class load."

"You're already close to the max. Why would you want to pile more meat on a plate that's already overflowing?"

"If I take extra classes, I can graduate a year early."

"I see."

"You sound skeptical."

"And you sound like you're doing everything you can to avoid Rebecca once she's baptized."

Dylan allowed herself a smile. "Am I that obvious?"

"Your middle name should be Crystal, because I can see right through you."

"You always have."

"Living with your father and your brothers has helped me hone my bullshit meter. Talk to me, honey. Tell me what you're really thinking."

"When I was younger, I used to question how Rebecca could place others' needs ahead of her own. Now I have to follow her example. She didn't leave me for some*one*. She left me for some*thing*. There's nothing I can do about that. I can't compete. She needs the church and her family more than she needs me. I have to let her go. But I love her so much, Mom." Dylan's voice broke. She squeezed the water globe to keep from crying. "I've watched her walk away twice—when she first made her decision and when she confirmed it the night before we left Provincetown. I can't watch her walk away again. Because this time it will be forever."

"Then don't take any extra classes. You're already on track to graduate ahead of schedule. Go to Ireland a year early. Find your roots. Do some healing."

"The application deadline has already passed. I needed to get my paperwork in before spring break if I wanted to go to Galway in the fall."

"You pulled a rabbit out of a hat and got into Albany for the summer, didn't you? Work your magic again. Talk to your advisor and see if there's anything she can do. If she says yes, your problems are solved."

"It's official. I have the coolest mother ever."

"Remember that when you write your memoirs."

"As if anyone would want to read a book I wrote."

"I'd be first in line."

"That's because you're my biggest fan. I love you, Mom."

"I love you too, honey. See you in a bit."

Dylan felt marginally better when she ended the call. She normally felt most at ease when she had a mission to accomplish—a task she needed to achieve. The monumental challenge she now faced—letting go of Rebecca—gave her no sense of peace.

CHAPTER SIXTEEN

Rebecca didn't know what was taking so long. It had been weeks since she had written Sarah. Plenty of time for Sarah to receive the letter, absorb what was in it, and compose a response of her own. Sarah wrote her parents all the time, but she had not responded to the letter Rebecca had written in April or the ones she had sent every week since then.

Rebecca had so many questions. Questions she could ask only Sarah and only Sarah could answer. Nearly three months had passed with no word. From Sarah or Dylan.

Dylan had looked so hopeful in Provincetown. Especially after they had made love. Rebecca had watched that hopeful look fade when she told Dylan she still planned to join church. By the time they returned home, the look had disappeared completely. But now hope burned in Rebecca's chest. Rebecca prayed it smoldered in Dylan's as well.

She headed back to the bakery after another fruitless trip to the post office. Mrs. Dunham was flipping through the sports section of that day's edition of the *Inquirer* when Rebecca walked in. With baseball season in full swing, the Phillies' quest for another division title was dominating the news.

Rebecca remembered going to see the Phillies with Dylan, Willie, and the Mahoneys the first year of her *rumspringa*. She remembered that day as if it were yesterday. The excitement of the game. The thrill of new discovery. The joy of being with friends.

But she didn't want to relive old memories. She wanted to make new ones.

"Anything?" Mrs. Dunham asked hopefully.

"Does junk mail count?" Rebecca held up the solicitations she had received from two cell phone providers and a cable company, then tossed them in the trash. Disconsolate, she put her head down on the counter. "Waiting is killing me."

Mrs. Dunham stroked Rebecca's hair as if she was comforting one of her children. "Is there a phone at the school where Sarah works?"

"Even if there is, I don't have the number. We don't have a telephone at home. Sarah probably figured we'd never call. Sarah should be there, though. She said she planned to help with the Summer Bible Study program."

Mrs. Dunham pushed some buttons on the computer and hopped on the Internet. "Oregon is three hours behind us, but Sarah should be at work by now." She pulled up a search engine and typed the name of Sarah's school. "Here it is."

Rebecca watched in amazement when a picture of the school appeared on the screen. The school's address and phone number were displayed underneath the picture. Mrs. Dunham wrote the number down and handed it to Rebecca.

"Call her. You can use the phone in my office."

Rebecca perked up for the first time in weeks. "When the bill comes, let me know how much it is and I'll pay you back."

Mrs. Dunham waved her hand dismissively. "I know times are tough, but I think I can afford a two-dollar phone call."

Rebecca went into Mrs. Dunham's office and sat behind the small metal desk. She picked up the phone and punched in the numbers Mrs. Dunham had written on a slip of paper.

One ring. Two rings. Three. On the fourth ring, someone said, "New Hope School. May I help you?"

New Hope. Would the name prove prophetic?

Rebecca's tongue stuck to the roof of her mouth, which had suddenly gone dry. "May I speak to Sarah King? I mean Sarah Lapp." After the divorce, Sarah had reverted to her maiden name.

"Who may I say is calling?"

"Her sister Rebecca."

"Hold, please."

The phone clicked and a hymn began to play. Halfway through the song, the line clicked again and the singing stopped.

"Rebecca?" Sarah panted as if she had run a great distance. "Is something wrong with Mama, Papa, or Uncle Amos? Did something happen to one of my boys?" Her voice was high-pitched and panicked.

Rebecca hastened to ease Sarah's fears. "Nothing has happened." *Yet.* "Did you get my letters?"

"Yes." Sarah's voice changed from concerned to wary.

"Why haven't you written me?"

Sarah sighed deeply. "Matters of the past are best left in the past."

"But your past can help me decide my future."

Sarah was quiet for so long Rebecca thought she had lost the connection.

"The questions you asked make me think you have already decided your future. Why would you want to live in the world? You would leave Mama and Papa alone? You would force them to lose another daughter?"

"They would not lose me."

"If you go into the world, you will leave them no choice. If you leave our faith behind, you will be shunned. It's the loneliest, most miserable existence you can imagine. I wouldn't wish that fate on anyone, let alone my sister."

"You survived being shunned."

"I had you to help me through it."

"Would I not have you?"

"I would give you all of the support you have provided me, but I would prefer if I didn't have to. Don't make the same mistakes I did. Don't pay the same price I did."

"You ended your *rumspringa* early because you had to. If you had not been with child, how long would you have waited to decide if you wanted to live among the English?"

"Living in the world was never an option I considered. I never fit into the English world. I was more comfortable in ours."

"Now you make your way in both."

"I enjoy modern conveniences and I love learning new things, but I'm not in the world every day. I spend most of my time here at the school. If I do leave, I am always with our people. That is not what you would do. You would live among the English. You would make their traditions yours."

Sarah's comment sounded like a personal attack. Rebecca wished she could see Sarah's face to see if she meant her words to be as harsh as they sounded. It was so strange hearing Sarah's voice without being able to see her. Rebecca tried closing her eyes and imagining Sarah was in the same room with her, but that didn't help.

"I would remember my own traditions. It is what I have done during my *rumspringa*. It is what I would continue to do if I were to leave."

"At all times or only when it's convenient?"

"Evidently, living in the world is not all bad. You could come home but you have chosen to stay where you are," Rebecca said defensively.

"It is best for all concerned if I remain where I am."

"Best for everyone or best for you? Isaiah and Moses miss you. Mama and Papa miss you. I miss you. Do you not miss us?"

"More than you'll ever know." Sarah's voice cracked as she said the words.

"Then why don't you come home? In one of your letters, you said you dreamed of being reunited with your boys. How is that going to happen if you don't take the first step?"

"I will when the time is right."

Rebecca could hear the fear in her voice. Sarah was not unwilling to come home. She was afraid to. She was afraid that even though she had been forgiven, she would not be accepted. Nothing could be further from the truth. But Rebecca could not convince Sarah of that until Sarah convinced herself.

"You are welcome to return at any time," Rebecca said. "I would not be unless I agreed to leave half my life behind."

"Is there something in the English world you cannot get from your own people?"

"There is...someone."

"Are you in love with an English?"

"Yes." Rebecca didn't have to see Sarah to sense her disapproval. "Half my heart is in the English world and the other half is in ours. If I leave, I'll lose Mama, Papa, Uncle Amos, and Moses. If I stay, I'll lose Isaiah and...the one I love."

Rebecca couldn't tell Sarah that the person she loved was Dylan. Sarah hadn't recovered from the shock that Rebecca was involved with an English. Telling her the person was Dylan would have been too much too soon.

"Whichever world you choose, you'll always have me. Do what makes your heart feel whole, Rebecca. No matter what the cost."

"Thank you, Sarah. I will."

Rebecca hung up the phone and returned to the counter. When she absently wiped her face, her fingers came away wet. How long had she been crying?

"I hope those are happy tears," Mrs. Dunham said.

"They are."

"So you had a good talk with your sister?"

Rebecca nodded. "Now I have to talk with my parents. I have to tell them how I feel about Dylan. I have to tell them about me. Uncle Amos is too fond of me to ask me to leave his home, but I would rather leave than force him to avoid talking to me or eating with me. Unfortunately, I can't afford to live on my own right now."

"Your boss should give you a raise," Mrs. Dunham joked.

"A big one."

"I would love to help, but with two kids, a husband, a cat, two ferrets, and three dogs, all the cages in my zoo are full. I'm sure the Mahoneys would take you in if you needed them to."

Rebecca waved through the window at her father, who had come to pick her up. "I cannot accept charity. It is against our beliefs."

"I doubt Grace and Thomas will see giving you a place to stay as charity. They made a similar offer to Sarah, didn't they? Their daughter loves you. They do, too. Now get back in there, call Dylan, and give her the good news."

Rebecca remembered how nervous she had been talking to Sarah on the phone. Her mind had been muddled and she had barely gotten some of the words out. She didn't want to be that way with Dylan. She wanted to sound as confident as she felt.

"Let me gather my thoughts first. Maybe practicing what I want to say will help me remember it when the time comes."

Never had she had looked forward to something so much.

Dylan adjusted the angle of her computer monitor to lessen the glare of the sun that beamed down on her grandparents' patio. She looked over what she had written and pronounced herself satisfied. Temporarily. Her opinion could change after she saw her grade. The Albany classes were even harder than she had thought they would be. She had received a B+ on her last paper, an okay result but not the A she had come to expect. Her instructor's critique had been succinct: *Great story. Technically, very well written. But an article is not supposed to be an opinion piece. Next time, show me, don't tell me.* Dylan thought she had done a much better job maintaining her objectivity this time.

Grandpa Malcolm looked up from the sudoku puzzle he was struggling with. "Is it a Pulitzer Prize winner?"

"We'll see." Dylan ran a spellcheck and clicked the Save icon.

"Soup's on." Grandma Siobhan pushed the back door open with her hip. In her arms, she carried a huge tray laden with big bowls of homemade beef stew.

Grandpa Malcolm tossed a wink in Dylan's direction. "What's this? Dinner's ready and the fire department hasn't shown up yet?"

"Keep that up and I'll feed your portion to the neighbors' dachshund."

"Don't do that. I always liked that dog." Grandpa Malcolm took the tray out of Grandma Siobhan's hands—after giving her a flirtatious pinch on her rear end.

Dylan watched the exchange with a smile. Her grandparents had been married for nearly sixty years but they still acted like newlyweds. Her parents were the same way. Her dad said it was genetic. Perhaps, one day, she'd be lucky enough to find out if he was right.

Grandpa Malcolm set the tray on the patio table.

"Almost forgot the salads," Grandma Siobhan said. "Back in a jiffy."

"I'll get them, Grandma. I have to charge my computer, anyway."

Dylan tucked her laptop under her arm and headed to the house. She plugged her laptop into the outlet in the kitchen and grabbed the salads off the counter. She whistled happily as she returned to the patio.

"Someone is in a good mood," Grandpa Malcolm said.

Dylan affected a thick Irish brogue. "Because someone is going to Ireland next month."

Her academic advisor had come through, helping to secure her a spot in the study abroad program. Dylan would leave for Ireland in three weeks to take up residence at the Gort na Coiribe student village in Galway, the cultural capital of the Emerald Isle. She would spend the next year learning about Ireland's rich heritage—and learning to live without Rebecca.

Rebecca's father organized a trip to the bowling alley one Saturday afternoon in late July. Rebecca volunteered to help Esther look after the younger members of the congregation. The group gathered at Peterli's farm and boarded a rented van. During the ride to Lancaster, while the rest of the group sang songs of praise, Rebecca rehearsed what she would say to Dylan when she told her that all the obstacles that prevented them from being together had been overcome.

I'm sorry if I hurt you.

No, that wouldn't work. If *I hurt you? There's no question I hurt her. More than once. I hurt her and I'm the only one who can heal her. Maybe she can heal me, too.*

Dylan, my life is incomplete without you.

That was better.

My life—No, my world *is incomplete without you. I would like for us to make a home in your world. My heart is yours. Is your heart still mine?*

Perfect. The rest would depend on Dylan's answer to her question. Would her answer be yes or no?

Rebecca lifted her eyes to the heavens. *Please, God, let it be yes.*

❖

"No," Dylan said firmly.

"What do you mean no? You're seriously not going to try to hook up with anyone while you're away?" Willie sounded incredulous.

"The thought never crossed my mind. I'm going to Ireland to learn, not add more entries to my little black book."

"Why don't you write Erin's name down instead? Dani and I ran into her the other day. That girl is seriously hot."

"Does Dani know you're lusting after my roommate?"

"It was Dani's idea."

"For you to lust after my roommate?"

"No, for you and Erin to hook up."

"We tried it once. It didn't work. There wasn't any chemistry. We're buds. I'm not going to ruin a good friendship because you think I need a girlfriend."

"Well, don't *you* think you need a girlfriend?"

Dylan sighed. *I need Rebecca.*

❖

Do what makes your heart feel whole, Sarah had said.

As she looked at the faces of her family and friends, Rebecca felt her heart fill with love. There was Papa giving Uncle Amos advice on the proper way to hold a bowling ball. There were Tobias and Naomi holding hands in a quiet corner. There were Joshua and Marian laughing at Moses, who was trying to crawl down one of the lanes. And there was Esther re-enacting the story of Jonah and the whale for a rapt audience of children from the school where she worked.

Rebecca smiled, remembering the water globe Dylan had bought in Provincetown. The one with the tiny whale inside. Esther's choice of stories was a sign. So was the name of Sarah's school. Everything in Rebecca's life seemed to be leading in the same direction—to Dylan.

"That is the smile of a woman who is at peace with her decision."

Rebecca, wrapped up in her thoughts, had not seen her mother approach. She sat next to Rebecca and took one of her hands in hers. "When will you be leaving us?"

Rebecca had not shared her decision with anyone. How did her mother know what she was planning to do? "Leaving?"

"To take your place in the world. To take your place with... Dylan."

Her mother's hesitation to link her name with Dylan's let Rebecca know how foreign the idea was to her. Rebecca tried to pull away—to retreat into a protective shell that would protect her from the slings and arrows that were surely about to be sent her way, but her mother squeezed her hand tighter, holding her in place. "How did you know?"

"A mother knows her child. And your uncle Amos is not the only one who has eyes."

"He told you?"

"He didn't have to." She patted Rebecca's knee. "I don't want you to have to struggle with the consequences of your decision the way Amos has these many years. I don't want you to suffer the way Sarah has and continues to do. Do what you feel is right, Rebecca.

Papa and I will learn to live with your decision, whether we agree with it or not."

Rebecca struggled to breathe. She felt as if a vise were clamped around her chest. The conversation she had tried to avoid was finally taking place. "Papa knows?"

Rebecca followed her mother's gaze. Uncle Amos had just bowled a strike and her father was patting him on the back. He glanced in their direction. His smile faded ever so slightly. Her mother nodded at him and he dipped his head as if providing confirmation to the unspoken question she had asked.

She turned back to Rebecca. "He knows. He is not allowed to say he approves. Neither am I. But know this: you are loved, Rebecca. Your happiness is ours."

"I don't want to leave you, but I can't live without her. I have tried." Rebecca wrapped her arms around her mother's narrow shoulders and rested her face against the side of her neck. Tears flowed freely down both their faces. "I will miss you."

Her mother's grip on Rebecca's arms was surprisingly strong.

"And I will miss you. I will dream often of your sweet smile and loving ways. But you are free to live your own life. You are free to make your own choices. Go with God and live in love."

Dylan was right. Their parents *were* more alike than Rebecca had thought.

❖

Rebecca sat behind the desk and took a slow, deep breath to settle her nerves. She could sense the enormity of the moment. What she had to say was too important to say over the phone, but she didn't want Dylan to go on thinking they had no future. Their future was now. Her life depended on the outcome of the letter she was about to write. How would Dylan react when she told her that the impossible had become possible? Would she be as happy as Rebecca was or was it too late? Would she accept the love that Rebecca was now free to give or had she hardened her heart? There was only one way to find out.

So she did what Dylan did every day: she put her feelings into words.

❖

"Dylan! Phone for you!" Grandma Siobhan called up the stairs.

"Thanks, Grandma! I'll be right down!"

Dylan zipped her suitcase and looked around the room to make sure she hadn't forgotten to pack anything. She was cutting it close. When she got back to Philadelphia, she would have only a couple of days to complete all the errands she had put off during the summer. Good thing Michael and her parents had spent the last two weeks in Albany with her, because she wouldn't see much of them before her flight took off on Monday afternoon.

She turned off the lights and closed the bedroom door. When she got downstairs, her dad carried her suitcase out to her car. She and her family weren't fond of airport good-byes, so they had said their tearful farewells in Albany the night before. Dylan was about to drive back to Philadelphia to pack up her apartment. Her parents planned to remain in Albany for a few more days.

Dylan picked up the cordless phone in the foyer and pressed it to her ear. "Hello?"

"Your mail's piling up, Lancaster," Erin said. "What do you want me to do with it?"

Dylan could hear Erin shuffling envelopes. The action reminded her of the letter she had placed, fittingly, in the pocket over her heart. She pulled the envelope out of her pocket and set it on top of the neat stack of outgoing mail Grandma Siobhan had placed on the console table near the front door.

"Does any of it look important?"

"Nah, just the same old same old."

"Then keep it there and I'll pick it up when I get home. It will give me something to read on the plane in case I need help falling asleep."

"You sound rushed."

"Last-minute details are kicking my ass."

"Do you have time for a farewell dinner with your favorite roommate ever?"

"Barely."

"Then hurry back. There are a bunch of people who are waiting to say good-bye to you before I drive you to the airport. I hope you haven't packed your dancing shoes yet because you're going to need them."

Dylan shook her head. Erin was probably going to have half the people in their apartment building lined up waiting to yell, "Surprise!"

"It's going to be a long night."

Rebecca pulled the envelope out of the box and looked quizzically at the postmark. The round stamp read Albany, New York. She didn't know anyone in Albany. Wait. Didn't Dylan's maternal grandparents live in Albany? Grandpa Malcolm and Grandma Siobhan? Was that where she had been all summer? In Albany, not Lancaster or Philadelphia or any of the other places Rebecca had imagined her in?

Rebecca looked at the handwriting on the envelope. The script was as familiar to her as her own. It was Dylan's handwriting.

Rebecca tore into the envelope and pulled out the one-page letter that was folded inside.

Rebecca,

I leave for Ireland on Monday. I have said good-bye to everyone I know. Everyone except you. I couldn't leave without telling you one more time how very much I love you. When I return from my trip, I will be a year older, a year wiser, and, most likely, still in love with you. I hope that admission doesn't make you feel sad or cause you pain. It is my cross to bear. I will carry its weight with honor and I will carry you in my heart for the rest of my life.

The decision you have made is the right one for you. Time will tell if the one I have made is the right one for me. I wish you were embarking on this journey with me, but you are about to begin one of your own. Enjoy the adventure.

I am a better person for having known you. Thank you for allowing me into your life—even if for only a short time. I wish you nothing but the best.

I love you.

Dylan

Rebecca lifted her hand to her mouth to stifle the sobs that threatened to rip her body apart. She had made up her mind too late. Dylan was leaving. Leaving town. Leaving the country. Leaving her.

Fate had brought her and Dylan together. Now fate seemed to be keeping them apart. Rebecca had always heard that you couldn't fight fate, but she was sure as hell going to give it a try.

She ran back to the bakery and called the only person who could help her now.

"You told me once if I ever needed anything, I should call you. You said you'd be there for me. I need you, Willie. I need you to take me to her."

"Her flight's boarding right now. By the time we get there, it's going to be too late."

"We'll never know unless we try."

❖

Dylan sighed impatiently as the maintenance crew continued to work on the plane. Her departure time had come and gone. She and her fellow passengers had been waiting in the terminal for over an hour while a problem with the ventilation system was repaired.

The ticket agent provided regular updates over the P.A. system, but Dylan had stopped paying attention fifteen minutes ago.

She was already fifty pages into the book she had brought to read during the nearly ten-hour flight to Dublin and she hadn't even boarded the plane yet. If the repairs took much longer, she might miss her connecting flights.

She was having the worst day ever. First, she had overslept and nearly missed her check-in time. Then the guard at the security checkpoint had seemed to enjoy running his wand over her crotch just a bit too much for her comfort. And now this interminable delay. She was starting to wonder if the snafus had been signs of things to come.

The ticket agent keyed the microphone and began to speak. Dylan cocked her head to decipher the garbled words. "Ladies and gentlemen, the maintenance crew has completed its repairs. As soon as they tighten a few screws, we will begin boarding our flight to Chicago with continuing service to Dublin, Ireland. Thank you for your patience."

"Yes."

Dylan marked the page she had been reading, then reached into her messenger bag. When she returned to Philadelphia, she hadn't had time to even glance at the pile of mail Erin had bundled for her. She removed the rubber bands and sifted through it. Erin had paid all the bills and Dylan had reimbursed her for her share, but Erin had left her copies of the invoices as supporting documentation. They were mixed up with the many magazines, subscription renewal reminders, and assorted pieces of junk mail that Erin had thoughtfully arranged in chronological order.

Best roommate ever. I hope the one I have in Galway will be even half as good.

The ticket agent announced it was time for all first-class passengers to begin boarding.

It's about time.

Dylan was in Zone Three. Another five minutes and she would be able to strap herself into her seat. As the first-class passengers filed through the gate, she continued to flip through the mail. An envelope rested between a form letter from her cable company and a two-week-old copy of her favorite entertainment news magazine. The only name on the envelope was hers. The delivery address was her box in the university post office, the box she had given up when she moved out of her dorm. A bright yellow forwarding sticker was affixed to the front of the envelope. The return address was a post office box in Lutz. Rebecca's post office box. Dylan shoved the rest of the mail aside and tore into the envelope.

"Now boarding Zone One. Now boarding Zone One."

The letter was short. Not much more than a note. But the thirty-three words that composed it spoke volumes.

> *Dylan,*
> *I choose to be true to myself and to the one I love. I choose to honor the commitment my heart made the first time I saw you. I choose you.*
> *Rebecca*

"Now boarding Zones Two and Three. Passengers seated in Zones Two and Three, please have your tickets available when you approach the gate area."

Dylan held her boarding pass in one hand and Rebecca's letter in the other. Which path was she supposed to take?

❖

Willie screeched to a stop in the short-term parking lot and began running to the airport entrance, Rebecca hot on her heels. Rebecca craned her neck as a jet roared overhead. Was that Dylan's plane?

When the electric doors slid open, Rebecca followed Willie to the wall of monitors that displayed all the incoming and outgoing flights. Her eyes scanned the screens but she didn't know what she was looking for.

After a few minutes, Willie punched the air. "Damn. We're too late. The flight left ten minutes ago. Ten freaking minutes. If we had one or two more green lights, we would have been here."

Rebecca stumbled to a nearby bench and sat down hard. She was too numb to cry. Willie sat next to her and put a comforting arm around her shoulder.

"Sorry, teach." Willie's cell phone buzzed. She looked at the display and typed a quick text message. Then she turned back to Rebecca. "It's going to be okay."

Rebecca buried her head in her hands. "How?"

"Just trust me."

"A lot could happen in a year. She could meet someone else and forget all about me."

"I doubt that."

Rebecca's eyes were downcast. Her vision swam as her eyes finally begin to fill with tears. Through the haze, she saw a familiar pair of black tennis shoes.

"Is this seat taken?"

Rebecca looked up. She blinked rapidly to clear her vision. She had to make sure the blurry figure in front of her was real and not an apparition. "Dylan."

Dylan dropped her bags and opened her arms. Rebecca flew into them. Dylan lowered her head and pressed her lips to Rebecca's, welcoming her into the last home she would ever have. The last home she would ever need.

EPILOGUE

Dylan looked around the room. She nodded at all the friends and family members who had come to wish her and Rebecca well. She couldn't get over how much love radiated from their faces.

"What did we do to deserve this?"

"Just lucky, I guess."

Dylan looked at Rebecca and grinned. "You don't believe in luck."

Rebecca returned Dylan's smile. "But I believe in us."

It had been ten months since the scene at the airport. Nearly a year had passed since Dylan had forgone her trip to Ireland in order to follow where her heart led her. Now she and Rebecca were about to take the trip to her ancestral homeland together.

After she obtained her GED, Rebecca planned to enroll in college. She wanted to earn a degree in library science so she could become a librarian. She had the life she wanted, she would soon have the job she wanted and, most importantly, she had the love she wanted. She had Dylan.

"I love you," she said.

"I love you, too."

Rebecca leaned forward and gently pressed her lips against Dylan's. Given freely and openly, it was the sweetest kiss they had ever shared.

A few people broke into scattered applause, but it was Willie's cry of "Get a room!" that caused Rebecca to blush.

Dylan brushed her lips across Rebecca's reddened cheeks. "I've said it before and I'll say it again. You're so cute when you blush."

Michael, who had been visiting with Sarah and her new husband Emmanuel, ran up to them. "Give me some skin," he said loud enough for the people in the back of the room to hear him.

Grinning, Dylan bent and slid her palm across his.

He snapped his fingers (or what passed for it) and said, "Lookin' good, dude."

"You, too, little man." Dylan had almost forgotten she had taught him the move. Just like his aunt Rebecca, he never forgot anything he learned. She ruffled his curly hair and watched him run back to talk to his mother and stepfather. Her parents and Rebecca's uncle Amos were deep in conversation on the other side of the room.

Rebecca's official announcement that she was leaving the church had not come as a surprise. Uncle Amos's had, however. He had sold his part of the farm to Rebecca's father and used the proceeds to buy himself a smaller piece of land he could call his own. After joining a small Anglican church that was accepting of gay and lesbian members, he began to take some tentative steps out of the closet. He found dating too daunting a prospect after forty years away from the scene, but he had met several people his own age with similar experiences and was enjoying spending time with them and getting to know them. If he met someone, that was fine with him, he often said. If he didn't, that was fine, too. But at least he had his freedom.

Dylan took both of Rebecca's hands in hers. She wanted to share what she was feeling. Since that day in the airport, she made sure nothing was ever left unsaid.

"I knew from the day I met you that this is where I wanted to be, but I never thought we would get here. I promise to make the journey worthwhile. I promise to cherish each moment as if it were our last. I promise to never let you forget how much I love you. And last but not least, I promise to go off list every now and then."

Her comment elicited an amused chuckle from Rebecca. Both women were well aware of The List and its prominent role in their love story—a role that would continue to grow. Dylan waited for Rebecca's laughter to subside before she said, "Thank you for choosing me."

"You have shown me things I never thought I'd see," Rebecca said. "You have taken me places I never thought I'd go. You have given me the courage to be myself and the strength to be more than I thought I could be. You make me feel like nothing is impossible. I thank you for that. I love you for that. I love you for being patient, for being kind, and for being understanding. I love you for being eager to learn and willing to teach. Most of all, I love you for being you. Thank you for choosing me."

Dylan pulled Rebecca into her arms. They slowly swayed to the sound of the music softly playing in the background. "You and I have been planning this trip for so long. I can't believe it's finally going to happen. I feel like a chapter of our lives is coming to an end."

"It isn't ending." Rebecca slid one hand across the nape of Dylan's neck and buried it in her upswept auburn hair. "It's just beginning."

Recognizing the hungry look in Rebecca's eyes, Dylan wished they could sneak away for a few moments to kindle the passion that always lurked just below the surface. "Really?" She trailed her fingers across Rebecca's forearm and felt familiar goose bumps form beneath her fingertips. "Do you have something special in mind?"

"Every day is going to be special from now on. Because we'll get to spend every day together."

About the Author

Yolanda Wallace is not a professional writer, but she plays one in her spare time. She has written dozens of short stories, which have appeared in multiple anthologies including *UniformSex*, *Body Check*, *Bedroom Eyes*, *Best Lesbian Love Stories: New York City*, and *Best Lesbian Love Stories: Summer Flings*. She and her partner of nine years live in beautiful coastal Georgia. They are parents to four children of the four-legged variety—a boxer and three cats. A writer since childhood, Yolanda has also become an avid photographer. She can often be found wandering the world trying to capture on film the elusive images she sees in her head.

Books Available From Bold Strokes Books

Chasing Love by Ronica Black. Adrian Edwards is looking for love—at girl bars, shady chat rooms, and women's sporting events—but love remains elusive until she looks closer to home. (978-1-60282-192-7)

Rum Spring by Yolanda Wallace. Rebecca Lapp is a devout follower of her Amish faith and a firm believer in the Ordnung, the set of rules that govern her life in the tiny Pennsylvania town she calls home. When she falls in love with a young "English" woman, however, the rules go out the window. (978-1-60282-193-4)

Indelible by Jove Belle. A single mother committed to shielding her son from the parade of transient relationships she endured as a child tries to resist the allure of a tattoo artist who already has a sometimes-girlfriend. (978-1-60282-194-1)

The Straight Shooter by Paul Faraday. With the help of his good pals Beso Tangelo and Jorge Ramirez, Nate Dainty tackles the Case of the Missing Porn Star, none other than his latest heartthrob—Myles Long! (978-1-60282-195-8)

Head Trip by D.L. Line. Shelby Hutchinson, a young computer professional, can't wait to take a virtual trip. She soon learns that chasing spies through Cold War Europe might be a great adventure, but nothing is ever as easy as it seems—especially love. (978-1-60282-187-3)

Desire by Starlight by Radclyffe. The only thing that might possibly save romance author Jenna Hardy from dying of boredom during a summer of forced R&R is a dalliance with Gardner Davis, the local vet—even if Gard is as unimpressed with Jenna's charms as she appears to be with Jenna's fame. (978-1-60282-188-0)

River Walker by Cate Culpepper. Grady Wrenn, a cultural anthropologist, and Elena Montalvo, a spiritual healer, must find a way to end the River Walker's murderous vendetta—and overcome a maze of cultural barriers to find each other. (978-1-60282-189-7)

Blood Sacraments, edited by Todd Gregory. In these tales of the gay vampire, some of today's top erotic writers explore the duality of blood lust coupled with passion and sensuality. (978-1-60282-190-3)

Mesmerized by David-Matthew Barnes. Through her close friendship with Brodie and Lance, Serena Albright learns about the many forms of love and finds comfort for the grief and guilt she feels over the brutal death of her older brother, the victim of a hate crime. (978-1-60282-191-0)

Whatever Gods May Be by Sophia Kell Hagin. Army sniper Jamie Gwynmorgan expects to fight hard for her country and her future. What she never expects is to find love. (978-1-60282-183-5)

nevermore by Nell Stark and Trinity Tam. In this sequel to *everafter*, Vampire Valentine Darrow and Were Alexa Newland confront a mysterious disease that ravages the shifter population of New York City. (978-1-60282-184-2)

Playing the Player by Lea Santos. Grace Obregon is beautiful, vulnerable, and exactly the kind of woman Madeira Pacias usually avoids, but when Madeira rescues Grace from a traffic accident, escape is impossible. (978-1-60282-185-9)

Midnight Whispers: The Blake Danzig Chronicles by Curtis Christopher Comer. Paranormal investigator Blake Danzig, star of the syndicated show *Haunted California* and owner of Danzig Paranormal Investigations, has been able to see and talk to the dead since he was a small boy, but when he gets too close to a psychotic spirit, all hell breaks loose. (978-1-60282-186-6)

The Long Way Home by Rachel Spangler. They say you can't go home again, but Raine St. James doesn't know why anyone would want to. When she is forced to accept a job in the town she's been publicly bashing for the last decade, she has to face down old hurts and the woman she left behind. (978-1-60282-178-1)

Water Mark by J.M. Redmann. PI Micky Knight's professional and personal lives are torn asunder by Katrina and its aftermath. She needs to solve a murder and recapture the woman she lost—while struggling to simply survive in a world gone mad. (978-1-60282-179-8)

Picture Imperfect by Lea Santos. Young love doesn't always stand the test of time, but Deanne is determined to get her marriage to childhood sweetheart Paloma back on the road to happily ever after, by way of Memory Lane—and Lover's Lane. (978-1-60282-180-4)

The Perfect Family by Kathryn Shay. A mother and her gay son stand hand in hand as the storms of change engulf their perfect family and the life they knew. (978-1-60282-181-1)

Raven Mask by Winter Pennington. Preternatural Private Investigator (and closeted werewolf) Kassandra Lyall needs to solve a murder and protect her Vampire lover Lenorre, Countess Vampire of Oklahoma— all while fending off the advances of the local werewolf alpha female. (978-1-60282-182-8)

The Devil be Damned by Ali Vali. The fourth book in the best-selling Cain Casey Devil series. (978-1-60282-159-0)

Descent by Julie Cannon. Shannon Roberts and Caroline Davis compete in the world of world-class bike racing and pretend that the fire between them is just professional rivalry, not desire. (978-1-60282-160-6)

Kiss of Noir by Clara Nipper. Nora Delaney is a hard-living, sweet-talking woman who can't say no to a beautiful babe or a friend in danger—a darkly humorous homage to a bygone era of tough broads and murder in steamy New Orleans. (978-1-60282-161-3)

Under Her Skin by Lea Santos Supermodel Lilly Lujan hasn't a care in the world, except life is lonely in the spotlight—until Mexican gardener Torien Pacias sees through Lilly's facade and offers gentle understanding and friendship when Lilly most needs it. (978-1-60282-162-0)

Fierce Overture by Gun Brooke. Helena Forsythe is a hard-hitting CEO who gets what she wants by taking no prisoners when negotiating— until she meets a woman who convinces her that charm may be the way to win a battle, and a heart. (978-1-60282-156-9)

Trauma Alert by Radclyffe. Dr. Ali Torveau has no trouble saying no to romance until the day firefighter Beau Cross shows up in her ER and sets her carefully ordered world aflame. (978-1-60282-157-6)

Wolfsbane Winter by Jane Fletcher. Iron Wolf mercenary Deryn faces down demon magic and otherworldly foes with a smile, but she's defenseless when healer Alana wages war on her heart. (978-1-60282-158-3)

Little White Lie by Lea Santos. Emie Jaramillo knows relationships are for other people, and beautiful women like Gia Mendez don't belong anywhere near her boring world of academia—until Gia sets out to convince Emie she has not only brains, but beauty…and that she's the only woman Gia wants in her life. (978-1-60282-163-7)

Witch Wolf by Winter Pennington. In a world where vampires have charmed their way into modern society, where werewolves walk the streets with their beasts disguised by human skin, Investigator Kassandra Lyall has a secret of her own to protect. She's one of them. (978-1-60282-177-4)

Do Not Disturb by Carsen Taite. Ainsley Faraday, a high-powered executive, and rock music celebrity Greer Davis couldn't be less well suited for one another, and yet they soon discover passion has a way of designing its own future. (978-1-60282-153-8)

From This Moment On by PJ Trebelhorn. Devon Conway and Katherine Hunter both lost love and neither believes they will ever find it again—until the moment they meet and everything changes. (978-1-60282-154-5)

Vapor by Larkin Rose. When erotic romance writer Ashley Vaughn decides to take her research into the bedroom for a night of passion with Victoria Hadley, she discovers that fact is hotter than fiction. (978-1-60282-155-2)

Wind and Bones by Kristin Marra. Jill O'Hara, award-winning journalist, just wants to settle her deceased father's affairs and leave Prairie View, Montana, far, far behind—but an old girlfriend, a sexy sheriff, and a dangerous secret keep her down on the ranch. (978-1-60282-150-7)

Vieux Carré Voodoo by Greg Herren. Popular New Orleans detective Scotty Bradley just can't stay out of trouble—especially when an old flame turns up asking for help. (978-1-60282-152-1)

http://www.boldstrokesbooks.com

Bold Strokes
B O O K S

victory
EDITIONS

Drama

LIBERTY
EDITION

AEROS
e
BOOKS

Mystery
C CRIME

Sci-fi
Sf SPEC FIC

e-Books

HE erotica

BSB
SOLILOQUY

Young Adult

BS
BOLD
STROKES
BOOKS

Erotica

MATINEE BOOKS
Romance

WEBSTORE
PRINT AND EBOOKS